# BENEDICT'S BRIDE

# BENEDICT'S BRIDE

Bereaved Amber Hartford is betrothed to an unknowing Viscount Costain, with Amber's dowry used to secure his estates by her plotting grandfather. The betrothal is news to the Viscount but is preferable to handing over his estate. Fate places Benedict in the position of rescuing Amber, when her cousin, the heir to Hartford Estate makes Amber the object of drunken amusement. Benedict falls madly in love with Amber only for her to be abducted and held to ransom. Once again Benedict comes to her rescue, a duel is held between the two men. It is then Amber realises her true feelings and that Benedict does truly love her.

# Benedict's Bride

*by*

Janet Woods

**Magna Large Print Books**
Long Preston, North Yorkshire,
BD23 4ND, England.

British Library Cataloguing in Publication Data.

Woods, Janet
    Benedict's bride.

    A catalogue record of this book is
    available from the British Library

    ISBN   978-0-7505-3801-5

Published in Large Print 2013 by arrangement with
Janet Woods, care of Kate Nash Literary Agency

Magna Large Print is an imprint of Library Magna Books Ltd.

Printed and bound in Great Britain by
T.J. (International) Ltd., Cornwall, PL28 8RW

# ONE

'I cannot say who will look after you now your grandfather is dead, Miss Hartford. But you're twenty-one years of age now and old enough to fend for yourself until the new owner of the manor arrives.'

'Won't you please stay just a little longer, Mrs Tranton?' Amber begged. 'The other servants have been dismissed and I'll be here by myself.'

'I'm sorry, Miss,' she said firmly. 'I didn't grow up in luxury and I'm not responsible for your welfare. I need to earn a wage and I have a new position to go to. You'll have to talk to that lawyer who dealt with the estate.'

'But he came all the way from London. Even if I knew how to get there I don't know where his office is or what he looks like. I was ill and confined to bed when he visited. Why did nobody think to mention me?'

'I told him you were indisposed with an infection and couldn't be disturbed,' the housekeeper said. 'The servants were more concerned with finding themselves new positions.' Her voice softened. 'Perhaps you should consult with the new reverend and his wife. They might be able to advise you.'

Amber shuddered. 'Reverend Winter is such a misery; his face is as long as an eel.'

'The poor man has a scold for a wife. A proper

busybody is Mrs Winter.'

'I've never seen either of them smile.'

'Saving souls is a serious business. I doubt if you'll be alone for too long, though. I imagine that solicitor is making arrangements for you at this very minute. Just carry on as normal.'

'But who will cook my meals?'

Mrs Tranton became brisk and impatient. 'Goodness me, Miss Hartford, you'll soon learn how to do that for yourself once you're hungry. You've got the new stove in the kitchen to cook on and there's plenty of coal to keep it going. Likely you can use one of the stew-hearths just for yourself. There are vegetables in the garden and the fruit will be ripe for picking next month. The hens will supply you with eggs, and there are plenty of dry goods left in the larder – enough to last for many months.'

Mrs Tranton picked up her bags and smiled cheerfully. 'Well, I'll be on my way then, Miss. Samuel is giving me a lift into Dorchester so I can catch the coach to Bristol, and I hear his cart coming up the lane. I'll ask Samuel to drop in on you now and again to see how you're managing. No doubt he'll bring you a fresh trout or a rabbit, so you can make a tasty stew for yourself. Try not to worry too much.'

'I won't. Good bye Mrs Tranton, and good luck.'

As she watched the woman walk away Amber was forced to gulp back her tears. She'd never felt so forlorn in all her life.

After Mrs Tranton had disappeared from her sight Amber went inside. There, she stood in the hall and felt its emptiness, as if the life had gone from it. Hartford House had never been any less than welcoming to her. Now she felt alien to it. She was not used to such quietness. Each sound was separated from the other into strands. The long clock in the hall tocked to a stately walking pace, the carriage clock in the morning room had a more frivolous tick while the one in drawing room clock made a muffled knocking sound. But it also had an authoritative, tinkling chime to remind those in residence of the hour.

Amber was so used to her time being accounted for that she automatically turned towards the music room when the carriage clock chimed half past the hour of ten. She slid the dust sheet from the instrument. Two hours of practise took her mind off the questions laying in wait in her mind, and the dilemma they'd cause her if they weren't answered to her satisfaction.

After piano practise she smoothed the creases from her skirt. It was a pretty gown of white muslin dotted with cornflowers, and fashioned in the latest style with small puff sleeves and detachable long ones for when the day was cold.

From habit, she took a book from the library shelf and began to read. Her concentration was spoiled by the sound of hammering. She flew outside, to where two men were fixing shutters across the windows. There was a cart filled with planks, and a horse between the shafts flicking the flies away from his flanks with his tail.

'What are you doing?'

The older man whipped off his hat. 'Sorry, Miss. We were told the place was empty and

9

instructed to board up the lower floor. This is Hartford Manor, isn't it?'

'Yes, but as you can see, it's not empty. I'm Miss Hartford.'

The two men gazed helplessly at each other, then the younger one told her. 'We're following orders. Miss. It's a precaution against gypsies and those who might think to gain entrance to rob the place.'

'Then how am I to get in or out if the house is boarded up?'

The younger man scratched his head, then grinned. 'Can you climb up a ladder to the second floor?'

'Certainly not ... it's unladylike.'

She relaxed when he chuckled and said, 'In that case you'll have to use either the front or back doors, for there's no need to board them up. And we'll leave small gaps between the boards on the window to allow some light in.'

By the time the men left it was late afternoon and the light on the lower floor was effectively painted in stripes of light and shade that crept across the walls and floor with the passage of the sun. It looked quite pretty swirling with dust motes.

As she made her way to the kitchen she realized she hadn't kept the fire going. But the ashes glowed red when she stirred them and she lit a candle from them. There was bread and cheese in the larder and some ham. After a makeshift meal washed down with watered wine she went out into the garden to enjoy the evening sunshine.

The house seemed odd without people in it.

Usually at this time she sat opposite her grandfather in the library and read to him for half an hour before they went in for dinner. His eyesight had been poor towards the end. How quickly things had changed. She didn't want to sit there in the library by herself, so went up to her room. Once again the quiet overcame her.

There were no horses clattering on the cobbled yard, no jingling of reins or whinnies and squeals as they gave voice.

It seemed a long time until night time and she didn't know what to do with herself as the evening stretched into dusk. She went to bed early and as she lay in bed in the empty house she felt small and vulnerable, like a tiny kernel trying to hide inside a very large nut.

When the candle stump sputtered into darkness the spaces around her were filled with whispers and shadows. Every crack and creak woke her, and the wind in the chimneys sounded like a moaning ghost.

When she'd been been very young her grandfather had shown her the secret passage. His ancestors had been smugglers, he'd told her, the tunnels led to a trapdoor in the stables and had been built in case they needed to escape easily. The place had smelled of sour earth and was lined with bricks, but water dripped from the roof and unseen creatures scuttled off into the darkness, so she'd pressed close to his side.

'Sometimes a draft comes through the tunnel and makes the house doors rattle, but you mustn't be afraid,' he'd said.

They were rattling now. Perhaps the kindly old

man who'd taken her under his roof when she'd been orphaned was rattling them all to remind her of him. Amber smiled at the thought of Barnaby Hartford haunting her, though she'd welcome his presence and advice, for she sorely missed having someone to talk to.

He'd told her that when he'd gone to the orphanage in Italy to collect her, at first the holy sisters had declined to hand her over. But he'd refused to leave without her. The remembered snippets of his accounting of the event tumbled through her mind.

'Ambra Rosa's mother was Italian,' the good sisters had said to him. 'She has relatives here. Two aunts.'

'Neither have stepped forward to lay claim to her in the past six months,' her grandfather had replied.

'It is difficult, the church, you see ... in her aunts' eyes the girl is a ... problem. They think it best that she stay in our care, then in time...'

'Enough!' Her mild grandfather had thumped the desk fiercely with his fist – at least, that's how Amber had always imagined it, and she inwardly tossed her head and mimicked her grandfather's gruff tone. 'Ambra Rosa is English, the daughter of my youngest son, Oliver. She will not be brought up to serve some religious order.'

The head sister had then spread her hands. Amber did the same and her voice took on the imagined accent of an Italian woman. 'But ze bambino cannot speak your language, Lord 'artford.'

Her voice became gruff, like her grandfather's

had been. 'Neither does she speak Italian, since she is too young. She will learn English and we will start with her name. Amber Rose, if you please.'

By all accounts he'd beckoned to his servant who'd stepped forward with a satchel and placed it on the table. 'This is a donation to your sisterhood. It will compensate you for the care that's been expended on Amber Rose and for her loss to your religious order. Now, kindly fetch my granddaughter so I can make her acquaintance. Then I shall deliver her to her nurse, who is waiting outside in the hall to take charge of her.'

Amber smiled, because grandfather had been taken with her right away, he'd told her. As for her, she'd grown to love the kindly old man so much, and could only be glad that he hadn't suffered. He'd gone to bed on that last night of his life filled with plans, and had been taken quickly and unexpectedly in his sleep. She missed him and his wise counsel.

There was another grandchild, her cousin, the heir. Patrick Hartford was the son of her late uncle, who'd been the black sheep of the family and who'd died in a duel.

Her grandfather had always shaken his head if Patrick's name had been mentioned. 'If it was up to me you'd inherit everything, Amber. But provision has been made for you, as you'll discover in time.'

Amber remembered meeting Patrick once. She'd been nine when he'd come to stay. He'd been a small, weedy youth of about sixteen years with grey eyes, a sullen mouth and brown hair that flopped over his forehead. He'd been mean to her, pinching her or pulling at her hair. She gave a faint smile, imagining that age would have brought about some improvement in him.

She held her breath when she heard a scratching noise. Her bedroom door opened with an almost imperceptible creak, swung open, to rebound against a chair. It then closed again with a gentle, but definite click. Blood pounded in her ears. She'd forgotten to lock it and somebody had come into her room. She was too afraid to get out of bed. 'Who is it?' she quavered, and trembling, pulled the blankets over her head when there was no response.

When something landed on her stomach she gave a frightened squeak, until two paws started to knead and a cat began to purr loudly.

'Tansy,' she said, sighing with the relief of having a kindred spirit for company, for the housekeeper's cat must have been left to fend for itself as she had been. She was out of bed in an instant to turn the key in the lock.

The thoughts she'd suppressed earlier intruded into her mind to worry her when she scrambled back into the bed. If the staff had been dismissed didn't that mean that the new master of Hartford Manor had no intention of taking up residence in the near future? And if Patrick didn't move in, what would happen to her then?

She cuddled the cat against her. 'We'll manage,' she said out loud. 'We'll learn to look after ourselves and we'll survive until he does put in an appearance.'

*Then what?* she asked herself.

'Oh don't be such a wilting lily,' she snapped. 'We'll simply face that problem when it arrives.'

When Amber rose the next morning it was to find that one of the chickens was missing. She followed a trail of flattened footprints in the dewy grass, which led around the corner to the stables. Finding a door open she looked inside and surprised an unkempt boy plucking the last of the feathers from the limp bird.

The lad was about ten. Small and thin, he had brown eyes and hair. His mouth fell open when he saw her and he said without apology, 'I thought the place was empty and I was hungry.'

'How did you intend to cook the hen?'

'I was going to light a fire on the cobbles and cook it on one of those shovels.'

Amber shuddered. 'They've been used for shovelling horse dung.'

The boy shrugged and shuffled to his feet. A closer look revealed the weariness written on his face. Her heart went out to him and her voice softened. 'You're not from these parts, are you?'

'I came here from London. I thought I could get work on a farm but all the positions were filled. So I went to the reverend's house to see if he would give me a meal. The woman who answered the door said he wasn't there, and she was his wife. She gave me a lecture and said I didn't belong to the parish. Then she called me a dirty little sewer rat and sent me packing with a smack around the ear.'

Amber began to burn at the thought of such treatment. 'And your parents. Where are they?'

15

'Dead and gone, Miss, along with my elder brother. Cholera took them and I'm on my own now.'

There was no self-pity evident in the lad's voice and he was well spoken, something that raised Amber's curiosity. 'What was your father's occupation?'

'He was a teacher, Miss. My mother was a seamstress. But the rooms we lived in belonged to the school and were needed for the new master so they turned me out.'

'I'm all on my own too,' Amber said, suddenly feeling an acute sense of grief for the loss of her grandfather.

'But you're grown up and you have a big house to live in and food to eat, and nobody will turn you away from here,' the boy reminded her.

She sincerely hoped not, for where else could she go? 'Yes … yes, I do have those things, for now.' Amber was of a mind to share this fortunate state of affairs while it lasted. It was possible she might end up in the same position as this boy and would also need someone's charity to survive. The Reverend Winter had preached that those who gave would receive their just reward in heaven. Obviously his wife didn't practise what her husband preached if she'd turned this unfortunate lad away from her door. She voiced her next thought out loud. 'I do hope I'm never obliged to steal from others.'

The boy shrugged, but dejection was apparent in the droop of his shoulders. 'I'm sorry, Miss. My parents taught me to be honest.' He held out the chicken. 'I'll be on my way, then.'

16

She hadn't meant it as a reprimand. 'On your way to where? Goodness, boy, by your own admission you have nowhere to go so it might be better if you follow me to the kitchen with that fowl. Perhaps we can get a fire going in the hearth and cook a proper meal between us, though I've never cooked anything before. And I'm sure I can find you somewhere to sleep.'

'I don't want to be any trouble to anyone, Miss...'

'Miss Hartford. And your name is?'

'Jake Selby, Miss Hartford.'

'I'm here alone, Jake. All the servants have gone and I'll be glad of your company. Follow me.'

Amber secured the stable door behind them and set out. When she looked back Jake was still standing there, the chicken dangling from his hand. He appeared undecided.

'You really won't be any trouble, Jake. We can look after each other, and you might be able to get a job in the district. Perhaps when the new owner comes he'll employ you.'

And she might be offered employment, too, though she didn't think she possessed any skills that would be of interest to anyone in the district, since she'd been brought up to be a companion to her reclusive grandfather and eventually ... some man's wife.

She had a vague recollection of talk of a dowry set aside for her, an agreement signed. She must look through her grandfather's strong box, where his papers had been kept. A chill went through her at the thought of leaving Hartford and marrying a stranger.

## TWO

Benedict Costain handed his hat and gloves to a waiting servant and headed for his father's study, his long legs carrying him up the stairs two at a time.

It was good to be back at Laconbridge, where he'd spent a happy childhood, but he'd wondered when a message had arrived from his father requesting him to return home.

The last few weeks had been spent in London with friends. They'd attended balls, gambling establishments and theatres and he'd enjoyed several house parties on the way home. There, he'd cast his eye over the available females, encouraging only those who were willing to help him enjoy his single status without expecting commitment.

Most of his nights had been spent in the company of women who lived for pleasure. He liked the way women purred and writhed like cats when they were being pleasured. He loved the scent and taste of their warm flesh – the pain that came with their involuntary nips, bites and scratches.

And when he wanted to get away from such sensuous pleasures, there was always Brierly House, the luxurious home in the Hampshire countryside that he'd inherited from his maternal grandfather. Adjoining it was his horse stud, which by his own efforts contributed nicely to his wealth. Though most credit belonged to his stallion, he thought with a grin.

The stud was not far from the modest manse where his mother had grown up under the strict guidance of the Reverend Andrew Brierly. Not that her pious upbringing had ensured her safety once his father had set eyes on her. Besotted by love, his father had persuaded Imogene Brierly to elope with him a few weeks after they'd met. Because his father was an earl and his mother had returned to the district a countess, her reputation had remained unsullied.

He broke into a smile when he saw her waiting for him on the landing at the top of the stairs, her face full of love and pride at the sight of him. From his father's own account she was perfection – a woman whose love had tamed him, for he'd never looked at another since the day they'd wed.

'Mother ... how lovely to see you again.' He swept her up into a hug and whirled her gently around before setting her back down on her feet and gazing into eyes as blue as his own. She was an elegant woman, nearing fifty, her dark hair stranded with grey. 'You're still the most beautiful woman in the world. No wonder my father carried you off. I'd be tempted to do the same myself if you didn't happen to be my mother.'

'You're just as eloquent as your father is, Bennet,' she said, laughter filling her eyes, and using their informal name for him. 'The one who wins your heart will be a fortunate woman, indeed. Welcome home, my beloved son.'

'How are my sisters?'

'They're well, and will be coming to visit with the children over the weekend.'

'So the summons isn't because of anything they've done. I was worried.'

'Were you, my dear? You needn't have been. The pair of them are happily married to the most delightful men, who cherish and adore them, and who have the sense not to keep them apart for too long.'

His father's study door opened and a head remarkably like his own – except the thatch of hair on top was grey – was thrust through the gap. 'Is that Bennet I can hear?' The bulk of him followed his head, his face now wearing a wide smile. 'Of course it is. My son, I'm so happy to see you.' He was pulled into a rough, but brief embrace.

Benedict found himself grinning from ear to ear, for it was a pleasure to belong to a family where there was so much honesty, respect and love to share around. He liked being at the family estate.

His father tipped up his mother's chin and stole a kiss from her lips.

'Not in front of Bennet, James,' she scolded with a slight blush.

His father chuckled. 'My dearest Imogene, Bennet will not be embarrassed since he knows how much I adore you. You'll not mind if I take him from you for a short while, will you?'

The blush still in place, Imogene shook her head and turned away. 'I'll be in the garden if you need me. I'm going to pick some roses for the drawing room.'

The two men watched her walk away then went into the study, where his father offered him a brandy. Benedict tugged on the bell-pull. 'I'd prefer tea at this time of day.'

There was approval in his father's smile. 'Then I'll join you before we discuss the business in hand.'

Benedict knew better than to push his father before he was ready. Affable though the earl was his word was law, and Benedict always respected his position as head of the family when they were together. So he waited while the footman poured their tea and they'd spoken of the state of the country, of their investments and of the estate in general. Benedict tried to rein in his curiosity all the while.

'So, Bennet, has your stud begun to pay its way?'

Benedict recognized one of his father's preambles when he heard it, but the smile he gave was full of satisfaction. 'Under the guidance of William Ross it's beginning to show a healthy profit. I've learned a lot from him, and I'm thinking of starting a second stud I can run for myself, if I can find the right sort of property further south. I've got a couple of young thoroughbred stallions I can put into service soon, and mares with good bloodlines aren't too hard to find. It's mostly a question of putting the two together at the right time and letting nature take its course.'

'Ah ... yes. So it is.' When his father placed his cup on the tray and went to sit behind his desk it was an indication of the gravity of what he had to say. 'Three days ago I received a letter from

Thomas Dunstan, Solicitor, of London.'

Benedict had never heard of him, but he nodded.

'It was to inform me of the demise of Lord Hartford, an elderly gentleman who resided near Bridport, in Dorset.'

'I'm afraid I was not acquainted with Lord Hartford.'

'Neither was I, Bennet.' His father's grey eyes came up to his in a rather searching manner as he said slowly. 'But it seems that you're betrothed to his granddaughter, Ambra Rosa.'

'Ambra Rosa!' Benedict stared at his father in complete bewilderment, racking his brain in a vain attempt to recall all the women he'd known – at least, those who'd made an impression on him. He was certain he'd never proposed marriage to any of them. 'The devil I am! I'd have remembered a name like that one.'

'If nothing else about her,' his father said drily.

Benedict gave a faint grin. 'It sounds like an Italian name. I assure you, Father, I haven't visited Italy since you sent me on the Grand Tour six years ago.'

'Only her mother was Italian. Gianna Puzo, her name was. Miss Hartford was fathered by an Englishman, Oliver Hartford. They fell in love and married outside the faith Gianna was brought up in. It appears you've been betrothed to Ambra Rosa for the last nineteen years.'

'Since I was eight?' A guffaw of laughter burst from him. 'Surely the girl would have married someone else by now. This is a jest.'

'Unfortunately not. The young lady will turn

twenty-one shortly.'

'And she says she's been promised to me since she was dangling from her mamma's teat. That's ridiculous!'

James chuckled at his son's answer. 'It would be ridiculous, except her mother died giving birth to her. Then there is this.' He slid a paper across his desk, a copy by the look of it, since it lacked an official seal. 'The agreement is dated August 1781 and was made between your maternal grandfather and her paternal grandfather. It seems that the Reverend Andrew Brierly borrowed a great deal of money from Lord Hartford – money with which he bought the house and gardens that you now inherit and enjoy. That was the girl's dowry, paid in advance to insure she would be cared for should she be left without a responsible guardian. A marriage bargain was struck.'

'Then it must be unstruck at once.'

'She will have expectations, Bennet. Apparently she's living in Hartford House alone. Thomas Dunstan said in his letter that he understood she was ill at the time he was there – not dangerously so, but indisposed with an infectious fever and rash that she caught from a sick child she tended in the nearby village. He's since learned that she survived.'

'How fortunate for me,' he remarked with a sense of irony.

'Dunstan carried out the wishes of the new Lord Hartford to dismiss all the staff, and left instructions for the place to be boarded up until the man can find the time to visit it himself.

Dunstan said he turned a blind eye to the existence of the girl, otherwise she would have been cast out on the street with nowhere to go. He also turned a blind eye to an amount of money found in her grandfather's strong box. It was just a few guineas so she'd have means to sustain herself for a short while. But he says it won't last long.'

The viscount raised an eyebrow. 'And now the old cove expects me to rescue this Hartford granddaughter, a young woman who doesn't have the sense to stay away from diseased children. And he expects me marry her?'

'Reverend Brierly was as sly as a fox. I often wonder how he managed to produce such a sweet natured daughter.' The smile that touched his lips was followed by a sigh. 'He was a man who would never forget a slight, or forgive it. He would have arranged this match to punish me for taking Imogene from him, but he was shrewd and thought so highly of you, his grandson, that I imagine it was more than just revenge on me. He loved you, and would have wanted you settled. You know, there must be a similar document amongst the reverend's papers. This copy could be a forgery despite being signed and witnessed. All the same, my enquiries have shown Thomas Dunstan to be entirely trustworthy and honest.'

'My grandfather's papers are stored in the stud manager's office. But you're my father, so you were my guardian at the time of this agreement. How could he have overridden that?'

'If I'd known about it and challenged it he couldn't have. But your grandfather knew it was unlikely that this document would come to light until Lord Hartford had gone.'

'But what if I'd married before?'

'It's a simple matter of family honour – especially for your mother. There's no escaping the fact that the estate you inherited was intended to be the young lady's dowry. Had you wed another we would be honour bound to return it to her. We owe her a debt, Bennet. There's also a possibility that Patrick Hartford might call in this debt if he finds out about it before she is wed. The agreement made between the grandfathers was not foolproof.'

A frown creased Benedict's brow as a noose seemed to tighten around his neck. 'It sounds as though you want me to marry this girl, Father.'

After a moment or two of deliberation, James nodded. 'I do think it's about time you settled down and produced a family. You've been on the loose for quite a while and there's been time enough to sow your wild oats. Having a wife can be a comfort to a man in more ways than one.'

Benedict managed a wry smile. 'Especially if the heart is involved. You must know that you've set me an ideal of what a marriage should be. I've always promised myself that I'd wait until I'm in love before I wed – as you love and respect my mother. You've always been so happy together.'

'I know, Bennet. I've been fortunate in my marriage. Your mother is, and always will be the centre of my life. Don't think your happiness is not dear to my heart, for I won't push you into marriage if you are against it. But I'm of the mind that being a husband and begetting heirs with a suitable woman is infinitely better for a man than him turning into an ageing roué with a tribe of unknown bastards laying claim to his name and fortune. And we both have the succession of estate and title to consider. The least you could do is make her acquaintance.'

Benedict winced. He prided himself on having had more sense than to get a child on any woman so far. 'Tell me what you know about her?'

'Ambra Rosa has been raised in the country as a companion to her grandfather, who was almost a hermit. She ran his household, but has not been accustomed to an extensive social life. Her birth name has been anglicised to Amber Rose, and is the name she's accustomed to using.'

'Even prettier,' he murmured. 'I promise to look the girl over. She sounds like a worthy creature who cares for old men, stray cats and sick children. Not my type at all.'

His father chuckled. 'Is this the Viscount Costain who gave a large donation to the parish benevolent fund last Christmas?'

'It was Christmas and there were orphaned children to consider. Besides, the money wasn't really mine, I won it at the card tables, a large portion of it from yourself and the squire, as I recall. The pair of you would never have forgiven me if I'd kept it.'

His father grinned at that. 'If you decide not to go through with the marriage Brierly House must be handed over to Miss Hartford, or a suitable cash settlement negotiated ... probably with her cousin.'

'Then what will happen to the girl?'

'She's not really our problem, Bennet.'

Benedict was loath to hand over Brierly House. Not because he was attached to it to any great degree, in fact, he was considering an offer on it. He found the classical lines of the place with its Grecian columns, marble floors and staircases, too pretentious for his more homely taste. But he'd lived there for the last eight years, while his adjacent horse stud was established.

He mulled over the problem. To compensate the girl would take a sizeable chunk of his fortune. If he gave her Brierly she wouldn't be able to afford to maintain it. But it wasn't his to give. Although the deeds were in his name, the agreement said it was built with her dowry. If he wed her there would no longer be a problem.

But what if she didn't want him? He almost laughed at the thought that the creature would scorn him. He had no doubt that he could bring the girl around. Even so, the thought of taking a virginal country mouse in marriage appalled him. 'Does my mother know about this?'

'Imogene and I have no secrets between us, but it will go no further.'

'What is her advice?'

'Naturally, she's concerned for the girl's welfare. Miss Hartford is alone in the house without support.'

'What about her relative. Surely he will not put her out?'

'I'm given to understand that the new Lord Hartford is a ne'r-do-well. Apparently the old man had supported him to some extent, hoping he'd mend his ways. It seems that he hasn't, for

27

he's heavily in debt by all accounts. He's already cashed in the investments and taken possession of the available money. Thus, the estate will soon be bankrupt except for the house. He'll have no means of maintaining it now, and shows no inclination to run the estate. Dunstan believes he'll sell the place as soon as he runs out of cash.'

Benedict's eyes narrowed in thought. 'I might take a look at it, it will give me an excuse to visit.'

'Dunstan believes the marriage agreement loan was made so his nephew couldn't get his hands on it. I have no doubt that the former Lord Hartford would have approached us on her behalf when the girl turned twenty-one.'

James stood and patted his only son on the shoulder. 'You're aware of her situation, but bear in mind that she might not be. Let me know your decision after you've made her acquaintance and thought it through. Now, I must go and help your mother to pick the roses. I don't want her to get thorns in her fingers.'

As he watched his father walk away Benedict couldn't help but laugh at the predicament he was in. 'Ambra Rosa,' he whispered, savouring the name on his tongue. It sounded like a bottle of wine fermented from sun kissed grapes ripened in an Italian vineyard. She would be sweet to the taste, warm and slightly musky.

He grinned at the thought. Then again she might be crisp and sharp. One thing was certain, the girl was all alone. He should seduce the maiden before he considered marriage to her. But then, he had his property to consider. He should wed her first to secure that. Then he could seduce her quite legally. His smile broadened at the thought that he was considering marriage, at all.

Grandfather Hartford's strong box was empty of his papers, but contained a number of coins. At least she had some money for essentials if she needed it, Amber thought with satisfaction.

She went in search of Jake, who a fortnight after his arrival was settled into the former butler's quarters. It was dark with the windows boarded up, but Jake didn't mind and there were plenty of candles in the store room.

Amber had grown used to the place being empty of servants. They just used their own rooms or the kitchen, with the occasional foray into the library for a book to read. Amber liked to sit in her grandfather's study sometimes because there was a portrait of him there, and his kind face brought her comfort.

All the clocks had stopped except the one in the hall with its stately tock, which she kept wound. She practised on the piano every morning, then schooled Jake at the kitchen table, setting him the same lessons as her tutor had set for her.

She soon learned that he understood numbers better than she did. 'You'll have to study them by yourself,' she said. 'But you can read to me for an hour every day, and you can write an essay once a week. I'll teach you to play the piano if you like.'

In return he helped her with any domestic work that needed doing and kept the kitchen garden free of weeds. Sometimes he went out for the day and came back with a few pennies in his pocket and a pleased smile on his face, saying. 'I walked into Dorchester and minded a gentleman's horse outside the Antelope Hotel.'

Jake would leave her if he found permanent employment for he needed to earn a living. Sad when the child had a good mind, plus a longing for scholarship. But he also had a wide streak of practicality.

She found him in the kitchen preparing breakfast, two boiled eggs apiece and the last two slices of smoked ham. She intended to use the bone to add flavour to some pea soup. Now she was getting used to it she quite enjoyed cooking, using a book of recipes she'd found in the drawer and reducing the amount of ingredients.

The kettle was steaming on the hearth.

'Have we no bread left, Jake?'

'No, Miss. I was going to try and make some. We have milk. I went to see the farmer. He's busy with harvesting, but said that if I milked the cow every morning and turned her out to pasture he'd allow me to fill the jug.'

'The farmer got the best of that bargain.'

'I know, but after he'd gone his wife promised that she'd make us an apple pie. We've only got enough tea to last a few more days.'

'We'll have to go without after that. It's too expensive.'

Tansy came in to weave about her ankles and Amber reached down to stroke her, saying, 'You feel plump, you must have provided your own breakfast.' She poured some milk into a dish and the cat began to lap, her eyes squeezed shut and her ears flattened against her head with the sheer enjoyment of it.

'Samuel's going to teach you how to catch some trout with your bare hands, Jake, so I'll try and make bread later. It can't be too hard.'

When Jake left with Samuel she washed the dishes, wondering if she could alter some of her grandfather's clothes to fit the lad, for his sleeves were too short and his trousers tight across his rump. Her grandfather had only been a small man. But then she remembered the clothes he provided for the staff.

In the laundry cupboard she found several pairs of trousers, shirts, a cloth waistcoat or two and a jacket. Her grandfather's wardrobe yielded a pair of nearly new short boots. His room was dusty, as were most of the rooms now. But there weren't enough hours in the day to keep the house clean.

She laid the clothes over the chair in Jake's room. If the trousers were too long she could easily turn up the hems.

Making the bread dough from flour and milk she placed two sticky lumps into pans and slid them into the oven they'd lifted onto the grid over the burning coals. The loaves didn't take long to cook, though the bottoms were burned. Her bread was stodgy, not light like the cook's used to be. Still, it would fill them up. Placing the loaves on the table to cool she wondered what to do next.

Her hair needed washing and so did she. Usually the servants brought a bath tub up to her room and filled it with kettles of hot water. But that couldn't happen now. It was too much work and she only had one kettle on the boil. A wooden laundry tub would have to suffice as a bath. She fetched her hairbrush from her bedroom, and a clean gown of blue cotton decorated with cornflowers.

It wasn't long before she was naked. She soon washed her hair, rinsing it in rose water. Standing in the pail she began to soap herself all over, then realized she'd forgotten to get the bath sheet. Once rinsed off she was obliged to pull her chemise over her wet body. The heat coming from the stove would soon dry both it and her hair.

Benedict had enjoyed the ride from the adjoining county into Dorset the day before. The countryside was golden with ripening corn. He'd taken a room at an inn at Bridport, which was a mere two miles away from Hartford House. The food had been excellent, the bed clean and comfortable.

Now he closed the wrought iron gates of Hartford House behind him and left his horse unfettered in the shade of an oak tree, appreciating the opportunity to stretch the back of his long legs as he strode off up the long carriageway.

Benedict was aware that he was as imposing a man as his father, both in height and looks. From his mother he'd inherited his blue eyes. From his father a dark head of hair that he wore fashionably short. He'd also inherited an abundance of intelligence, which was sometimes at odds with a heart that was too soft to be comfortable at times.

As he rounded the curve in the carriageway he stopped and gazed at the house. It presented as a solidly constructed country residence of faded red-hued brick with arched windows softening its facade. To the left, and separate from the house was a long, solid looking stable building.

He walked around the side of stables and a coach house of similar design as the house. The stables were large enough to contain a schooling area, he noticed. Six fields adjoined the gardens, the whole surrounded by a thickly wooded copse on the sea side. If it ever came up for sale it would suit him perfectly.

Four of the fields were given over to corn crops which were ripening nicely. The wheat would need harvesting in a few short weeks, he noticed. But the labourers must have been dismissed since he saw nobody about. He frowned, hating to see the results of any man's efforts allowed to go to waste.

He walked though a walled orchard where the trees were laden with ripening fruit. A door led into a kitchen garden. Beyond that was an open door that hung rickety on its hinges, and Benedict found himself in a yard.

The windows downstairs were boarded up, nevertheless there were gaps between the boards. Cupping his eyes with his hands he peered through the gap and found himself looking into a kitchen. A movement drew his glance and his gaze shortened. He was rewarded by the sight of a young woman dressed only in a chemise. Head bent forward she slowly pulled a brush through the long dark mass of her hair.

Mesmerized, he watched her straighten up. She was slender with a firm rounded backside and long, shapely legs. His throat dried when a toss of her head sent her hair tumbling back over her head and down her back. She took up the brush again. Her movement pulled the chemise against the jutting breasts revealing the dark, delicious nubs and the damp triangle of hair just below her belly where the material clung. She was exquisite, and he prayed that this was Amber Rose Hartford and not some kitchen maid.

Benedict couldn't tear his eyes away when she stepped into a gown, pretty with flowers that covered up her charms. She buttoned the modestly cut bodice up as far as it would go, which was almost to her neck. She then seated herself in a chair and began to braid her hair, her head to one side and facing him, her eyes filled with dreaming.

He stayed absolutely still in case she saw him and thought he was a peeping tom. Hell, he *was* a peeping tom, and just at that moment he was suffering for his sin! He'd just formed an impression of a lushly curving mouth and long eyelashes framing extraordinary greyish green eyes when those eyes suddenly cleared. For a moment she stared at him, a puzzled frown lightly creasing her forehead. Then her eyes widened. Springing to her feet she stood there for a moment poised for flight, then ran like a gazelle out through a door and into the interior of the house.

Benedict groaned to himself and turned away. If that enchanting morsel he'd seen was Amber Rose Hartford, then he intended to have her, and

34

as soon as possible. He might as well introduce himself now she'd seen him.

Giving himself a few moments to compose himself he walked round to the front door and knocked at it. He was being observed, he could feel her glance on him. A shadow moved between the boards when he looked towards the closest window. He imagined her standing there, her ears straining to discover what he'd do next – exactly as he was doing, he imagined and placed his ear against the door. He heard a faint shuffling sound on the other side of the panel.

'I'm Lord Costain,' he said. 'I'm here to visit Miss Hartford.'

No answer was forthcoming.

Benedict decided it might be a good idea to re-assure her, thus saving her the agony of maidenly blushes. 'I'm sorry to arrived unannounced. I thought I saw a maid in the kitchen, but couldn't be sure since it was too dark. When my eyes adjusted to the dim light I saw the room was empty. Nobody responded when I tapped on the door.'

He took his card from his waistcoat pocket, found a pencil and scribbled a time on the back before sliding it under the door with a loud sigh. 'I'm staying at the George Inn. Perhaps you'd tell Miss Hartford I'll be back tomorrow to see her. It's a matter of business.'

If he'd expected such a ruse to bring this cautious country mouse out of her hole he was disappointed. Instead, her footsteps pattered rapidly away from the door as if she was frightened he'd kick it down. He hoped she didn't see through the lie, otherwise he wouldn't have a chance in hell of making her acquaintance on the morrow.

Benedict moved away from the door. Going down the four wide steps to the carriageway, he placed his fingers in his mouth and whistled. A few moments later his horse came cantering up the drive and snuffled into his palm as he stroked him. Foot to the stirrup he mounted, and settled himself into the saddle before pulling the gelding's head around and walking him off down the carriageway.

The place could do with a gardener to tidy it up, he thought. There was a sense of order under the overgrown grass. The flower beds were a riot of purple harebells, blood red poppies, goldenrod and heather amongst the weeds. But even the weeds had a flowery summer charm at this time of year. Honeysuckle had extended streamers of flowers that waved in the breeze and carried their sweet tantalizing perfume to his nostrils.

Before he went around the curve he looked back and saw her watching him from an upper window, her hair a cloud of shining darkness around her shoulders.

When he tipped his hat to her the curtain fell across the window and hid her from his sight.

# THREE

Amber watched Lord Costain ride away. He'd given her such a fright that her heart still thumped in agitation. She was relieved beyond measure to learn that he hadn't seen her in the kitchen, and mortified to think he might have seen her in a state of undress, or worse, in nothing but her skin!

The manner in which his great black horse had come to his whistle like a well-trained, but oversized dog, and the way Lord Costain had gently caressed the beast's nose as a reward had made a fine impression on her. Only animals who were treated well would respond in such a way. The pair of them looked well-matched together, so powerful and handsome.

Her own dark bay had been sold along with the rest of the stable. She missed the mare, but had to admit she was relieved that she didn't have the responsibility of looking after her.

After the man rounded the bend she brushed the dust from his card and gazed at it. Gold embossed lettering stood proud of the white background. *The Right Hon. the Viscount Costain. Brierly House, Hampshire.*

What on earth did a viscount want with her, especially at such an early hour? She grinned and supposed she'd have to keep on wondering until he presented himself on the morrow. If she'd opened the door today she'd probably know the answer already. It was hard to know what to do when her grandfather had never encouraged her to act for herself.

'Then again, you might be dead if you had opened the door ... or something worse,' she murmured, giving a little shiver even without speculating on what that something worse might be. She'd made the right decision. At least Jake would be with her tomorrow.

Going back down to the kitchen she finished braiding her hair, securing the end with a blue ribbon she'd left there. She tipped the bath water over the flagstones. It would soon dry.

There was a skinned and cleaned rabbit Samuel had left on the table for them. She donned an apron, then quartered the beast, added vegetables and water to the pot then hung it from a hook over the stew hearth. Once it was tender she'd thicken the liquid with flour and drop some dumplings in it.

Her feet carried her to the music room and she began to practise. Soon she was lost in the music that Bach had composed for the organ. The musical pieces exercised the fingers while they soothed the mind. It also served to remind her that tomorrow was Sunday. Since she hadn't attended a church service over the past few weeks she'd better turn up in case the Reverend Winter thought to visit her with a lecture. Her eyes narrowed. She'd take Jake with her to remind the reverend's wife of her lack of charity.

Annoyingly, the Viscount came into her mind. The eyes she'd gazed into had been a deep, clear blue, and he had seemed aware of her. She suddenly remembered the hand that had stroked the velvety nose of the horse, the skin tanned, the fingers strong and a gold ring adorning the little finger. A blush ran up her neck and various parts of her body seemed to be stimulated by the thought of him, so she stopped playing, squirmed in her seat and pushed her palms against her tingling breasts. Goodness what was wrong with her when the thought of a man she'd barely seen could bring on such a reaction? She hoped she didn't come out in itchy spots like those caused by the stinging nettles.

Lord Costain was a gentleman. But what if he *had* seen her naked and had been spying on her. He might have lied to save her from undue embarrassment, or simply as a salve to his own. She giggled, wondering if he'd regard her a strumpet on the morrow.

'Well, what's done can't be changed. You must act as though the encounter had never happened, as he will,' she told herself practicably.

Jake came back early in the afternoon, a smile on his face and a couple of brown trout hanging from a string. She wrapped them in dampened muslin and placed them on the marble slab in the larder to keep them fresh.

'Thank you Sam,' she said to the carter. 'That's kind of you.'

He touched his forehead and smiled. 'They's from your own stream. Jake here did right good at tickling them up, and likely the lad can catch his own fish now. You should lock the door to your kitchen garden, Miss. I saw the reverend's wife come across the field with a basket of this and that on her arm t'other day. Through copse and over the fields into the back of the manse she went, as if she had the right.'

Amber didn't think there was a key to the kitchen garden door, but she'd look for one. 'I thought the rabbits had been at the vegetables.'

'Could be, Miss, though if you lock the door the rabbits won't be able to get inside, either. Next week I'll show Jake how to catch one of them varmints and skin it.'

Amber shuddered after Sam had gone. Eating rabbit meat was one thing, killing the animal another thing all together. They had such soft, shining eyes.

She sent Jake upstairs to try on his new clothes. Most of the garments fit him with room to spare. As she rolled his sleeves up she told him, 'I think those were meant for the stable lad. You'll grow into them, and there's another set to change into when those are being washed. You can wear the jacket when you take me to church tomorrow.'

His face fell.

She chuckled. 'Your parents were respectable and would want you to live up to their standards while you're able. They expected you attend church with them, did they not?'

He nodded resignedly.

'Then we will attend the morning service. At four in the afternoon I'm expecting a gentleman visitor who says he has some business to discuss with me. He is Lord Costain who resides in Hampshire. I don't know what that business might be, perhaps he's an envoy for my cousin

Patrick. I'll see him in my grandfather's study. As I haven't met this gentleman before I'd like you to stay within call, if you would. In case I have to send you to get help.'

'Yes, miss.'

She threw Jake's old clothes into a wicker basket in the corner. She'd wash them and put them away in case somebody else needed them in the future.

They ate their stew at the kitchen table, putting a portion of rabbit and gravy aside for Tansy. The cat ate it then hurried back into the house.

'Odd,' Amber said. 'She hasn't been outside all day.'

A few minutes later the cat came back with a kitten dangling from her mouth. She dropped it into the wicker basket and disappeared again. Amber and Jake smiled at each other. Three more trips and the cat settled down on Jake's discarded clothes, purring loudly as the helpless kittens squeaked and rolled over on their backs as they tried to suckle from her.

Kneeling by the basket Amber moved the ginger one into position and whispered to Jake, 'No wonder Tansy was getting fat. Look how sweet the kittens are. There are two tabbies, a black one and a ginger.'

'Before you know it there will be thousands of cats running around the place, Miss.'

'They'll keep the mice under control.' Despite Jake's gloomy prediction the event had quite cheered Amber.

The next morning she donned her bonnet and away they went to church. Heads turned at the

41

sight of her and people began to whisper amongst themselves.

Mrs Winter took a seat beside her, turned a mean eye her way and said in a rather affronted manner, 'We understood that you'd left the district Miss Hartford. And what's that boy doing with you? He doesn't belong in our parish.'

'I don't know what gave you the idea that I'd left. I've actually been ill for a while. As for Master Jake Selby, he's a guest in my home, Mrs Winter.'

'Your guest? At Hartford House? But the place is boarded up.'

'As a precaution against thieves until the new Lord Hartford takes up residence.'

'You want to watch that boy. He's from London and the placc is full of sinners and pickpockets. One of these days he'll disappear with everything he can lay his hands on.'

Which when all was said and done, were only small hands. Anger kept well under control Amber answered softly, 'Master Selby is the most trustworthy person I know. However, I've been forced to lock the door to the kitchen garden,' she lied, for she hadn't found the key as yet. 'Somebody has been observed stealing our vegetables and have also taken eggs from under the hens. If that person is seen on the property again I'll make sure they're charged with stealing. I imagine they'll be transported to Botany Bay along with the other felons. I understand it's a long way off and they'll probably never see their families again.'

Mrs Winter's face, which had turned a dull red

now paled.

Amber was not the late Lord Hartford's granddaughter for nothing. 'As for Jake Selby, you're wrong about him, Mrs Winter. He comes from a respectable scholarly background, and I'd be obliged if you'd apologize for your uncharitable attitude.' When the woman's lips pressed into a thin, flat line Amber stared hard at her. 'Well?'

'I'm sorry, I'm sure,' she mumbled.

'Thank you. Now, as you know, this is the Hartford pew. Kindly find somewhere else to sit, Mrs Winter. I find your presence to be quite irksome.'

Jake gave a soft snort when the woman went away. Amber tried not to laugh but her shoulders were shaking when she knelt to pray.

'What did you pray for, Miss?' Jake asked her afterwards.

'That I wouldn't burst into laughter, and that Lord Costain's business will be of benefit to us. Now, let's go and see the farmer before we return home. I want to come to some arrangement about harvesting our corn crops. It would be a shame to let them go to waste. I was thinking he might accept a quarter share as payment.'

He'd accept half. 'I'll have to provide the labour, and you never know what price the corn exchange will place on the crop. If this weather keeps up the wheat yield should be a good'un, and you'll do nicely enough, girl.'

'But what if the new Lord Hartford turns up and he doesn't like the arrangement.'

'Aye, well, I'm not used to dealing with the

twists and turns of a female mind, but I reckon I'd tell him the same as I'm about to tell you. He can take it or he can leave it. He won't be able to hire any labourers at this time of year and the corn will rot in the field, otherwise. Tell you what, Missy, I'll scarify the stubble after as a favour to the new Lord Hartford. It'll make the earth easier for ploughing. And as well as the milk from the cow I'll give that skinny London lad of yours sixpence every week for mucking out her byre on top. Just until the harvest is over.'

'What do you think, Jake? The work involved is dirty.'

'And I can earn twice as much money looking after gentlemen's horses in town while they go about their business.'

'Ninepence then,' the farmer said.

Amber decided to bargain with him. 'One shilling and a loaf of bread every other day as well as the milk. And Jake will need a smock to go over his clothes, and boots to wear while he's on the job.'

The farmer gave a throaty chuckle. 'Damn me, girl, only the full time labourers get boots and smocks. You'll have me giving him a bed for the night next.' He heaved a sigh when she put her hands on her hips. 'All right. I reckon my missus can manage an extra loaf, and I've got a smock and boots my own lad has outgrown, and some breeches as well, most likely. Tenpence is all I'll pay, though. And that's my final offer.'

Amber gazed at the lad. 'Jake? I'm sure you could put your brain to better use, but it's up to you.'

The farmer ruffled Jake's hair. 'There's not much call for brains around here, only brawn, and that's something the lad's short of. Reckon my woman won't be able to resist the urge to feed him up a bit. Could be he'll do quite nicely for his tenpence. 'Sides, my cow likes him. He's gentle with her.'

Jake grinned. 'I reckon I'll get used to it.'

Amber was relieved as she and the farmer shook hands on it.

They walked home together through the leafy lanes. It was a warm, lazy summer day. Rabbits loped across in front of them and startled mice summersaulted in the hedgerows.

There was a haze in the air, a slight humidity. In the leafy canopy of a blackthorn tree a song thrush warbled to his lady love.

'Thanks for looking after me, Miss,' Jake said abruptly.

Amber gazed down at him, so small for his age when compared to the country lads. The sun had spread a caramel tan over his pale skin. He had brown hair that curled, and large, sad brown eyes. How terrible to be left all on his own at that age. 'You must miss your family.'

He nodded and his eyes filled with tears. 'I was thinking of them during the service, and prayed that God was looking after them.'

'I'm sure He is. What did your mother look like, Jake?'

'She was pretty, Miss. When the sun shone on her hair it glinted like gold. And she had freckles on her nose and cheeks. My dad said the angels sprinkled them on her because she was special.'

45

He placed his hands over his eyes and his voice was choked with sorrow. 'I can't remember exactly what she looked like now ... or my father and brother.'

Her heart went out to him. How could one so small be so brave? 'I understand, Jake. I never knew either of my parents. But you have me. We'll be family for each other.'

When he choked on a sob she held him tight against her in a hug while he sobbed away the grief that had built up in him.

'I'm sorry, Miss, I didn't mean to cry,' he said, his voice muffled in the folds of her dress.

It must be hard to be manly when you were only ten years old, she thought, and kissed the top of his head. 'You needn't feel ashamed of your tears. Sometimes it's good to cry because the tears help to heal the sadness you feel inside of you.' She handed him her handkerchief and gave him time to compose himself. 'Now we're best friends you may call me Amber if you wish.'

'It wouldn't be proper.'

'Then you must call me whatever feels comfortable for you.'

They slipped into silence as they strolled up the lane together, following the imprint of some horses that had disturbed the soft leaf litter.

Jake tentatively slipped his hand into hers. She squeezed it and smiled when he said. 'My mother was kind, and so are you ... *Miss Amber.*'

Patrick Hartford was in a bad mood. He and his two companions had spent the night in Poole, where they'd drunk too much of the local scrumpy cider then got into a fight with a couple of seamen.

Today they'd lost their way. Luckily they'd happened on an inn where the landlord was persuaded to provide them with directions after several tankards of ale had slaked their thirst. By the time they'd found Hartford House they were tired and hungry, and the place was locked up tight.

Patrick let the horses loose in the pasture at the back where they ambled off towards a hayrick. A board wrenched from a set of french doors plus a heel against the glass gained them an entrance from the terrace at the back into the conservatory.

Remembering how well the cellars had been stocked in a past visit, Patrick called his companions and they stumbled down into the cellar and groped around in the dark, snatching bottles from the shelves and laughing when they dropped the odd one. They brought up armfuls of bottles each. Still affected by their excesses from the night before they didn't bother with glasses, just took their booty into the drawing room and proceeded to slake their thirst.

Dragging the dust sheets from the chairs the three men sprawled inelegantly on them in the stripes of light coming through the shutters.

Stephen Gould held his bottle aloft in a toast to Patrick. 'So this is your country seat, My Lord. A perfect hideout when one is tired of London, if one is fond of rusticity. But to my mind it's too far from the flesh pots of the capital. We need a willing milkmaid or three to keep us entertained.'

'One with a nice spread of hips, and breasts to match for me, like the woman in the painting over there. She's a beauty.' Jonas Carlton said and raised his bottle to her in a toast before taking a deep draught from it. He swore as he took more wine than his mouth could hold. It dribbled from the sides and over his chin to splash redly against his cravat.

Patrick said sullenly. 'That's my grandmother. She fell from a horse and broke her neck before I was born. That's my grandfather with her. He never married again.'

'You have his look.'

'But not his nature. He was a disapproving old sod, and even though he's dead I can still feel his disapproval of me in the house. Although he paid for my education and gave me an allowance he never encouraged me to stay. Well, this is what I think of him.' Pulling back his arm he threw the half empty bottle at the portrait. It smashed in a spectacular welter of shards and red wine. 'If he expects me to become a farmer, he's mistaken. I shall probably sell the place after I've stripped it of anything valuable.'

'Oh, good shot, Patrick. Now he does look disapproving. Shall I shoot his eyes out for you?'

'In this dim light?' Patrick laughed. 'Let's have a contest. We'll take it in turns. Whichever of us gets him through the top button of his waistcoat first, wins. If I win you pay me a guinea apiece. If either of you win you can have anything you like from the house. We'll toss for who has first shot.'

Laughing, the three men pulled out their pistols and began to load them.

'Can you hear shots?' Jake said as they turned into the carriageway.

The sounds were spasmodic, and muffled. 'They might be coming from the woods. Someone is after a brace of pigeons, I imagine.'

Jake put a hand on her arm. 'They sound to be closer than that.'

'It's nothing to be alarmed about, Jake. This is the country and people are always shooting at animals. Perhaps somebody is in the fields at the back. We'll go in through the front door, go upstairs and look.'

'There, it's stopped,' she said as she inserted the key in the front door.

As it swung shut behind her she heard someone say from the other room. 'Did you hear something, Patrick?'

'Only the sound of my stomach growling.'

Amber's heart sank. *Her cousin!*

'It's your shot, Jonas. Hurry up, the game's beginning to bore me and I need a piss.'

The resulting shot brought several cheers.

They were drunk! Aware of the danger she was in Amber placed a finger against her lips, then took Jake's hand. As they began to creep towards the staircase, she whispered, 'It's my cousin and his friends. We'll wait until they've sobered up.'

When they reached her room she carefully locked the door behind them, then heaved a sigh of relief.

Downstairs, the hall clock began to whir in preparation for sounding the hour.

Stephen Gould dropped a silver snuff box back on the table when he saw it was engraved. His eyes sharpened. 'Didn't you say the house had been unoccupied for the past two months, Patrick?'

'What of it?'

'Who wound the clock up?'

Patrick suddenly remembered he had a cousin. Amber her name was. There had been some scandal about her Italian mother marrying outside her religion, and her maternal family not recognizing the match. When Oliver Hartford had died of a stomach complaint, his wife had gone into a convent, where she'd followed him into the grave after giving birth to the girl.

Surely his cousin didn't live here alone, and without a chaperone? There was only one way to find out.

'It might be my cousin, Amber.'

'You have a cousin? What's the girl like?'

He remembered a thin girl with a pinched face, greenish eyes and a thick dark braid. She'd cried when he'd teased her. His grandfather had smacked him and locked him in his room instead of taking him out riding as he'd promised. In retaliation he'd thrown a stone at grandfather's dog the following day and had cut its head open. That was the last time he'd been invited here.

There was no sending his cousin away to school. She'd lived with their grandfather, beloved by him, being educated by a governess. Envy tore blackly at Patrick. If his grandfather thought he'd take responsibility for her he'd be disappointed. As far as he was concerned she could go back to where she came from.

Lifting his pistol he took aim. The shot went wide. 'The game's over,' he said.

'No, it's not.' Casually, Stephen Gould raised his pistol and shot the button from Barnaby Hartford's waistcoat.

'Take what you want,' Patrick said.

'Anything?'

'That's what I said, isn't it?'

'I'll let you know when I see something worth having. Everything's so old-fashioned, or it's engraved with the family crest. You haven't told us what your cousin is like.'

'Amber Rose is half Italian. She's as ugly as a frog, and bad-tempered with it.' He cheered up. 'If she's in residence she'll provide us with some sport. Let's search the place and ferret her out. We'll start at the top and work our way to the bottom. Jonas, you stand guard on the landing in case she tries to run.'

A lazy chuckle came from Jonas. 'I love playing hide and seek.'

The three men looked at each other and grinned when they went into the hall and Patrick shouted out. 'Amber Rose Hartford, my creepy little cousin. We know you're in here. Hide all you like, but we're coming to find you.' Amber's face paled as the men went hurrying past the door, noisily whooping.

'What will we do?' Jake said, his voice quavering nervously. It sounded like they were tearing the place apart, and she winced when she heard something smash.

51

'Be careful, you dolt,' someone said ten minutes later from almost outside her door when there was a louder crash. 'This house and the contents are all that I have left. If you break anything else you can pay for it.'

'Sorry, Patrick. I'll toss you for the house if you like.'

'Go to hell.' The door handle rattled then Patrick shouted. 'The door to this room is locked so I think I've run her to ground.' A shoulder thundered against the panel. 'Come out of there, cousin dearest.'

Amber pushed Jake inside her cupboard. 'Sit tight until the coast is clear. Then you can make your way outside and hide in the stable. Better still, try and fetch help from the farmer.' Not that he'd dare to defy his landlord, who was the lord of the manor, she thought. However, it would give Jake something to do other than worry.

'What about you?'

'My cousin won't hurt me,' she said with more confidence than she felt, and closed the door on him, taking care not to latch it. The door to the hall shuddered again and Patrick swore. Amber picked up the heavy iron poker from her fireplace.

'Here, let me take a run at it,' a different voice said.

The door hinges were already loosened from the frame. Quietly, Amber unlocked the door, then when she heard footfalls she swiftly swung it open. A man came flying through it, his momentum careering him into a chair, which promptly overturned. He slid across the floor tangled up in its legs and crashed into the wall, giving a foul curse.

Drawing back her foot, Amber kicked him as hard as she could, and snapped, 'Your language is disgusting, sir. How dare you crash into my room like this. Get out at once, else I'll brain you with this poker.'

Holding his stomach Patrick doubled up, roaring with laughter. He staggered around acting the fool. 'I told you she was a bad-tempered bitch, Stephen.'

Turning on to his back the man gazed up at her, his eyes narrowing. He smiled nastily. 'You also told us that your cousin was ugly, Patrick.'

'She is ... was.' The laughter was gone from Patrick as he reached for her.

She lashed out at him, catching him across the shoulder with the poker. Wrestling it from her hand he threw it aside, then slapped her face with the back of his hand. She yelped and started to struggle, but his grip just tightened. When she stopped struggling he forced her face up and smiled. 'Well ... well, how my little cousin has changed.'

'You haven't changed at all, Patrick. You seem to be the same spiteful bully you always were.' He was short like their grandfather. His eyes were grey and sullen, his hair a lank brown. 'What do you want with me?'

'My dear Amber. You live under my roof. What I want from you is some hospitality and respect for myself and my friends, as befitting my position in society.'

'I can have no respect for drunkards who display

53

such disgusting manners in front of women. As for your position, it seems to me that you're still the little worm you always were.'

Face contorting with rage he slapped her again, then when she tried to catch her breath he gripped her around her shoulders and shook her until her teeth rattled. It was the other man who put a stop to it, gently disengaging Patrick's grip. He seemed to be the leader of the pack.

'Don't injure this exquisite creature too badly, my dear Patrick. Personally, I'd like her to remain in one piece. Even though you might not have a use for her now, I can certainly think of one for later. In the meantime she can make herself useful and find us something to eat to go with our wine. I'm as empty as a corn barrel in winter. You said I could have anything I want from the house. I've decided I want her as my slave for the day.'

Amber began to tremble. 'Please, Patrick ... don't allow this. Make him release me. I'll leave the house and never come back.'

For a moment Patrick looked ashamed, then his eyes slid away from her when the other man said, 'Tsk, tsk, Patrick, you're not thinking of going back on your word are you? I'll cancel your considerable debt to me if you let me have her.'

Patrick nodded.

Taking her by the braid, the one called Stephen pulled her head back and placed a knee in her back until she was forced to her knees. 'I've always wanted a dog. Come along Amber Rose.' When she didn't move he yanked sharply on her braid, making her yelp. 'You must learn to obey your master if you don't want to be hurt.' Gently, he tugged her towards the door, with Patrick following after. On her hands and knees, Amber kept tripping on her skirt, and every time she fell flat on her face she was dragged up again and punched or pinched, on her arms, her breasts, her stomach. Although she tried not to cry out it was hard not to.

'Patrick, don't allow this. Help me,' she cried out, and when they got to the top of the stair she got a grip on the balustrade with both hands. 'I'm not going any further.'

Her captor tried to pull her away, and it wasn't until he poked her in the ribs with the point of his boot that she lost her grip.

They were joined by a third man, and she shuddered when he gazed at her and said, 'Why, hello, it's Patrick's little cousin.'

'She's mine, Jonas.'

'I never touch a woman who isn't willing. I do hope you don't intend to ruin her, Stephen. I won't be party to it. Patrick, do I have your promise?'

'Oh, Stephen won't go that far. She'll be his slave for a while and fetch and carry for him. I've been waiting for an opportunity to humiliate her. You're not so smug now the boot's on the other foot, are you, Cousin Amber.'

She kept her counsel, deciding not to do or say anything to inflame the situation further – unless she could get clear away.

# FOUR

Man and horse ambled along the lane, enjoying the silent comradeship as well as the countryside. Benedict was looking forward to his encounter with Amber Rose Hartford – if indeed it had been her he'd glimpsed. And if the sprite would deign to allow him the privilege of appearing in her presence.

He'd dressed in his comfortable black dittoes, the trousers tucked into short boots. A blue brocade waistcoat covered a shirt with a stand collar. Not the most suitable attire for one intent on courtship, but there was a limit to the amount of clothing that could be carried in his saddlebag. At least the inn had been able to provided a barber to remove his whiskers.

As he rounded the curve his reverie was interrupted by a small boy who tumbled out of a hole in the hedgerow, tripped over a bank and rolled in front of him.

'Whoa! Juniper,' Benedict soothed, thankful he'd been at a walk when the horse dug his front legs into the ground and came to a sudden halt, with only a faint snicker of complaint. Dismounting, he went to the lad, who'd had the good sense to curl in a ball and stay very still. He hauled him up by the collar. 'Are you hurt?'

'No, sir. Will you help me ... it's Miss Amber,' he blurted out. 'Her cousin and his friends have

56

arrived and I think they're going to kill her. I went to fetch the farmer but he wasn't there.'

'Are you referring to Amber Rose Hartford?'

'Yes sir.'

'Why should her cousin and his friends want kill her?'

'They're drinking, sir ... and they're shooting pistols. She ... Miss Amber made me hide in the cupboard and told me to fetch help when I could.' The boy's face was creased with worry. 'I've got a pitchfork in the kitchen garden I can use, but you have a pistol on your saddle holster.'

'So I have.' Benedict also had a smaller one in his boot. 'You have sharp eyes, lad. What's your name?'

'It's Jake Selby, sir.'

'How d'you do, Jake Selby, I'm Lord Costain. I was just about to call on Miss Hartford.'

Jake nodded. 'Miss Amber was expecting you.'

'How many men are there?'

'Three. One of them made her crawl on her hands and knees and they dragged her out of her room by her hair.'

Shock rioted through Benedict that anyone would treat a young woman so badly. Anything could have happened to her by now, and he feared the worst.

Jake said, 'We'll have to go through to the back garden if we don't want to be seen. I came out through the kitchen door and left it unlocked in case she was able to escape.'

'That was quick thinking. We'd better not waste any time then.' Closing his hand around the lad's arm Benedict swung him up on the horse and

57

mounted behind him. 'Hang on tight, lad,' he said and put the horse to the stretch.

Ten minutes later he left Juniper in the shade of a tree with strict instructions to Jake to stay with him. He surveyed the house, tempted to walk up to the front door and bang on it, but the boards could hide watching eyes and foolhardy, he wasn't. If they saw him coming they might shoot him out of hand.

Ducking round to the back he placed a cautious eye against the chink between the boards. There was his Aphrodite. A man had her by a leading rein that was looped around her neck. Benedict recognized him. It was Jonas Carlton, a man who came from a well-established family and was heir to his uncle's title. He wouldn't have thought Carlton was capable of such barbarism. He was also was acquainted with Stephen Gould, a different proposition altogether. Gould was the son of a lawyer, and a crack shot. He made his money from gambling, for he'd been disinherited.

Just at that moment the girl's eyes met his. He saw recognition come into them but she didn't acknowledge him, not even with the flicker of an eyelash as she turned to pick up a some plates from the table. Hard to tell if she was blushing, since her blood was up and her cheeks glowing as a result.

'Should I take these to the other two drawing room,' she said loudly.

'You don't have to shout, I'm not deaf, cousin Amber.'

'I'm not your cousin. Let me go free,' she said.

'I'll run away into the woods.'

'If I did that Stephen would hunt you down, and he's a bad enemy when he's riled. He'd probably kill you. Just do what you're told and say nothing. Everything will be all right.'

'And if I don't?'

For her pains Jonas impatiently flicked the leather rein across her fingers. When she jumped the plates slid from her fingers and smashed on the floor. She clawed at her neck when the noose tightened around it.

She'd put herself in danger by creating a diversion. Benedict was about to hurl himself through the door when Stephen appeared. 'Be careful with my slave, Jonas. I want her to last the day.' He loosened the leather, took a firm grip on her chin and kissed her on the mouth.

She must have bitten him, for he gave an oath and took a step backwards. Blood seeped from his lip before he staunched it with his handkerchief.

'You vicious little vixen!'

'And here's something else for you.' She picked a wicked looking knife from the bench and held the business end towards him. Gould took several steps backwards and tripped over a cat that had chosen that moment to streak into the kitchen. The cat disappeared with a spitting hiss into a basket in the corner, while Stephen Gould sprawled on his back on the flagstones.

Tearing the rein from her neck she lashed Jonas Carlton with it. 'Get away from me, you cowardly cur.' Carlton turned and headed out of the room at a run when she waved the knife in his direction. She turned and gazed down at Gould, who was rising to his feet, and she had such hate and intent in her eyes that Benedict began to quake.

He wasn't about to allow her to kill anyone, however much the victim deserved it. But three men against one girl was rather uneven odds Even though the girl was doing quite nicely, Gould would easily disarm her, and would probably use the knife on her if she got any closer.

Opening the door he thrust through it and positioned himself between the protagonists. What he saw was that Amber Rose Hartford was at the end of her tether. Her hand was trembling, but her eyes smouldered with a barely concealed rage.

'Give me the knife, Amber Rose. You might think he deserves it now, but believe me, you won't enjoy the sensation of slicing that knife through human flesh or paying the penalty for murder. The man's scum, and his death is not worth the price you'll have to pay for it.'

She shuddered, and he was relieved when good sense penetrated her anger. When she handed the knife over to him he threw it out into the garden, then put an arm around her trembling body and drew her against his side. 'Miss Hartford ... are you all right?'

Stephen lumbered to his feet. 'Well, if it ain't Benedict Costain, just in time to rescue the fair lady from a fate worse than death.'

'Seems to me it was the other way round,' Benedict drawled.

'It's been a long time, My Lord. You might

recall that you pipped me at the post for the Beddington purse. You were a worthy adversary, as I recall.'

Benedict nodded. 'Yours was an unlucky shot.'

'Yes, I thought so too. That damned bird flying up from behind the target distracted me.'

Patrick came in, pistol in hand. 'What the hell's going on here? Who the devil are you, Sir?'

'I'm Viscount Costain, heir to the the Earl of Laconbridge. I'm also Miss Hartford's affianced. Perhaps you'd care to introduce yourself.' When the girl stiffened against his arm, he thought, So ... she hadn't known about the arrangement.

'I'm Lord Hartford. Miss Hartford is my cousin ... and my ward.'

'A damn fine job you're making of protecting her,' Benedict said. 'I caught your companions mistreating her.'

'You can release my cousin now,' Patrick said. 'It was a bit of fun that went too far, that's all. Go up to your room, Amber.'

The young woman moved closer against him for protection. Normally Benedict would encourage such a move from one so fair, but she was blocking access to his pistol and Patrick's weapon was still aimed in his direction.

'I had no idea my grandfather had made a match for her. I don't think Amber knows of it either. She looks rather surprised.'

'Of course I know,' she said with surprising spirit. 'I was expecting Lord Costain today. We were going to discuss the arrangement in view of my grandfather's death.'

'So, the old man's ambition was to turn you

into a countess so the Hartford blood could be bred into future earls,' Patrick sneered.

'Your vulgarity in front of a young woman does you no credit,' Benedict said.

Patrick's eyes were red-rimmed and he was swaying. Stephen Gould was edging around the side, trying to get behind him, but he and the third man were unarmed.

Amber must have sensed the danger too. She edged away from him, then drew his gun smoothly from his holster and moved back, holding the pistol between them. When his fingers closed around it she stepped back slightly, giving him room to bring the weapon up. 'I hope you have no intention of using that weapon, Lord Hartford,' he said.

'On you, no.' Patrick turned and aimed it at the basket in the corner. The pistol discharged. Something exploded in a welter of fur. A few seconds later the wild-eyed cat slunk out of the basket with a kitten in its mouth and streaked through the open door.

Patrick went pale and gagged before he was able to take control of himself.

Giving a scream of dismay Amber dashed across the room. On her hands and knees, now, she searched through the rags and brought out a couple of tiny kittens, their fur and her hands covered by their unfortunate sibling's blood. Tears streamed down her face. 'How could you be so cruel, Patrick. You've killed one of them.'

'It was an accident. I saw something move and thought it was a rat.' He shrugged, exchanging a glance and a grin with his two companions that seemed more like bravado than anything, for he was as white as chalk. He recovered quickly. 'It's only a cat. Put your pistol away, Costain. I suppose you want to talk to your *betrothed*. You do have proof of this betrothal agreement, I imagine.'

'Not on me. I came to make arrangements with Miss Hartford for a time to collect her tomorrow, to take her to my parent's home in Hampshire.'

The girl's head jerked up.

'The invitation arrived, did it not?' he said.

She was quick-witted for she nodded, then stammered, 'It was kind of the earl.'

'They didn't want you to be left alone in an empty house and they wanted to make your acquaintance before the marriage takes place. Perhaps you know where your grandfather kept the copy of the agreement.'

'Mr Dunston took all grandfather's papers away,' Amber said. 'There's nothing left in his strongbox except for a few guineas.'

Interest came into Patrick's eyes. 'My cousin is under my protection, and will not be going anywhere at the moment.'

'I'm old enough to please myself where I go, and with whom,' she said.

'You'll defer to my authority. I intend to go to London and see Dunstan, to make sure this agreement is above board. We should be back before the week is out. Gentlemen, let us go about this business now. Costain. No doubt you can be trusted with my cousin for a short time. But make sure you leave the premises before nightfall. If any harm befalls her we'll know who

63

to look for, and I'd hate to see you swinging from the end of a rope. And I suggest that you think twice before pulling a gun on me in my own home, again.'

Jonas turned his snigger into a cough when Stephen gave him a warning look.

A little while later Benedict watched the three men canter off. A few minutes and one piercing whistle later, Jupiter came trotting up the carriageway, with Jake came running after him.

Amber heaved a sigh of relief when she saw Jake. 'I was worried about him.'

Benedict turned to her, noting that her mouth was still tense, so he longed to kiss the softness back into it. 'I'm more worried about you.'

'But they've gone,' she said.

'They'll be back tonight, after dark. They mean you harm, Miss Hartford, and they intend to place the blame on me.'

Her face paled and she began to tremble again. Gently he touched the purpling bruise on her face and anger rose in him. How could they treat such an exquisite creature so badly? 'Go and pack a travelling bag with all you can carry, then head across to the woods. I'll meet you at dusk, hopefully with a carriage of some sort.'

She held the wriggling kittens against her cheek, an altogether charming gesture. 'But we've never met before, Lord Costain. Why should you help me to escape? Besides, I've got nowhere else to go. I'd better take the kittens back to the kitchen in case Tansy gets over her fright and comes for them.'

He took them from her. 'I'll do that. You go and

pack. It'll be dark soon.'

The eyes that came up to his were puzzled. 'Thank you for your intervention on my behalf, My Lord. I must ask though, what was your business with me? And where do you intend to take me?'

'The first has already been adequately stated. As for the second, I intend to take you to the home of one of my sisters, who lives in Hampshire. Now, will you go and pack. We haven't got much time.' Hearing a faint sound behind them he turned and said, 'Everything's all right, Jake. You can trust me. I want you to get your mistress away over the fields.'

Jake placed the outsized pitchfork he was carrying against the wall and came to stand by Amber, who said, 'He's not my servant. Jake is my family. Where I go, he goes.'

'I didn't know you had a brother.'

'I haven't. Jake and I are best friends, and look after each other.' Benedict didn't bother arguing with her since she had the same stubborn expression on her face as his sisters did when they argued with him.

He smiled at her and nodded to Jake, who appeared to be pleased by the young lady's revelation, and gazed at her with worship in his eyes. But although his rival for Miss Hartford's affection had got to her first, Benedict didn't let it bother him. Experience would stand him in good stead.

'Which way did they go, Jake?'

'Towards Bridport.'

'They'll stop at the nearest inn, the Red Hart,

probably. They'll return to the house when night falls. Why are you still here, Miss Hartford?'

'I don't know if I can trust you.'

That was straightforward enough. He chuckled. 'I don't know if I can trust me, either. Let me put it thus. It's either me or them. Take your choice, I know which I'd prefer.'

She shrugged and walked towards the staircase, turning at the bottom only to say, 'I can't believe your business with me was marriage, since we've never met. Why were you here, really?'

A half-truth was better than a lie, he thought, and he didn't want to waste time debating the marriage agreement with her. 'I was looking for a property to buy and thought Hartford House might have been up for sale. I was hoping you'd show me around while I was in the district, but I've seen enough of the building to know that I like it.'

Was that disappointment he saw on her face; hard to tell in the dim light. If it was the expression had disappeared when she stated, 'Good, because my grandfather never mentioned a marriage agreement to me. He knew I wanted to be in love with the man I marry.'

Exactly his sentiments. 'And if he had made an agreement?'

'I'd obey his wishes. I loved my grandfather dearly and he always acted in my best interests.'

You've just cooked your goose, little lady, he thought and smiled at her.

They had something in common he could work towards. It would be preferable if the girl was in love with him before she learned of the marriage agreement, and Benedict would aim his efforts towards that goal. He'd never had trouble attracting women, and enjoyed the game of courtship, especially when the women concerned knew what the likely outcome would be. He'd hazard a guess that this one didn't.

Either way, Amber Rose Hartford would give him no trouble.

## FIVE

Amber and Jake waited by a milestone. By Amber's side was a large wicker basket, which contained as many clothes as it could hold. In a bag she had her hair brushes and toiletries, and a small amount of jewellery, trinkets her grandfather had given her on various birthdays, which had once belonged to her grandmother.

On her other side a picnic basket contained the cat, who'd returned shortly after the three men had gone and seemed not to have noticed the loss of one of her kittens or the change of bed as she set about cleaning them.

It had been a struggle to carry the luggage across the fields and through the copse between them.

The night held magic. A purple dusk began to fill with flying moths and black swooping bats. A bright, three-quarter moon sent light spilling across a field of wheat that swayed and whispered in the breeze, turning it into liquid gold. The first star had appeared. She wondered where the viscount would take her and felt regret at leaving the place that had always been her home.

'What a pretty night it is,' she said quietly to Jake.

'What will we do if Lord Costain doesn't come?' he said.

'He struck me as being a reliable man.'

'But what if they laid in wait and killed him?'

She refused to give in to the flare of fear that came with Jake's words, and being careful not to trigger the safety mechanism, fingered the viscount's small gun, which was now in her pocket. 'Don't say such things, Jake. Lord Costain has the intelligence to out-think those men, and the strength to overcome any danger they may represent.' *If the ruffians could be called men!* 'He's brave, but not foolhardy.'

She was hungry, and she guessed that Jake was too. There was some bread and a small hunk of cheese in the basket Jake carried. Also a bottle of wine. But it would have to be shared between the three of them.

The carriage arrived a few minutes later, following the viscount on his horse. Both arrived with hardly a noise on the little used and over-grown track. His smile mirrored his relief when he saw them by the side of the road. 'I could have sworn I said a travelling bag. If we'd been compelled to travel by horseback that basket would have had to be left behind.'

She smiled at the laughter in his voice. 'Then it was lucky you had the foresight to hire a carriage.

As it is I had to leave most of my wardrobe behind.'

She'd stolen a couple of guineas from her grandfather's strongbox and had thrown the key into the stream on the way across the fields, mostly out of mischief. A pity she'd mentioned it to Patrick in the first place. But now he'd have the devil of a job opening it, unless he found the spare key, which was well hidden inside a hollowed-out book.

'Miss Hartford?'

Amber came out of her reverie to realize that Jake and the luggage was already in the carriage, a rather shabby vehicle drawn by two dark horses. The driver was a silent shadow, who was now lighting the lanterns on his vehicle.

Lord Costain's hand was warm and strong around hers. 'I was lucky, the carriage was on its way back to Poole and the driver has agreed to take us. The driver's name is Matt. We can stay the night there and go on in the morning. Are you recovered from your fright?'

'Yes, thank you, Sir. You're welcome to ride with us in the carriage if you wish. We have some bread, cheese and wine for our supper.'

'It would be better if I used my horse, in case your cousin realizes they've been tricked and try to follow us along the coast. If you'd pass some bread and cheese through the window it will suffice. And I'll have my little pistol back, unless you feel safer with it.'

'Indeed I do, but I'd prefer not to have to carry a weapon since I've never been taught to use one, except for your brief instruction a little while ago.' When she handed the pistol over it disappeared back into his boot.

Hand closing around hers he helped her up the step and into the carriage then gently kissed her palm. 'Never fear, little lady, I promised to get you away to safety, and I will. Try to enjoy the adventure of it.'

'Adventure?' A nervous laugh left her mouth. 'To be quite honest I'm so frightened that I keep trembling. I must be insane to pack my bags and run away with a complete stranger.'

'I'm doing the very same thing. Don't you find the concept of running away together just a little bit daring ... and a little bit romantic perhaps?'

If he had any ideas in that direction she must dispel them at once. 'Romantic ... certainly not!' *Liar! Liar!* If only he knew the excitement churning inside her. She fizzed with it, as if her blood was filled with fireflies. The voice of reason prevented her from enjoying the feeling. Her reputation would be shredded when her flight became public knowledge.

As it would have been if she'd stayed there, she reminded herself. Patrick would have made sure of that. She shuddered as she thought of the way his companions had treated her. He'd made no real effort to stop Stephen Gould. Only this man – a complete stranger – had come to her aid. She felt as though she'd known him all her life and softened towards him.

'I admit I do find my flight a little adventurous. This morning I was just an ordinary young woman who'd spent her life as an obedient companion to a grandfather I loved. Now, not only am

I homeless but I'll have a tarnished reputation I don't deserve by morning.'

'Cast aside the notion that you're ordinary. In fact, you're breathtakingly unexpected. And I'd really prefer my honour not to be measured against the likes of your cousin and his companions.'

'Please accept my apology. If I did measure you against them I'm certain you'd stand so tall in my estimation that I wouldn't be able to look you in the eyes.'

His smile was a joy to her. 'Prettily put, Miss Hartford.'

*Such beautiful blue eyes,* she thought, and brought him down a little. 'I will also have to say that I fear there's absolutely nothing that's safe about you, Lord Costain. You can take that as you will.'

'Then I'll believe it to be a compliment. As for you, Amber Rose, the sight of you warms me considerably, so perhaps you're right to feel scared. In all sincerity, would you prefer it if I returned you to Hartford House?'

It was she who felt warmed now, and thank goodness he couldn't see her blush. She felt quite disgruntled by her inability to reply with drawing room wit. Flirting with young men was something she'd never been given a chance to learn. The best she could manage was, 'Since there was nothing at all sincere about that question I shall ignore it. And despite my suspicions that you're not quite the gentleman you lead me to believe you are, I do trust you ... I think. You may let go of my hand now, then we can be on our way.'

71

'A pity to allow such a soft hand to escape.'

So saying, he gave it another kiss and set it free. Gently he confined her in the dark interior of the carriage with Jake and the family of cats by closing the carriage door. She would rather be riding with him in the soft moonlit night, she thought, as he gave a low whistle and the carriage lurched forward.

The journey was uneventful. Either Patrick Hartford and his companions had drunk themselves into a stupor, or they had taken the more popular road.

The moon was shining brightly now. Their own driver took them across the heath, following the bone white ribbon of a path with a surety of one totally familiar with it. Benedict wouldn't have taken such a risk, since he'd never been across the heath before and knew the heathland would be full of traps and bogs for those without local knowledge.

It was after midnight before they reached the harbour town of Poole. It was not a good place to be in at night, for danger lurked in the shadows. The town was swarming with seamen, lightskirts and lawless smugglers who brought kegs of brandy and other goods ashore.

Suspecting that the coaching inn might be watched, Benedict asked the driver, 'Do you know of other lodgings that are more suitable for a lady, Matt?'

'Aye, my sister has a room and takes in boarders now and again. She'll give you a good breakfast.' He took them to a house on the edge of town –

one that was owned by his sister, a plump creature called Meg who came downstairs grumbling at being disturbed and rubbing the sleep from her eyes.

'Oh, it's you, Matt. And you've brought boarders this late? Well, I won't say we can't do with the money.' Her eyes softened when she saw Jake asleep in Benedict's arms. 'The nipper's fair tuckered out. I reckon I can find you a room, at that.'

'Two rooms,' Amber said primly. 'We're not man and wife.'

Gazing from one to the other, Meg nodded. 'Well, I hope you know what you're doing, Miss, running off with him in the middle of the night, though I don't blame you. He has a right lusty look to him. I've always liked a man who knows what he wants and how to go about getting it.' She poked a finger in Benedict's chest. 'You make sure you put a ring on her finger before you bed her, mister. No creeping up the stairs during the night.'

'I intend to wed her and bed her as soon as I get the opportunity.' Or the other way round. Having now met Amber, Benedict wasn't bothered over which event happened first.

He grinned when Amber turned a pretty shade of pink, opened her mouth to retort then shut it again. Her naivety amused him. You haven't begun to live, little bird, he thought.

'I daresay the gentleman can make do with the chair in the parlour and a blanket. 'Tis all I've got.' She eyed the basket with the cats. 'The cat can have to run of the kitchen for tonight. I'll give her a dish of milk, and she can catch herself a mouse or two in return for her lodging. Pesky creatures, mice are. Matt, are you staying or going?'

'Going. I've got some business along the coast.'

'Take our Tom a meat pie then, and put one in the basket for yourself. Stable the gentleman's horse first, then be off with you. Be careful, and tell my Tom to be careful, too. 'Tis a bright moon out there.' She took Jake from Benedict's arms and said to Amber, 'Follow me, Miss.'

'My thanks. If anyone asks I'd appreciate it if you haven't laid eyes on us,' Benedict murmured to the coachman a little while later, and slipped him an extra guinea with the fare he'd been quoted.

'I imagine you mean those three men in the inn who were plotting the young lady's downfall, and your own.' He held out a hand. 'Matt Striker, revenue man at your service.'

Benedict chuckled. 'I thought you were a rogue. Those men are Miss Hartford's cousin and his cronies. They're a bad lot. I'm Lord Costain.'

'Aye. They mentioned your name and the girl's when I overheard them talking. I thought I'd give you a hand, since two guns are better than one. How far are you going? I can send a trustworthy man with a rig in the morning to take you there if you like, and I might be able to make arrangements for your pursuers to be delayed meanwhile. A few hours in a cell while you get away might do the trick.'

'On what charge?'

'Could be we'll find a bottle of smuggled brandy

in their saddlebags when we search them.'

'I was right, you are a rogue,' Benedict said with a chuckle. 'I'm going to Lyndhurst, where I'll be leaving Miss Hartford at my sister's house. She'll be safe there for the time being.'

'She's a sweet one, if you don't mind me saying. A real lady.'

'She most surely is. Thank you for your help, Matt. I hope I can do you a favour in return one day. Good luck in whatever you're involved in tonight.'

'Thanks.' The two men shook hands, then giving a secretive grin Matt slipped the money back into Benedict's hand, touched his hat and disappeared into the darkness.

The few hours sleep had refreshed Amber and the delicious smell of cooking woke her. It seemed like months since she'd eaten a well-cooked meal.

Washing her hands and face in a bowl of warm water someone had thought to leave her, she brushed out the length of her hair and braided it before pulling on the gown she'd been wearing the day before. It was looking grubby, and she'd have changed into a fresh one if the wicker basket hadn't been downstairs.

It was early, the sun just coming up over the horizon. There had been some light rain during the night and the air was filled with a pearly, drifting mist.

Her mouth watering she followed the smell of cooking down to the kitchen, where two young girls were cooing over Tansy and the kittens. Meg gave her a broad smile. 'The girls are hankering after a kitten, but they're too young to leave their ma just yet. If you want a home for the litter I'll take them off your hands. I can place the kittens in homes when they get older. Your man told me to ask you.'

He wasn't her man, Amber thought crossly, but said, 'That's kind of you, Meg. I couldn't leave them behind because they would have starved to death.' Or worse, she thought, remembering the result of Patrick's stray shot. 'Is Lord Costain about?'

'He's at the pump, taking a wash. Have you made yourself comfortable, Miss?'

'Yes, thank you.'

'Then sit yourself down.' A plate appeared, laden with eggs, ham and tomatoes. And there was a thick slice of bread fried to a crisp on both sides.

She'd never eaten such a large breakfast and had just swallowed the last delicious morsel when Lord Costain came in, his shirt open at the neck. Her heart lurched and her breath left her body when she set eyes on him, his hair damp and curling and his eyes as blue as summer cornflowers.

He set a pale pink rose on the table in front of her and offered her a smile that warmed. 'Good morning, Miss Hartford. I hope you feel rested.'

Meg beamed a smile at him, and then at her. 'There you are then,' she said to nobody in particular.

Amber was sure her face turned as pink as the rose as she picked it up and breathed in its fragrance. She lowered her eyes to the cup of steaming tea Meg had set before her. 'Thank you, Lord Costain. I do feel rested.'

The huge breakfast Meg gave the viscount had the addition of sausages. He set to with gusto while Amber sipped her tea. She suddenly remembered the lad. 'Have you seen, Jake?'

'He had his breakfast with my girls, earlier. Your brother thanked me. I like a child who knows his manners.'

Amber exchanged a smile with the viscount over Meg's mistake, but didn't bother putting her right. He told her, 'You needn't worry about Jake. He's keeping a look out for the transport. We must be away as soon as possible.'

'Thank you, My Lord. I'll not hold us up.'

It wasn't long before they'd said their goodbyes. As the viscount helped her into the chaise he whispered to her, 'You needn't be so unfailingly polite with me. My name is Benedict, but my family call me Bennet.'

'I'm not your family. May I remind you that up until yesterday we were complete strangers, Lord Costain.'

If he was upset by the curt rebuff he didn't show it, apart from a tincture of hurt in his voice when he said, 'So we were, Miss Hartford, but we've shared so much together that it seems longer. I beg your pardon for being so forward.'

Guilt tore at her. This man had rescued her from a fate so degrading she couldn't even imagine it. She was treating him like a pariah. She reached out, placing a hand on his arm to detain him. 'No, it's me who should beg yours. I was too sharp, and I'm an ungrateful wretch to be so standoffish.

Thank you for being so kind to me … Benedict. Please continue to call me Amber, if that's your wish.'

'It is my wish. Amber Rose is such a pretty name it would be a shame not to use it.'

Because he was now on a level with her she leaned forward to kiss his cheek, but he turned his head and for one surprising moment his lips claimed hers in a clinging little kiss. Her eyes widened when he withdrew, but she couldn't help but smile as she scolded, 'You're an opportunist, Benedict Costain.'

'Indeed not. It was merely a fortunate accident.' He laughed and turned away, calling to Jake to join him on his horse, since there was hardly any room left in the chaise. It was full of her luggage.

They were in Lyndhurst by noon, a leafy lane leading them to the country residence of Lord and Lady Stratton, an ivy-covered manor house set amongst the trees.

Emma Stratton burst from the front door, her face wreathed in smiles as Benedict paid the chaise driver and sent him on his way. Her ringlets bobbed as she gave him a tight hug. Her eyes were as blue as his, her hair a lighter colour.

'Bennet, how wonderful to see you. Archie's not here at the moment, he's in London but should be home tomorrow.' A speculative glance went to Amber and Jake, and her smile widened even more. 'Will you introduce me to the young lady?'

'This is Miss Amber Hartford. Amber, this is

my elder sister, Emma. She has the title of lady, but rarely acts like one.'

'Nonsense, Bennet. Miss Hartford I've decided to take a leaf from my brother's book and call you Amber. And I insist you call me Emma. Welcome to my home.' She reached out and ruffled Jake's hair. 'Is this lad your brother? He doesn't look much like you.'

Amber took Jake's hand. 'We've decided to look after each other, so I rather think of him as my family. His name is Jake Selby, his mother was a seamstress and his father was a teacher by profession.' She exchanged a smile with him. 'Jake is clever with numbers.'

'Goodness. How frightening in one so young.'

Emma eyed the clothes basket, saying drily, 'Well, Bennet, am I to have unexpected guests?'

'If you wouldn't mind for a short time. Through no fault of their own Amber and Jake were forced to escape from an unpleasant situation with a relative. If it will set your household at odds then Caroline will make room for them, no doubt. I don't want to take them to the family home because that will be the first place her cousin will enquire.'

'And if he enquires for her here?'

'You have only to look at the bruise on her face to know you must lie. No doubt she has more on her body. Patrick Hartford and his friends must not be underestimated and I'll stay here with you until Archie returns.'

Emma's voice softened. 'Did you help them abscond from this bully? Really, Bennet! What-ever will you think of next? But, by absconding with Miss Hartford you've compromised yourself as well as her.'

Amber stammered. 'It's not what you think, My lady. Lord Costain just happened to be there at the time. He had no choice but to rescue me from the situation, which was not of his making, nor mine. For that I'll be forever grateful. My Lord, perhaps it is not a good idea to burden your sister with my presence.' She hauled in a shaking breath, for the ramifications of what had occurred were being forced home to her. 'I know you acted out of chivalry. Pray, do not think you must ... that I'd expect, or even contemplate...'

He chuckled. 'See what you've done, Emma ... you've scared the young woman into going all formal on me again, and she's losing her tongue into the bargain. The word you're struggling to avoid Amber Rose, is marriage.'

'Is it?' she said vaguely.

'Indeed it is, and you might as well know that I have every intention of proposing to you. It was the *raison d'être* of my visit to Hartford House in the first place.'

'Oh! But you said–'

'I know what I said. Looking over the property was the other reason.'

Amber didn't know whether to laugh or cry so she did neither, just stared at him, her mind struggling with the enormity of it as she said faintly, 'I cannot marry a man I've only just met.'

Her protest was lost in Emma's exclamation of pleasure. 'You are to be married, Bennet. Why didn't you tell me?'

He kissed his sister on the cheek and laughed. 'I just have, but it must remain a secret until after the event, which will take place as soon as Amber turns twenty-one in two weeks time.'

Marriage? To Benedict – this titled stranger with his pleasing manners and looks. But he couldn't be that perfect, else some other woman would have claimed him by now. 'My Lord,' she said, 'Do you have any imperfections I should be told about?'

'Not one.' And he laughed when Emma snorted.

'I haven't agreed to this yet,' she said in a tired voice, for she felt rather strange.

Benedict caught her as her knees buckled, and his voice came from far away, 'When you've thought it over I'm sure you will...'

## SIX

As Benedict had requested of his parents, the reason behind his decision to wed had not been revealed, even to his sisters.

It was better for Amber Rose to think he was attracted by her charms, which he couldn't fail to be, than for her to know that the initial approach had stemmed from something entirely mercenary.

Amber been orphaned at birth. She'd recently lost her grandfather, her home and most of her possessions, which from necessity had been left behind. She'd also taken on the responsibility of a child. Jake would need feeding, clothing and educating for the foreseeable future. Benedict had appeared at the precise moment she'd needed help, and he knew she felt beholden to him. There could be no objection to the marriage on her part. Not only was he a desirable suitor, one of higher social standing than she'd have expected to marry, but her back was now to the wall. She'd be a fool to turn him down.

He smiled as he reasoned: If he allowed Amber to think she brought nothing to the marriage she'd be grateful when he redeemed her reputation through marriage and offered her the security of a comfortable home. Amber Rose Hartford needed him. It would also make life much more pleasant if she fell in love with him.

Now Benedict had made his mind up to the course he was about to embark on nothing was going to change his mind. He paced up and down at the bottom of the stairs like an expectant father. What the devil was going on up there? Surely the girl had recovered from her faint by now.

It was another twenty minutes before Emma came down, her face set to scowl like a thunderstorm. '*Men!*' she scorned as she flew past him.

He caught her by the wrist on the way back, allowing a maidservant carrying a box of medicines and unctions to go on alone. 'What's the matter with her, Emma?'

'The girl's body is so bruised you can hardly see her flesh. She must have been in extreme discomfort. The person who did this to her should be flogged.'

'She didn't say anything.'

Emma snorted. 'Of course she didn't. You're a man and a stranger to her, she could hardly have revealed her body to you. It wouldn't have been circumspect. Really, Bennet. Knowing the girl had been mishandled, you should have *guessed*.'

When he'd thought of Amber Rose's body it was always the picture of dainty, curvaceous perfection he'd spied through the kitchen window in the first place.

'Bennet, this is serious business. You should have shot those felons out of hand. If they come here I'll certainly give them short shrift. Now, will you please stop hovering like an expectant father, and leave. And why are you wearing that ghastly grin?'

'A stray thought amused me, nothing more.'

'Which was?'

He lied, and teased, 'I was thinking what a scold you're becoming. I do believe you would give them short shrift. But, Emma dearest, these men are no respecters of women. You've seen what they can do, so I beg you ... do be cautious.'

She touched his face. 'Don't worry on my account little brother, that's Archie's job. You know I'm more bark than bite. Amber will be more comfortable when she's bathed and has rested. No doubt she'll recover in time for dinner. I'm not quite sure what to do with Jake. I've put him in the nursery for now and he can take lessons with my children and be part of their routine while he's here. As soon as Amber is settled I'll find him something more suitable to wear. There will be some garments John has outgrown.'

She hesitated, then said. 'Amber has made it clear that she's attached to the lad. If I may be frank...'

He nodded. When had she been anything less?

'Worthy and polite though Jake is, he is not one of us. Do you intend to make him part of your household staff eventually, or will he be your ward?'

'I haven't given it any thought.'

'Then you should, Benedict. I gather the pair of them have only known each other a little while. It would be easier and kinder to both of them if you decided on his future before the bond between them strengthens, and before you venture into matrimony.'

'Amber seems fond of him.'

'She's guided by a soft heart. But you and she will have children of your own to consider in time, and they will take precedence. Jake will then be the odd one out.'

'The cuckoo in the nest?'

'Exactly. Such situations can be troublesome because they're a breeding ground for envy. If you intend to provide for Jake then take my advice and send him to a school that will educate him in a manner that will enable him to earn his living. He can spend time away from his studies with you, and later, you'll be able to use your contacts to secure him employment. Such an arrangement will allow him to grow up looking upon you as his benefactor rather than his father. He will be much happier for knowing his place.'

Her advice made good sense to Benedict. 'Thank you, Em. I'm sorry to be such a nuisance.' His humble tone brought a suspicious glance from her and he was hard put not to laugh.

'What use are sisters if brothers can't put upon them?' she said loftily, and kissed his cheek. 'Now, stop loitering in the hall. Go and find Archie's man; tell him he's to raid my husband's wardrobe and tidy you up in time for dinner. You resemble a ruffian at the moment.'

Emma organized her household efficiently. Reassured, as well as given a definite purpose in life, Benedict ambled off to carry out her instructions.

Lying in a bath, the warm, scented water was a soothing balm against her bruised skin. It was heaven, Amber thought. All her worries and cares, along with the ache from the journey were seeping away from her. Patrick seemed like a world away. Two maids bustled about, one making the bed up, the other unpacking her toiletries.

'It's wonderful to be so pampered,' she said to her hostess, who was inspecting the clothes that the maid had taken from the wicker basket. 'I never want to emerge from this bath.'

'I'm afraid you will have to if you want some dinner.' Emma glanced at the little clock on the mantelpiece. 'You can have ten minutes more, then we must dry you and tend to your bruises.' She tut-tutted. 'Your gowns are quite grubby.'

'I'm sorry. All the servants were dismissed from Hartford House, and although I've been doing my best to keep my clothing clean I'm not very good at it.'

'That's because you were not raised to be a maid. Jessie, take these gowns away and tell the laundry maid to see to them. Miss Hartford will wear the grey silk with the blue embroidery and puff sleeves tonight, since it appears to be clean, and that sweet little matching fringed stole with it. See if you can get rid of the creases.'

'Yes, My Lady.' Jessie departed with Amber's clothes.

As a guest in Emma's house Amber was in no position to protest at her host's high-handed manner, even if she hadn't been naked. But she forgave the woman when she said. 'I'm so glad Bennet brought you here, Amber. What a trial you've been through.' She gave a little smile. 'My brother has just told me I'm turning into a scold, so I must watch my tongue.'

'Do you always do what Benedict tells you?'

Emma gave a huff of laughter. 'He'd never stop laughing if he heard you say that. He was teasing. He said that Caroline and I bullied him so much as children that he couldn't breathe without orders after we married. Not true, of course. Bennet is a law unto himself despite his quiet demeanour. He is like our father so I'm sure he'll make you an affectionate husband. He must have fallen in love as soon as he set eyes on you, since he's showed no inclination to wed up until now.'

And that must have been when he looked

though the kitchen window and saw her standing in nothing but her skin. Already pink from the warm water, Amber hoped Emma didn't notice her blush. Goodness, did he intend to wed her because he'd inadvertently compromised her!

She certainly didn't believe Benedict's statement that he'd visited Hartford House to propose marriage to her in the first place. A man like him would have women swooning at his feet, and she had neither property or dowry enough to attract a man of his status, or even tempt one to pursue such a union. But why *had* he visited? Burning with curiosity she knew she must see him alone and have an answer from him before he left.

*Benedict would make an affectionate husband?* Emma had said. Amber's glance fell on the blush pink rose he'd unexpectedly presented her with that morning, and even though it was beginning to wilt she felt warmed by the gesture. He was a man of great charm, and it had been a sweet gesture from him.

The clock chimed the hour, enabling Amber to change the subject. 'Time to get out of the bath, I'm sad to say.'

Emma signalled to the older maid who advanced with a large white bath sheet held up for her to step into. 'This is Annie who works in the laundry. Annie previously worked for a theatrical lady, so will be your maid while you're here. She will see to your injuries. I'll return for you in an hour or so. We will visit the children in the nursery and say goodnight to them before we join Bennet in the drawing room before dinner.'

'Is that where Jake is?'

'Yes, my dear. He will have my daughters for company. I daresay they'll enjoy the novelty, since their elder brother John is away at school. Ah ... here comes Jessie with your gown. Let me see it, Jessie. Yes, you've made an excellent job of it. Place it carefully over that chair. I need you to help me change and do my hair before you go back down.'

The pair swept from the room in a stir of air.

As Annie gently patted her dry, Amber asked her. 'Did you enjoy working for a theatrical lady?'

'No, Miss Hartford. She had a lovely voice, right enough, but she put on airs and graces in public. When we were alone she was very coarse in her ways. She had a dreadful temper and threw pots of powder and stuff, at me. It would go over everything and she'd expect me to clean it up.' Annie lowered her voice. 'She entertained men ... in private ... for money.'

'She sang to them in private? How odd.'

Smothering a grin Annie hastily spread a towel on the bed and picked up another. 'Would you lie on the sheet please, Miss Hartford. I'll place this one over you for the sake of modesty, while I see to your injuries. Just in case anyone comes in.'

Annie had a soothing, gentle touch as she applied witch hazel to the smaller bruises, and soothing salve to the grazed areas of skin. Amber's knees were bruised and scratched from crawling, and they ached. Annie massaged aromatic oil into the rest of her body.

Then it was into her darned hose, a clean chemise and her gown. With a deft touch the maid dressed her hair, drawing the length of it up to the crown and fashioning it into a fall of ringlets. 'You have lovely hair, Miss,' she said, tying the last decorative blue ribbon in place. 'It's so dark and lustrous. Will you wear your pearl necklace?'

'Thank you, Annie. I appreciate what you've done. You're very talented.'

Annie deftly attached the earrings, and smiled at Amber's reflection in the mirror when she fastened the pearls around her neck. 'It's my pleasure, Miss. If you don't mind me saying so, you have lovely features.'

As Annie began to bustle about putting things away, Emma came to collect her to take her to the nursery. Emma's eyes mirrored approval of her appearance. 'That's better. A pity about the bruise on your face and the scratches on your neck. No doubt they will soon fade, though.'

The nursery was on the upper floor. Jake was resplendent in a sailor suit. His hair had been trimmed and was brushed neatly to one side. He smiled with relief when he saw her.

Two adorable-looking blue eyed girls, one older than the other but wearing identical gowns, hugged Emma, then curtseyed to Amber when she was introduced.

The older one was called Charlotte, and she trilled, 'Jake told us you were kidnapped by bad men and he helped our uncle rescue you, Miss

Hartford. How thrilling that must have been.'

Jake assumed a look of casual self-importance and Amber smiled at him. 'They were both very brave.'

'I would have been scared,' Susannah lisped. 'Do you want to see our dolls' house?'

'Yes, I'd love to see it.'

But before she could Jake sidled over to her and whispered, 'Do I have to sleep here, Miss Amber?'

'The arrangement is part of Lady Stratton's routine for her own children. So yes, while we are guests here you must try to fit in, and do everything the nursery maid says. Tomorrow you'll have lessons. You'll like that.'

His eyes brightened.

They stayed for half an hour and Amber could see that Jake felt a little out of place.

To excuse any quirk of behaviour he might display in advance, she said on the way downstairs, 'Jake used to have a brother, they attended the school where his father taught. He's grown used to having his independence since he lost his family, and is mature in his thinking.'

'Nevertheless, the boy has retained the good manners of his class, and he has an honest air about him. He's of an impressionable age, something which could work against him if he fell into the wrong hands. He's lucky you've become his benefactor, Amber. A boarding school will be the making of him.'

'I had not thought ... I cannot afford school fees.'

A glance came her way. 'You should discuss the

90

situation with Bennet. It might be a good idea to send Jake to board at the school he attended previously. He will feel familiar with it, and therefore be more comfortable in the position he finds himself in.'

Discuss it with Benedict? She hadn't even decided to marry him yet. But what other option did she have? School for Jake was an ideal solution if she did marry him. But he might not want to support Jake! Besides, it would be crazy to marry a man she'd only just met. She'd be crazy not to, she thought as she entered the drawing room and set eyes on him again.

Benedict had been sitting at the long windows gazing out into the garden. He turned and rose to his feet when they entered, looking breathtakingly handsome in a dark blue cutaway coat, grey trousers and tied cravat. Her heart did a rather odd dance and she smiled with the pleasure of seeing him so resplendant.

He crossed the floor in half a dozen strides, took up her hand and kissed it. His glance sought hers. 'You look entirely exquisite, Amber Rose. Have you recovered completely from your collapse?'

She had, but was now in danger of him taking her breath away. 'Thank you, yes. It was tiredness, that's all. The last day or two have been stressful.'

'Then you'll now have time to relax.' He offered her his arm, the other to Emma.

A smile flitted across his sister's face. 'I need to go to the kitchen, so you will have to entertain Amber in my absence. I have the feeling there will be two extra guests for dinner.'

He nodded, seemingly not in the least surprised by his sister's remark. As for Amber, she welcomed the few moments she'd have alone with him as he seated her on the little blue velvet sofa, and himself next to her, so his warmth became hers and the lemony scent of his skin was drawn into her body with every inward breath.

'What shall we talk about, Amber?'

'There's something I wish to ask you ... two things really?'

'I thought there might be. Go ahead.'

'Did you see me in the kitchen when I was ... was...'

'As naked as the day you were born?' he said, giving a faint grin as he helped her out. 'In all truthfulness, yes I did. But I don't make a habit of peering through windows in case I come across a naked woman. Fortune happened to favour me that day for she delighted me with a glimpse of what was available to me.'

'Oh, I was certainly not on display, nor am I available to you!' Blood rushed to her face and she hung her head.

'Forgive me, it was a bad choice of words, and I'm sorry if I offended your sensibilities.' A finger inserted under her chin lifted her face up to his. His eyes were compelling in their blueness. 'You needn't be ashamed that I saw you thus. You have a flawless body, my Aphrodite, and your modesty is laudable. All the same, I look forward to the day when I can take advantage of what you have to offer a man.'

'Oh, you grow more impertinent by the second.'

'Would you prefer me to lie to you?'

Her eyes widened when he grinned. Would she? 'No, I would not, but you are too familiar on so slight an acquaintance.'

'And were we to marry today I'd be even more familiar.'

No doubt he would. 'Why did you say you'd come to Hartford House to propose marriage to me?'

'Ah yes, I admit that was a lie.'

Dismay rushed through her. Vexed by her own inconsistencies, she thought: Make up your mind, Amber. Do you want him or do you not?

'But not that much of a lie. I had actually gone to Hartford House to see if I liked you enough to propose marriage. When I saw you standing there in nothing but your little pink skin I knew I did.' The eyes that held her gaze were brimming with laughter. 'There, milady ... the truth, the whole truth and nothing but the impertinent truth. Your derriere bobbed so prettily when you took fright and ran away.'

She tried not to giggle but didn't quite succeed. 'You are outrageous. You know very well that by the time I ran I was dressed.' She was laughing now. 'And if you tell anyone of that incident I shall strangle you with my bare hands. Why did you tell Patrick there was an agreement between us?'

He chuckled. 'A slip of the tongue to distract him. Actually, it was an agreement made by our respective grandfathers when we were children. They took it upon themselves to arrange a match between us. His glance slid to her mouth and he smiled. 'May I kiss you?'

'Certainly not, I've never been kissed.' She remembered Stephen Gould forcing his mouth on her and shuddered as she added, 'At least, not willingly.' But Benedict wasn't forcing her, he was using persuasion. She wanted to be kissed by him, and yet she didn't. She whispered, 'I didn't enjoy being kissed the first time, so I doubt if I would enjoy it the second time.'

He moved so there was only a fraction of space between their mouths and his breath shivered against her lower lip. 'Are you quite sure you don't want to find out?'

How would it feel if their mouths were touching one to another? The anticipation was excruciating and the need to continue forward to the next intimate step sent a strong thrill of excitement through her.

'No, I'm not sure, at all.'

His hands cupped her face, the fingers splayed across her cheekbones, his thumbs lying along her jaw. His little fingers caressed the contours of her lips then gently rested against the corners, keeping her mouth parted slightly. His lips touched against hers, soft and tender. Closing her eyes in quivering delight she savoured the magic of the awakening inside her. The tip of his tongue flicked against her bottom lip like the lash of a tiny whip designed for pleasure rather than pain.

She opened her eyes when the kiss came to an end.

'How do you feel about it now?' he said, his

voice like smoke.

He'd shown her what desire was and she'd never felt more alive in her life. A tiny smile played around her mouth. If this was being courted, she liked it! 'Your kiss is a tease, an invitation to sin, Benedict. It has warned me I could acquire a craving for more, and eventually you might become an addiction.'

'Amber Rose, for one who has led a sheltered life you've turned out to be a delectable hussy who tells a man exactly what he wants to hear.' He laughed and gently kissed the bruise on her face before he let her go. 'But by teasing you I'm teasing myself, and now is not the time to pursue this course. May I offer you a glass of sherry?'

He rose and strolled over to the decanter when he heard the patter of footsteps on the tiles in the hall, and filled three glasses from the decanter.

Emma called out. 'Here's Caro. I knew she'd come.'

There was the sound of a carriage and snorting horses. The front door opened and shut. Children's voices fluted a greeting and a woman's voice cried out. 'Emma darling! Where is the young woman Bennet has chosen? I'm dying to meet her. What's she like?'

'Shush, not so loud, Caro. She'll hear you.'

The voice lowered just a fraction. 'What a sly dog that brother of ours is. I'll never forgive Bennet for bringing her here first, will I Kitt, darling?'

'So you say, my love,' a deep voice rumbled. 'Is Bennet in the drawing room, Emma?'

'Do go on in, Kitt. Come, bring the children, Caro. I'm sure the nursery maid will be able to find room for them. Edward, there's a boy of your age staying, and I want you to be specially nice to him because he's lost his entire family.'

'Then who will look after him, Aunt Emma?'

'Your Uncle Bennet will.'

'Can I see Uncle Bennet?'

'In the morning. It's way past your bedtime. You must come and see the girls before they go to bed, Caro, otherwise they'll never forgive me. You are staying the night, aren't you?'

'Of course. It's ages since I last saw you. We have so much to catch up on.'

'I could have sworn you saw each other a week ago,' Kitt said.

'Nonsense, Kitt. It's been at least ten days.'

'I stand corrected,' he rumbled.

Benedict had a smile on his face as the door opened and the man in question poked his head around the door. 'Ah, there you are Bennet. I'm not interrupting anything am I?'

Benedict flicked her a smile that spoke of the intimacy they'd just enjoyed. 'Not at the moment.'

'The girls have gone up to the nursery. No doubt they'll gossip for half an hour before they come down,' the man rumbled. 'I do hope that sherry is the amontillado I gave Archie for his birthday.'

The reason for the three glasses became clear.

'It is,' he said. 'May I introduce Miss Hartford. Amber Rose, this is my brother-in-law, Kitt Foster. Wine Merchant.'

A man of medium size with soft brown eyes and matching hair took her hand in his and kissed it. He smiled as he let it go. 'I say, Bennet, what an absolute charmer.'

'Yes, I'm inclined to agree.' He handed them both a sherry.

Kitt raised his glass. 'I understand congratulations are in order. Welcome to the family, Miss Hartford.'

She hadn't agreed to the marriage yet; indeed, Benedict hadn't even proposed to her in a manner she'd consider to be acceptable. A quick glance at Benedict found contemplative, but confidant eyes resting on her. He was too used to having things his own way, she thought and smiled slightly as she answered, 'Thank you. You're most kind, if a little premature, Mr Foster. Nothing is settled yet, for a proposal has been neither made or accepted.'

Benedict sighed.

A little later Caroline and Emma came into the drawing room together. They were arm in arm and wore gowns in a similar shade of pale lavender.

There was a chuckle from Benedict when the pair came straight to where she was seated. One of them said, 'Amber Rose, may I introduce my sister, Caroline Foster.'

Their eyes were rounded with innocence, but there was an air of repressed excitement about them.

They were identical twins; how disconcerting. But no, this was something they must have done hundreds of times, for how would they have been able to resist it. And there had been a small clue.

She said to the speaker, 'Forgive me if I'm wrong, but I do believe it's you who is Caroline Foster.'

The pair looked at each other and grinned before Emma said, 'And of course, you're right, Amber. Hardly anyone can tell us apart. What gave us away, that little brown freckle on my forehead?'

She'd remember that for next time. 'I thought it would be something twins might do, but mostly it was because Benedict laughed and alerted me.'

'Amber Rose must have read my mind,' Benedict said.

'Not entirely. I remembered admiring the lace on Emma's sleeves earlier, and the lace on your gown is slightly different in design, Caroline.'

'See how compatible Amber and Bennet are,' Emma said to Caroline. 'I saw it straight away. A sort of empathy exists between them.'

Caroline hugged her. 'You must allow Emma and myself to help organize your wedding.'

Now it was Amber's turn to sigh. As if one of the twins wasn't formidable enough, now there were two to contend with.

# SEVEN

Although she was not used to a social life Amber soon relaxed, drawn by the warmth and friendliness of Benedict's family.

Dinner was a welcome event, for although she'd eaten a huge breakfast at the inn she hadn't had anything since.

Between them, Benedict's sisters and their husbands managed to bring her out of her shyness as they entertained one other, mostly with chatter. But Amber was more of a listener than a participant.

The twins were irrepressible as they acted out an amusing skit.

Amber was persuaded to play the piano and sing. She chose a John Dowland song, *Sorry, Stay*, and was sure her nervousness showed in her voice.

Benedict surprised her by sliding into the seat beside her. He said, 'That was a little melancholy. Do you know *My Beautiful Amaryllis?*'

She nodded and began to play while he sang. His voice was pleasing as he sung the love song in his deep voice. '*Amaryllis, my beautiful one, do you not believe ... that you are my beloved.*'

Caroline sighed when the last note died away. 'I wish you'd sing to me like that, Kitt.'

'Do you, dear? Perhaps I'll take singing lessons.'

'I didn't know you could sing so well, Bennet,'

Emma cried out in amazement.

Benedict led her back to the sofa, took a seat beside her and chuckled. 'Neither did I.'

Outside, darkness began to draw in and the candles were lit. The family began to talk about their youth.

'Do you remember when Bennet hid a frog in his governess' bed?' Caroline said, grinning at Emma.

'And Miss Grimley told papa he deserved a flogging.'

Benedict's deep voice cut in. 'While father whacked the stuffing out of the back of the chair I screamed as loud as I could. I can't remember him ever thrashing me, but when he chastised me his voice was always so stern that he scared me witless.'

'Our mother would never have forgiven him if he'd thrashed any of us. Lordy, Bennet, you used to try his temper at times though. When you were six you stood at the nursery window and threw a dish of water over the head of Bishop Quilby, who was talking to papa in the garden.'

'If I did, I imagine one of you must have put me up to it.'

'It was her,' they said together, grinning as they pointed at each other.

Benedict shook with laughter. His closeness was disconcerting, Amber thought, for it enticed her to move closer. She could feel his warmth, and she kept remembering the kiss they'd shared ... oh, how she remembered it, she thought, closing her eyes to savour the soft touch of his mouth against hers, over again.

She smiled to herself as the conversation continued with their childhood misdemeanours being brought out and aired. She wondered what it would have been like to have been raised with siblings by two loving parents instead of a grandfather who was unable to provide the female guidance a young girl needed. She'd often felt lonely, for she'd been schooled at home and had never been given the opportunity to make friends of her own age.

It could have been worse, she supposed. If her grandfather had left her in Italy she'd being spending much of her day in religious contemplation and prayer. Would the training have been enough to dampen her streak of rebellion and her new-found desire to savour life to its fullest? If she wasn't in love with Benedict now, she thought she soon would be. It was a problem not knowing how to behave in his presence.

Her thoughts were too pleasant to let go of and she allowed them to drift where they would. Gradually, the voices faded away to a pleasant buzz...

'Amber Rose,' somebody whispered against her ear.

Benedict, she thought, and smiled. Then her eyes flew open and she discovered that her head rested comfortably against his shoulder and he'd slid his arm around her for support. He was looking down at her. Her instinct was to turn her face up to his to be kissed. Just in time she remembered where she was. 'My pardon.' Jerking upright she gazed at her hostess, mortified. 'How rude of me to fall asleep. I'm so sorry.'

'Don't be, Amber dear. I should have realized you'd be tired after all you've gone through. We were about to take coffee and play cards, but if you'd prefer to retire we'll quite understand.'

'Thank you. I would like to retire if I may.'

'Then Bennet will escort you to your room and place you in the capable hands of Annie.'

Amber rose a fraction after Benedict. 'Thank you all for a pleasant evening. I hope to be more lively company tomorrow.'

'Can you forgive me?' she said when the door closed behind them.

'For what?'

'You know very well for what. I fell asleep.'

'I can forgive you for anything.' He took her hand in his and they walked up the staircase together.

She pressed against his side. 'After what happened to me at Hartford House the shadows seem full of menace. I had not thought to feel so vulnerable now the danger has passed.'

He seated himself on the top step and pulled her down beside him. 'Try not to worry. The house will be locked up tight and armed men will patrol the ground floor at night. Now, there's something I need to ask you.'

'What is it?'

'I've come to the conclusion that I've been presumptuous, expecting you to wed me when we've only just met.'

All noise was drowned out by the loud beating of her heart. She realized she was holding her breath, so expelled it and gently drew in another. 'If that's what my grandfather really wanted, then

I'll obey his wishes.'

'I'd rather you married me because you held me in some regard.'

'I hold you in great regard, but we've only known each other for two days so you can't expect a miracle.'

'Why not?'

She laughed. 'My Lord, did you not state that you came to take stock of me, as if I was a mare you were selecting for the horse stud you told me about? This was with the view to offering matrimony. Then when you saw me you were overcome by your desire for me.'

Laughter filled his eyes. 'My pardon for making such a crass statement.'

'You know very well that you didn't make it. You were a little more subtle. Is it the truth?'

'That I desire you? It most certainly is.'

'Have you offered marriage to any other women you've desired?'

He shrugged, uncomfortable with the thought of discussing anything quite so personal with her. 'Now you're talking of love rather than desire. Desire doesn't attract love, and I'm well aware that it can be satisfied without love. I do believe that love invites desire, though.'

'But that hasn't happened in your case, yet.'

'Hasn't it? I can't recall saying that I've never been in love.'

'Oh!' She felt unreasonably miffed at the thought that he might have loved a woman. 'Obviously there's more to choosing a wife than just desirability. I must point out that I have nothing. No dowry, no property or title, just the

103

clothes on my back. Would you offer me marriage because some misguided gentlemanly code of conduct suggests that you may have compromised me? If so, please allow me to release you from it.'

'The agreement between our grandfathers–'

'Ah, the agreement. I cannot understand why you believe an agreement between our grandfathers is binding. In fact, I'm doubting that such an agreement exists. Will you not show it to me?'

'When I return I'll bring it with me.' He stood, pulling her to her feet. 'You're overwrought, and it's my fault, for my intentions were not made clear to you. I do want you to be my wife, but I was premature in thinking you were ready to accept such a proposal. Now, I must go down to the drawing room. There's the door to your room, I'll wait here until you're safely inside.'

'Thank you for your proposal. Will you not kiss me goodnight?'

Surprise came into his eyes and even in the shadows she saw the smile the played around his mouth. 'Do you want me too?'

'Does it surprise you to realize I can also feel desire ... although I must admit, I didn't know what it was until I met you.'

He chuckled and drew her close. 'You're the damnedest creature, with a talent for tying me up in knots I've been looking at your mouth all evening, longing to take a bite from it. So, yes, I certainly will kiss you goodnight.'

If she'd thought she'd experienced desire before, he now proved her wrong. His mouth scorched her, so fire ran through her veins to heat every portion of her body. Then, as he let her go his head dipped down and he breathed a kiss against each breast bringing each nub pushing against her bodice. Lord, every part of her was asking for more, she was moist at her centre and her thighs were trembling so much she could hardly stand.

'Oh, that was so unfair,' she said, and for her own survival was about to push him away when he straightened and took a step back, saying, 'Goodnight, My beautiful Amaryllis. Sleep well.'

'You know I will not, you wretch,' she scolded, and she removed herself to the door of her room. When he began to descend the staircase she whispered, but loudly enough for him to hear, 'I'll consider your presumption.'

Turning, he gazed up at her. 'Did you say something?'

Entering her room she closed the door behind her and leaned against the door panel, a grin on her face and her finger against her mouth so Annie wouldn't talk and interrupt the moment when her words sank in.

'I'll be damned,' he said, and after a moment of silence he began to laugh.

After Archie arrived home the next afternoon, and he'd greeted his wife, his children, and had been introduced to Amber, he then disappeared into his study with Kitt and Benedict. Benedict placed the problem of the marital agreement and the loan before his brothers-in-law.

105

From his position behind the desk, Archie said, 'Now let me get this straight, Bennet. Amber Rose Hartford – a young woman you met just three days ago – has accepted your proposal of marriage.'

'Yes ... well almost. She has little choice, since it's the best thing for her.'

'And you disregarded the wishes of her guardian and have absconded with her? Now the pair of you are being pursued by her guardian and two companions, who sound to be an unsavoury lot.'

'Exactly. Except Patrick Hartford has not been appointed her guardian by any court. He cares nought for her. He's assumed her wardship because I thwarted the attempt of himself and his friends to ruin her by using her as sport.'

Kitt rumbled, 'Is the girl wealthy?'

'She has nothing. At least ... nothing she knows of. It's a rather complicated affair.' He explained. 'Now her cousin has got wind of it, I'm afraid. All my fault, of course.'

'Ah, I see. You stand to lose your home and horse stud over this.' Archie grinned cheerfully at him. 'If you'll take my advice you'll obtain a special licence from a bishop and wed her as soon as possible. At least when this cousin of hers gets around to shooting you, her widowhood will be a comfortable one and she'll get her just dues. And it would serve you right.'

'You'll change your mind when Emma tells you of the damage Miss Hartford sustained. No woman should be treated so badly. While Patrick is at large I fear for her – and my livelihood, of course. There's a possibility that Hartford can lay claim to Brierly House. And I need to speak to my father and inform him of the actions I've taken, and the likely outcome. I can't take Amber there because it's the first place they'll think of after they've been to my home. It's possible they're lying in wait for me along the road, though I'm hoping to get to Laconbridge before them, then on to Brierly House.'

Archie chuckled. 'Will your father believe you've fallen in love at first sight.'

'He'll probably think history has repeated itself.' Benedict grinned broadly. 'I can't recall saying I'd fallen in love with Amber Rose Hartford.'

'You didn't have to. It's written all over your face every time you speak of her, for her name slides off your tongue like a caress. As for the lady in question...'

Now it was Kitt's turn to grin. 'The girl is dewy-eyed over you, like a peach ripe for the plucking.'

'And I intend to pluck her from the tree as soon as possible, Kitt. Once she's mine Patrick Hartford won't have a leg to stand on. The man's a wastrel.'

'Have you told Amber that the reason behind the proposal is entirely mercenary?' Archie inquired, one eyebrow arched.

Benedict gazed at his brother-in-law, his eyes revealing the trouble he had absorbing such a concept. 'Oh, hell, I suppose I must sound mercenary, and it may have been that way to start with, but it's hardly that now,' he protested.

'Amber Rose stands too high in my estimation. You were right, Archie, I have fallen in love with her, but I'm still growing used to the idea. Damn it, I've never felt about any woman like this. She's robbed me of a brain and I'm acting purely on instinct.'

Kitt's laughter was a deep, warm rumble. 'Women have a tendency to train men like dogs. Eventually, we jump over a stick every time they snap their fingers and we end up drooling and wagging our tails like fools when they tickle us under the chin.'

Benedict grinned at the thought of any woman turning him into a slave. It would be the other way around when they were wed! If Amber Rose wanted to learn what desire was all about he'd tie her to the mattress for the first week or so.

He grinned, placing the agreeable thought to one side. 'Nevertheless, a man must protect his property and I've had a good offer for Brierly House. Be damned if I'm going to allow Hartford to profit from it. In fact, I'm after the property he's just inherited if it comes on the market. I'll make a fair offer for it. I haven't informed Amber of the business reason behind this, and neither will I.'

'Let's hope she doesn't find out then.'

'Besides myself, only you two, my parents and the lawyer, Dunstan, know about the loan arrangement at this time. Let's hope it stays that way. I must be off.'

Archie held out his hand to him. 'Don't worry, Bennet I'll make sure your lady love is kept busy and adequately guarded in your absence. Just take care of yourself.'

Words echoed by Kitt, who slapped him on the back.

Then he had to run the gauntlet of his sisters, who parted with him with tears in their eyes and words of wisdom, as though he'd be gone for a year instead of a few days.

Amber Rose stood back a little way, as if she wasn't sure of her place. 'We've hardly spent a moment alone together. Walk with me to the end of the carriageway,' he said, taking her hand in his.

His sisters burst into laughter when she said drily, 'Then you'll have to walk me back to the house, and we'll be walking up and down the carriageway all day.'

Such a delicious sense of the ridiculous should be captured in a bottle. He grinned, then kissed her hand and gazed awkwardly at her, holding it, palm against his chest.

The trouble with being part of a family, he thought, was that a man wasn't given any privacy – couldn't do his courting without everyone look-ing on, giving advice and making him look like a fool for feeling like he did.

All he wanted to do was kiss that soft mouth, long and hard enough to heat and crush the honey from her lips. Then he could taste the essence of her against his tongue on his journey.

Acting on a whim he took the ring from his little finger and placed it on her middle one. 'A keepsake until I can replace it with something better.'

Unexpectedly, she stood on her toes and kissed

him, a dry dusting of her mouth against his like the wings of a butterfly. So chaste it was that it brought the urge to ravish her into awareness. And her mouth so teasing he knew that even in her innocence she was aware of him and would react to his attention with a pleasing passion when the time came.

When she whispered in her prim, country mouse voice, 'You may release my hand now, Benedict. I shall look forward to your safe return,' he could only smile at her before he mounted the impatient Juniper, who danced prettily and whickered in anticipation of the exercise.

Benedict pulled the beast's head around and set him to the walk, then, because he was pulling at the reins, into a canter. He turned to wave at Amber, and she blew him a kiss to take with him.

It was a fine morning. The air was perfumed and the verdant landscape displayed a kaleido-scope of shining flowers, as though they'd come down with a shower of rain and speared into the earth.

He'd never seen the beauty of the place so clearly before. Everything was clean, fresh and new to him. He ignored the road and cut across the heath. He'd take the path through the forest, he thought, there was less chance of being accosted.

Amber had watched Benedict go, a man dressed in black on a horse of shining darkness, a man still a stranger to her, but one she felt part of. She didn't know what she'd done to deserve him. He'd arrived at the moment when her future had

110

looked bleak and had taken her life and future happiness and made it his quest. It was as if fate had preordained them.

'God, keep him safe,' she whispered and caressed the ring he'd placed on her finger.

Emma and Caroline had come up, one either side of her. They slid their arms around her waist. She reciprocated by doing the same to them, making them all part of each other.

'If I seem reserved at times I hope you'll forgive me,' she said. 'I've been living with my grandfather since I was a baby. He entertained infrequently, and then it was with older people. I'm used to a life of solitude and have learned to be content with my own company.'

'Oh, my dear, we're as garrulous as geese when we're together, so you must get over your shyness,' Caroline told her. 'We're only family, after all, and you are almost one of us. Our mother has longed for the time when Bennet decided to settle down. You're perfect for him, and I'm sure our mother and father will adore you as much as we do.'

Identical kisses landed on each of her cheeks, then Emma said, 'You mustn't worry about anything. We're going to play a game of cricket with the children, then have a picnic in the pavillion. Will you join us?'

The warmth of the welcome and the effort they were making to take her mind off her troubles brought tears to Amber's eyes.

'Yes ... that would be lovely,' she said.

Patrick was still at Hartford House. He'd been

furious when he'd discovered that the girl had fled. He'd wrecked her room. Smashing the mirror on her dressing table against the wall, he'd then ripped the lacy bed hangings to shreds and had torn asunder every item she'd left behind.

Stephen Gould picked up the remains of a lace chemise, and in a way which made Patrick feel sick, inhaled the scent of her body like a bloodhound. Slipping it inside his waistcoat he said softly, 'I want this cousin of yours at any cost, Patrick. She's a beauty, and she has spirit.'

Patrick's conscience needled him. Stephen was unstoppable once he'd set his mind to something. Yet he sensed an opportunity in his companion's words.

'You'll have to wed her first, and without dowry. And you'll have to cancel my debts. You know how I'm situated.'

Stephen's eyes narrowed, then he began to laugh. 'When I said any cost that referred to her. Your cousin's virginity is not worth such a sacrifice on my part and you will not shed your debt to me that easily. The game will be in hunting her down and running her to earth. I wonder where Costain has taken her. What about the Italian aunts? Would he have taken her there?'

'To Italy? As I recall there's only one of the black widows still breathing. They disowned Amber when she was born. Family honour and all that.' Which reminded Patrick his own honour had been tarnished by Amber's flight. 'I'll kill Benedict Costain for absconding with her when I get hold of him, challenge him to a duel,' he muttered with more bravado than conviction.

112

'Do that and you'll die,' Stephen drawled. 'Stop being such a bore, would you. There's nothing to do here now your business is finished. Come on, let's drag Jonas off that poxy tavern wench and go back to London to consult with your lawyer. If there's a marriage agreement between your cousin and the viscount he'd be aware of it.'

'Then why didn't he inform me of it?'

'Because there isn't any agreement. Costain tricked you. He's the type of man who puts some women on a pedestal while he cavorts with the more willing types. I hear he's quite popular with the society trollops, so I doubt if he feels the need to marry just yet.'

'But what was he doing at Hartford House in the first place? And where has he taken my cousin?'

'I imagine he was acquainted with the old man and he was here to offer his condolences. As for hiding your cousin – providing she went with him, Costain has a family and a wide circle of friends. She could be staying with any one of them.'

'*Providing* she went with him? It's obvious that she did.'

'Is it? She might have borrowed some money from him and fled to Italy, there to throw herself on the mercy of her mother's family. Or she might be hiding out with some local yokels.'

'If she was hiding locally, that thin-faced crow who's married to the churchman would know it. She's got eyes and ears everywhere and tells me that Amber has taken a London orphan into her care.'

'I'll send the sewer rat packing when we catch up with them. Thomas Dunstan can draw up an agreement of wardship between the girl and myself. Once I'm armed with that we'll go and find her.'

'And talking of money.' Taking aim, Patrick fired his pistol at the strong box. The ball dented the surface, then ricocheted back past Stephen and buried itself in the woodwork.

'You fool, Patrick, that just missed me. Come on, let's get out of here,' Stephen shouted, heading for the door.

Patrick swore, because, although he'd sold off everything of value he could fit into the carriage, including the monogrammed silver, he didn't like to leave the cash behind. He hesitated, then reluctantly followed Stephen out through the door. He brightened. When he reached London he intended to make good his losses at the gaming table. Lady luck favoured the brave and he couldn't remain unlucky for ever.

As the door slammed behind them the dusk stirred and eddied though the striped light of the empty spaces, then gradually drifted into the more quiet air currents. All that was left was the deep tock of the clock. Its tongue fell silent two days later when the eight day span of its mechanism wound down and there was nobody there to rewind it.

# EIGHT

Consolata Puzo received the sacrament, then took her last breath as the consecrated oil sealed the cross on her forehead. There was a smile on her face as she went to meet her maker, for the guilt she'd lived with for the past twenty-one years had been absolved by her penance. The resulting absolution had wiped her conscience free of stain, like a sheet emerging from the wash-tub.

The priest left the sister praying by her bedside and joined Alfredo Dominico by the window while the doctor pronounced absence of life. The churchman and the lawyer left together, stopping to briefly discuss the woman's will. The priest was satisfied that the orphanage would benefit from Consolata's death by the gift of the Puzo villa outside of town, which the orphans could run as a farm under supervision.

He didn't need to enquire as to where the rest of the estate would go. He'd received the contessa's confession. Despite his disappointment that the church hadn't inherited more, he conceded that it was a just legacy, even though his bishop might not agree with him when he was informed.

'She was a generous woman, the village will miss her,' the mayor said to the lawyer two days later as Consolata joined her husband in the Puzo family tomb. The event had been witnessed by most of the villagers. They had followed the flower-covered coffin, carried on the shoulders of several men. The cortege had been preceded by the village band down a winding hill of shops, the hills behind them littered by small farms and white villas.

The cemetery overlooked the sea, which was overlooked by the village of Cessina, which in turn was overlooked by the church. The village was not far from Turin.

'A pity there were no children to inherit. Strange that neither she nor her sister Orsola managed to breed before their respective husbands died. There was a rumour that they were still virgins when they were widowed.'

The mayor laughed. 'I wouldn't be surprised.'

The lawyer told him. 'Consolata named her niece as the main beneficiary. She is Lucia's daughter, after all, and the only surviving member of her family.'

'Lucia's daughter? *The Inglese bastardo!* But Consolata would never allow her to be mentioned in her presence.'

Alfredo smiled. 'Guilt is a powerful force, my friend. Ironic isn't it? The girl's name is Ambra Rosa Hartford, and she's no bastard. Her father died before she was born and her mother lived long enough to give the girl life before she followed him to the grave. The child was destined for the church before her English grandfather arrived to claim her. The late Lord Hartford has kept Consolata informed of her welfare all these years, and brought pressure to bear on Consolata

116

regarding her duty towards her niece. Now he is dead. By his own account, his successor is not a worthy man.'

'The Bishop thought Consolata's money would go to the church. She was very devout.'

'Most people did. She had two wills made out, both unsigned. One was in favour of the church, the other addressed her niece's needs. She signed the one in favour of the girl when she learned of the late Lord Hartford's demise. She said she regretted turning her sister away from her door and was grateful to the English lord for keeping her informed of the girl's progress.'

'A pity she was not acknowledged by her earlier.'

'Ambra Rosa is twenty-one years of age, so old enough to handle the fortune she's inherited. The contessa said she didn't want her niece to be at the beck and call of her English cousin – though an independent adviser is to be appointed. I thought her grandfather's lawyer could be retained for the purpose. He's old enough to be her father, by all accounts.'

'You'll go to England then?'

'I depart tomorrow. England is a miserable place when it rains, so I'm hoping for some fine weather.'

Benedict was surprised that Patrick Hartford hadn't caught up with him. Perhaps he'd thought better of pursuing Amber. She was, after all, of an age to make her own decisions.

The rain had started shortly after he'd set out from the Laconbridge estate. His horse had thrown a shoe and the pair of them now trudged through the mud and puddles. With still another mile to go before he reached Brierly House the weather had cooled considerably. Thunder rumbled in the distance.

Juniper whickered anxiously. He didn't like thunderstorms. 'It's all right, lad,' Benedict said, soothing him. 'We should be home before it catches up with us.' But the foliage suddenly started to rattle and Juniper shied as small balls of ice began to pepper down on them. Leading the horse under the shelter of the pines Benedict swore soundly.

The storm of hailstones was short-lived, but the sky was darkening ominously. It looked as though it was going to settle in for the night. Taking a chance, Benedict headed out into the grey, gusting day. He kept his horse on a tight rein, for the slightest sound sent him crabbing sideways and his muscles bunching with tension.

It wouldn't take much for the horse to attempt to buck him off. As they reached the gates Juniper whinnied loudly as the familiar smell of his stable reached his nostrils. Benedict dismounted in case there was ice on the cobbled yard. As he did there was a loud crack of thunder. His normally well-behaved horse squealed, then jerked his head and nearly pulled the rein from his hands as he bucked powerfully several times, his ears flattened to his head.

'Whoa ... no you don't.' Benedict handed the rein into the expert hands of one of the two grooms who came hurrying out. 'He's cast a shoe, and the storm has panicked him. He's ready to bolt.'

'Yes, My lord. A rub down and a good feed will settle him down, won't it Juniper?' They took a grip on his bridle either side and led him into his quarters, where he was greeted by his restless stable mates.

Benedict made a run for the house, jumping when a jagged arrow of lightning speared to the ground in the direction of where he'd been sheltering. Sparks and smoke shot skywards and there was a crack as a tree fell.

A footman opened the door and took his hat from him. The house was gloomy from the storm, the marble cold and uninviting. 'Light some lamps, Ben. Tell George I've gone to my room. I need a brandy and a warm bath, in that order. I'm soaked through.'

'Yes, sir.'

George joined him within a few minutes. He put a taper to the fire then helped peel the wet clothes from Benedict's body before handing him his robe. Sinking into his chair, Benedict sipped at the brandy, feeling it relax him right down to his toes as maids began to bustle in and out from the corridor with with kettles of hot water for the adjoining bathing room.

Soon he was immersed up to his shoulders, and he murmured with the sheer bliss of it. George smiled as he placed a second brandy on a table within reach of Benedict's hand, then removed himself to the bedroom to lay out fresh linens and clothes.

'Have there been any visitors in my absence,

George?' Benedict called out.

'Reverend Avery left his card,' George said, coming in with bath sheets to warm around the fire.

'He wasn't after my soul again, was he?'

'No, sir. He said the Bishop had told him you'd applied for a marriage licence. He wanted to congratulate you, and to tell you he'll be standing by to perform the ceremony at a moment's notice.'

'Damn it, that was quick. I only applied for a licence this morning before I visited the earl.' He thought of Amber and smiled ... why wait and allow her charms to go to waste?

'May I ask who the fortunate lady is, My Lord?'

Benedict gave a faint smile. 'When the young lady becomes my wife you'll realize that it's me who has the good fortune. In the meantime I'd be grateful if the rest of the staff were kept in ignorance.'

George Fildew was a neat, handsome man of middle years and fussy habits. The former tailor who had once been second valet to a Marquess, drew himself up. 'It would be beneath my dignity to gossip about you to anyone, My Lord.'

'Which is why I'm going to tell you her name. The lady is Miss Amber Rose Hartford of Dorset. Because she's in grave danger, if anyone comes looking for her you've never heard of her.' He just hoped the rest of the staff remained in ignorance.

'Indeed, I have not.' George gave him a critical look, then tutt-tutted. Opening the mahogany gentleman's dressing cabinet he laid out his master's shaving dish, then took out his razor and began to hone the blade on the leather strop.

Benedict was beginning to wish that he'd brought Amber Rose back to his home, that at this moment they were lying naked together, his hands on the pale mounds of her backside as they rose from the water, better to position her over his rapidly rising...

His shaft subsided woefully when George took a grip on his nose and began to lather his chin in a vigorous manner. Just as well really, since he couldn't put the randy creature to any good use at the moment. He was sure though, that Amber Rose would be a very good fit.

Nasally, he said, 'Do you have a nady friend, George?'

'Indeed I do, sir. I visit a widow in the village on Monday and Friday nights for a small consideration. She meets my needs adequately.'

'And you've never considered narriage?'

'To Mrs Pethan? Good lord ... certainly not!' For a moment George looked shaken, then he drew the razor smoothly along Benedict's jaw line and said delicately, 'I'm given to understand that Mrs Pethen has other regular visitors.'

'Ah ... I see.' He twitched his nose when George released it, expanding it with a deep breath as a warm flannel was wrapped around his face. He congratulated himself as he realized he'd never again need to seek out a woman willing to satisfy his needs.

While he was here he intended to talk over the possibility of a second stud with William Ross, his estate manager – in case he was able to purchase Hartford House. He had no intention of dragging him out in the storm though, which seemed to have increased in intensity.

The storm didn't abate, and later he sat and watched the glory of it in solitude from the drawing window. If Amber had been here she could have played for him. She had a deft touch on the keys, and her voice was pleasing. After the sociable din of his sister's home the silence of his own company was less than entertaining. Not having Amber to flirt with was proving irksome. She may have led a sheltered life but she could hone her wit to match his on occasion.

Questions and answers raced through his mind. What if Amber had been plain, dull and awkward? There was no point in dwelling on it, since she was none of those things. Then he wondered, what had motivated the two grandfathers to make such a bargain? Had the late Lord Hartford devised the scheme to protect his granddaughter, as it seemed? If so, he'd been an astute gentleman, for he'd arranged for her to marry into wealth and family far greater that his original investment.

And why had he been less than honest with Amber? He must show her their grandfathers' agreement and allow her the option of withdrawing from an arrangement she'd been manipulated into. Would losing Brierly House to her be so bad? No, it would gall only if Patrick Hartford managed to take possession of it. Amber would understand when he told her the reason behind the agreement.

Benedict went to bed early, resolving to search

through his grandfather's papers in the morning. The last thing on his mind before he fell asleep was Amber Rose.

The first thing that drew his attention when he woke was the fact that his throat was extremely sore and he felt feverish.

'George,' he croaked. 'You'd better send for the doctor.'

Thomas Dunstan was hardly settled in his office at *Dunstan and James* when there was a scuffle in the outer office, where his two clerks were setting the office up for the daily business.

'No, I'm afraid you can't see Mr Dunstan without an appointment. Mr James might be able to see you. He has a cancellation, though he hasn't arrived yet.'

'I want Dunstan. Tell him it's Lord Hartford ... and be quick about it.'

Thomas had hardly had time to compose himself when the door burst open and his articled clerk was followed in by Patrick Hartford and Stephen Gould, who pushed through the door, all arrogance and swagger. 'Ah, there you are, Dunstan.'

Thomas tried to diffuse the situation with his usual calmness. 'I have an appointment in about ten minutes. How can I be of assistance to you, My Lord?'

'How? I'll tell you how. I believe there was a marital agreement drawn up between my cousin, Amber Rose Hartford and Lord Costain. I want to know why I wasn't informed about it.'

'I'm afraid you've been misinformed. I haven't

handled an agreement between the two parties you mentioned, though if they decide to wed they're old enough to do so.'

His visitor caught him by the lapels. 'You know very well I'm talking about the agreement between our grandfathers. I want to know what was in the agreement.'

'I'm afraid I cannot disclose what was in the agreement between your respective grandfathers, since it was a private matter. I carried out the terms of your grandfather's will exactly as he directed. That did not include relating to you anything he confided to me. In fact, I was specifically instructed not to consult with you over any matter regarding Miss Hartford. Now, unhand me sir, or my clerk will summon an agent of the law.'

'I want that agreement,' Patrick snarled.

He was an unpleasant young man, Thomas thought, jerking his jacket from the man's hand. 'I'm sure you do, Lord Hartford. But this is not the way to go about getting it. The matter has been dealt with as per the late Lord Hartford's instructions. Believe me there is no marriage agreement in my possession. The original papers were given to the parties concerned on receipt of their signatures. The copies were handed to a specific person after your grandfather's death, as were his wishes. I'm not at liberty to disclose that person's name.'

'I see ... and the deeds to Hartford House. Where are they? I want to sell the place.'

'The house deeds are in the strong box in my cellar. I have been waiting for you to collect them. My clerk will fetch them for you.'

Ungraciously, Patrick muttered, 'You might as well keep them until the place is sold. I intend to go to America to live, and I need a quick sale. Perhaps you might know of someone.'

'I have an agent in Poole who can make enquiries and handle the matter, if you'd care to sign a paper to that effect before you leave. It's a desirable country residence, if a little remote. Where can I reach you? At Hartford House?'

'I'm not sure where I'll be. If you'll give me the address of your agent there I'll deal with him when I'm in Dorset. Failing that, I'll be in touch. There is another matter.'

Thomas tried not to sigh. 'Which is?'

'I want to know where my cousin is residing. Her place is at Hartford House.'

'I'm unaware of her whereabouts. Besides, if you are to sell Hartford she might not wish to return.'

'She's my ward, and will do as I say,' Patrick protested.

'No, My Lord. Miss Hartford is not your ward, since you haven't been appointed by the court as her guardian. At her age she is responsible for her own decisions.'

'Where is she, Dunstan?' Patrick snarled.

'Your cousin was residing at Hartford House the last time I was there.'

'I believe her to have been abducted by Lord Costain.'

'*Abducted!* Choose your words with care, Sir, lest you be called to account for them, especially when your cousin's reputation is at stake. Lord

Costain is a gentleman. He would have offered her his protection, not removed her from her home against her will.'

'Are you saying she's his guest?'

'I am not. I have no idea where Miss Hartford is. I've never met the young lady. Lord Hartford,' he said with a sigh. 'You've stated your intention of leaving the country. Perhaps that's all to the good. I'll try and secure the sale of your estate as soon as possible.'

'Perhaps you'd allow me an advance on the sale.'

'I'm afraid that is not our policy, Lord Hartford. You might try a money lender. Timothy, do the necessary paperwork then show the *gentlemen* out, would you.'

'We might have to pay Costain a visit, and if she's with him, snatch her back from him.' The pair turned, laughing as they strolled off.

'That would be a very bad idea gentlemen,' Thomas muttered, and expelled an aggrieved breath. Stephen Gould's father was a good lawyer, and an honest man. His eldest son had turned out to be a rogue. No wonder he'd been disowned.

He'd hardly consulted with his first two clients when Timothy knocked at the door. 'A legal gentleman from Turin in Italy wishes to see you. He says he has some business with you. Alfredo Dominico is his name. He hasn't got an appointment.'

'Then I'm afraid I'm unable to see him. That other business has put us behind. Have you finished the correspondence to Cuthbert Harris regarding his overdue account?'

'I'll have it ready for signature by noon. As for the Italian lawyer. He understands that you're busy. If you cannot accommodate him now, he wonders if you might meet for dinner. He states his business as the estate of one Consulata Puzo. Your next client hasn't arrived yet, so you have a few minutes.'

Thomas didn't know any Consulata Puzo, but he supposed it wouldn't hurt to see the man now, rather then dine with him. After all, business was business. 'All right, Thomas, I'll see the lawyer. I hope he speaks good English, since I only have French as a second language.'

'His English seems perfectly understandable, sir.'

When the Italian was announced the two men shook hands. Alfredo Dominico smiled and opened the satchel he carried. 'I'm sorry to arrive unannounced, sir; I know your time is precious. I'm 'andling the last will and testament of the Contessa Consulata Puzo, who recently departed this world. Apart from an 'andsome property left to the church. She was a very devout woman, you understand. Her fortune has been left to her niece, one Ambra Rosa 'artford. I'm given to understand you were her late guardian's legal representative.'

'That is so,' Thomas said.

'Then you will not mind acting as advisor to her over this matter. The sum concerned is a considerable one. All the papers you require are in the satchel. They 'ave been translated into English for your convenience, but the originals are included.'

In fact, the estate turned out to be more than

considerable. Bemused by the turn of events Thomas regretted not meeting the girl before. There was now even more reason to find her before her cousin did, for if this got out every fortune hunter in England would be after her. He had a good idea of where she might be found, and she must be made aware of her worth before Patrick Hartford learned of it.

'There are some personal items the contessa wished the girl to 'ave ... some jewellery and some family papers and heirlooms, including a *miniatura* of her mother as a young woman.'

'If you would like to meet Miss Hartford perhaps you'd join me in the search for her whereabouts. It's important that she be informed of this legacy as soon as possible. It will offer you the chance of seeing the English countryside, and I will explain the urgency of the situation during the journey. If it suits you I will book tickets on the stage for tomorrow, and we can take the morning coach.'

Which might be an improvement on staying in a dirty city that teemed with people, was choked by unhealthy river smells and smothered in fog, Alfredo thought. Besides, he rather like this *Inglese* lawyer. And it wasn't as if he wanted to hurry back to his wife, or even his mistress. Both had become rather demanding of late. Spreading his hands in a manner that proclaimed his delight at such a notion, Afredo smiled broadly.

When the man had gone James called his clerk in. 'Timothy, I'll be going to Hampshire on company business the day after tomorrow. I'll be absent for a few days. You'll have to see my clients by yourself, since you're well aware of what's needed. Mr James will be on hand to advise you if there's anything you're uncertain of. Mostly they are all uncomplicated, routine matters.'

'Yes, sir,' Timothy said, a smile lighting up his face at the chance of practising the profession he aspired to.

Amber continued to enjoy Emma's hospitality after Kitt and Caroline had taken their brood back home. She would have preferred to be mistress of her own home, but alas, she didn't have one yet.

'I'm not sure if you will like Brierly House,' Emma told her. 'Benedict has always found the place too austere and impersonal. He's said that when he finds a property suitable to his needs he'll sell it. He wants to start a second stud, one he can run by himself.'

And Benedict had been taken with Hartford House! If it were for sale and she had the money to buy it she would give it to him for a wedding present – *if she married him*.

'At least the sun has come out now. No doubt he'll soon send word of what has been arranged. And even though the wedding is to be a quiet affair, our family will all be at the church, and family of family. And no doubt a few friends will turn up, and neighbours, for one can't snub people by ignoring them on such occasions. If there is anyone you wish to invite let me know, then you can leave it all to me.'

Amber smiled at the thought of being a married woman. Falling in love with a man she'd only just

129

met was totally ridiculous, yet exhilarating. One minute she was churning with excitement, the next she was scared out of her wits by the thought of becoming Benedict's wife. Sometimes it seemed as though she'd never been given the chance to sit and think things through properly. She wished she had a mother to talk to.

Two days later a rider approached the house. It was one of Benedict's servants with a message.

'Oh, poor Bennet has been taken ill!' Emma cried out, her hand flying to her chest.

Amber's heart sank. 'What's wrong with him?'

'A sore throat and fever. He begs us not to worry, since the doctor said he'll recover completely if he behaves himself and stays in bed. The illness was caused by the soaking he got during the storm, and in a few days the infection will have passed, then all he need do is rest and recuperate for a few more days.'

'Will he behave himself?'

'I rather doubt it. Bennet is not a person who enjoys being incapacitated. He goes all grumbly when he's ill, like a bear with a sore foot.'

Amber giggled at the thought.

A second piece of paper fell from the back of the first. Emma picked it up and handed it to her. 'It's for you.'

Amber would have liked to have read her note in private, but Emma was gazing at her with such an expectant expression that she couldn't help but smile when she said. 'Do tell me, what does it say?'

*Dearest Amber Rose,*

*I have arranged for us to make our wedding vows for 11am, in three weeks hence, the date then being Saturday the 20th day of September, and the event taking place in the church at Minstead.*

*I hope this arrangement will meet with your approval, for by which time I shall be fully recovered from my affliction.*

*Remember to remain vigilant at all times, my dear. Affectionately yours,*

*Benedict.*

'He still thinks I'm in danger from my cousin then.'

'It seems so.'

'But why should I be? Patrick has got nothing to gain by harming me.'

'Yet, he did seek to harm you.'

'He and his friends had been drinking. When they sobered I imagine they forgot all about me.'

'Bennet said you were terrified.'

'Yes ... yes, I was.' She had a sudden vision of being reined in by Jonas Carlton, and of Stephen Gould dragging her by her hair. That was followed by a feeling of vulnerability. She gazed nervously around her and shuddered.

'Oh, my dear.' Emma hugged her tight. 'What you must have been through. I have never seen Bennet so angry, or so protective of anyone. You must listen to his advice. We all must be vigilant.'

'He didn't seem angry to me.'

'His anger is deceptive, since he secludes it within quietness and reason. He's not one to take rash action which may give him cause to regret, but he won't allow a slight go past without apology, however long it takes. And he doesn't walk away from an altercation if he thinks the cause is just, however overwhelming the odds.'

'He will recover completely, won't he?'

'Goodness, yes. Bennet's extremely resilient, and it's only a cold on the chest. I remember when he was five and he caught scarletina...'

Amber smiled as she listened to Emma's chatter. She loved hearing tales about Benedict's childhood. It made her feel as though she'd always been part of his life.

## NINE

The two lawyers alighted from the coach at Lyndhurst, where Thomas took rooms at the inn.

The next morning found them bowling through the pleasant countryside towards the Earl of Laconbridge's estate in a hired rig. Both lost in admiration of the countryside, they missed seeing the two men who'd arrived during the night.

Stephen Gould had talked the tavern wench into imparting certain information to them, as well as allowing him certain favours. The pair had ridden out early to position themselves amongst the trees at either side of the road.

Jonas Carlton was no longer with them. He'd become bored of chasing around the countryside after Patrick's cousin. Ashamed of his part in humiliating the young woman, he'd decided to stay in London in the house of his uncle, a man renown for his generosity, hospitality, and his many lovers – and whose estate and title Jonas would one day inherit.

It was late morning when the two lawyers reached the Earl of Laconbridge's magnificent country estate. The earl himself came to greet them, a smile on his face and two elderly lurchers sniffing at his heels. 'Thomas Dunstan? Good Lord. To what do I owe the pleasure of this visit?'

'An urgent matter has cropped up regarding Miss Hartford. May I present Mr Alfredo Dominico from Italy. He is a lawyer acting on behalf of Miss Hartford's aunt, Contessa Consolata Puzo. Mr Dominico, this gentleman is the Earl of Laconbridge.'

Alfredo bowed from the waist and beamed a smile. 'My Lord, I am *onerato* ... honoured to meet you.'

'Thank you, Mr Dominico.' The earl looked puzzled. 'Miss Hartford has an aunt? I thought she was without relatives, except for her male cousin.'

'It is now correct,' Alfredo said. 'Consolata Puzo is at rest in her grave, and Ambra Rosa 'artford has inherited her fortune.'

'The late Lord Hartford was always in touch with the contessa, to keep her informed of her niece's progress, something which has paid off,' Thomas said approvingly.

'The contessa's position rendered it impossible

for her to recognize the girl while she was alive, of course,' Alfredo explained.

'I don't see why, when Lord Hartford was not ashamed to. The girl's parents were legally married, after all.'

'The church dictates–'

'Not in this country, Mr Dominico. The monarch is the head of our church, and he is advised only by his first minister, Mr William Pitt. However frowned upon certain religions are in this country, we would never disown the offspring of a union legally entered into.'

'Quite so, a different system altogether,' Thomas said hastily. 'Is Miss Hartford here?'

'I have yet to meet Miss Hartford. But you should perhaps be made aware that the young lady has agreed to my son's proposal of marriage, and is soon to become my daughter-in-law.'

'A good arrangement, one that is to prove even more advantageous now. However, I'm disappointed at not being able to see her, for we came to acquaint Miss Hartford with the fact of her good fortune. Also, I wanted to warn you that Patrick Hartford has been making enquiries as to the marriage agreement. He came to me with his companion, Stephen Gould, a young man who is as unsuitable as he is unstable. It would not do for either of them to lay eyes on the agreement.'

'Miss Hartford is the guest of my daughter, Lady Stratton, who lives only an hour's journey from here. My wife and I were about to visit our daughter for an overnight stay, so to make Miss Hartford's acquaintance. Perhaps you'd like to accompany us and present your business to her at the same time. It shouldn't take long to acquaint her of her good fortune, then you can be on your way.'

'That's kind of you, My Lord.'

'As for the marital agreement, I have the copy safe in my desk drawer. My son will look for the original after he recovers from his illness, which will not be for a fortnight, at least. He thinks it might be amongst the late Reverend Brierly's papers in his estate manager's office.'

Patrick and Stephen who'd been making their way through the shrubbery, arrived just in time to overhear the tail end of the conversation.

'So, there *is* an agreement,' Patrick whispered. 'I knew that lawyer was covering it up. There's something in it they don't want me to know about. Shall we go and shake it out of Costain while he's incapacitated?'

'Don't be stupid. He might appear mild mannered on the surface, but he's as dangerous as a snake. The only way I'd take him on was if he had his back towards me and both hands and feet were tied. We'll wait until dusk, then when the servants are eating their dinner we'll slip into the house, find the earl's study and read the agreement. The earl won't even know we've been in there.'

It was a plan that hadn't even occurred to Patrick. He felt like a fool as he said sullenly, 'I was about to suggest that myself.'

Stephen smiled pityingly at him. 'Of course you were. As for your cousin, at least we now know where she is, so we can bide our time.'

'What if she weds Costain?'

'He'll be ill for the next two weeks, probably longer. We'll stay out of sight and lull them into believing we no longer have any interest in the girl. We'll find out when the wedding is and snatch her from under his nose.'

Interest piqued, Patrick gazed at him. 'How will we do that?'

'They're bound to use the local church. Minstead is the nearest one. One of us will keep the reverend busy while the other slips into the office to look through the events register.'

'Where will we stay for all this time? I can't afford to waste money at the inn.'

'When we've done the business we'll go to Hartford House and lay low. You can play at being Lord of the manor.'

'I am the Lord of the manor.'

'As you say. In that case it will come naturally to you. The locals will support us for a while, no doubt. We'll go to church on Sunday and we'll ask the rector's wife to send one of the poor of the parish to clean and cook. And you can open accounts. But first, we must read that agreement – and as soon as possible.'

The obtaining of the marriage date and the agreement proved to be trouble free. As soon as the earl and the lawyers left, the villainous pair took the opportunity to climb through the open study window. The agreement was exactly where the earl had said it was, the objective easily achieved.

Straight away, Stephen Gould grasped what

Patrick didn't when he read it. 'The property Costain is living in was bought with your grandfather's money. It was tied to your cousin as a dowry. No wonder Costain ran off with her. The minute the marriage vows are said the debt will be rendered null and void.'

'But we can't prove the property is mine without a copy of the agreement.'

'I'm wondering if your delicious cousin is aware of the existence of the agreement. We should make sure by informing her of it. I could copy the papers and you could slip the agreement back into the desk before the earl comes back. We could then send a copy to her.'

Patrick had not enjoyed trespassing on another man's property or riffling through his desk. Life was getting too complicated with Stephen, and he felt like abandoning the chase. 'Why, Stephen, what would you get out of it?'

Stephen's frown said he didn't welcome the question. 'Your cousin and Costain made a fool of me. I want to ruin the pair of them, bring them down. Costain will offer you a cash settlement instead of the property. You still owe me a great deal of money, Patrick, and I'm not carrying the debt much longer.'

'I've promised to pay it when Hartford House has been sold. Plus there will be enough left over to go abroad with. I thought we'd agreed. There's no need to ruin my cousin. Marriage to Costain is the best thing for her.'

'So you're happy to let the viscount keep the estate that should rightfully be yours, knowing it was paid for with your grandfather's money, something you were entitled to have as his legal heir.'

Patrick stared at him, doubt mirrored in his eyes. When he was sober his conscience was easily pricked. Although he'd disliked the way the old man had treated him, that wasn't Amber's fault. 'As long as you understand that I don't want her to be physically hurt again. We'll toss for who goes back in. It won't take two of us.'

Patrick was a coward, Stephen thought. As for his cousin, the girl had mocked him, and had made him look a fool. So had Costain. He wasn't about to allow the bitch to get away with it. If Costain married her he would spend his wedding night with damaged goods.

A little later, their courage bolstered by the wine they'd consumed, the pair of them returned to the Laconbridge residence.

Stephen had lost the toss, something that had pleased Patrick, since his friend usually had luck on his side. He suspected Stephen made his own luck, though he'd never been able to figure out exactly how.

On this occasion Patrick wasn't far wrong. Stephen had made his own luck, with a two-headed coin. The first time he had been in the earl's study he'd seen the key to the strong box in the drawer.

Opening his lozenge tin he pulled down his kerchief and placed one in his mouth, sucking reflectively on it as he gazed around the study. Slipping the original agreement back into the drawer, he grabbed up the key and opened the strongbox. Inside, he found a purse heavy with gold sovereigns. What luck! He slipped it into the pocket inside his waistcoat. An enamel snuffbox on the desk took his fancy, so he took that, too.

But he wasn't so lucky leaving unobserved. He hadn't seen the dogs, two elderly lurchers who heaved themselves up from the rug in front of the fireplace, and came to where he stood. Tails wagging, the pair sniffed at his legs, then waddled over to the door and began to bark and whine, looking back at him every now and then.

They wanted to be let out. He crossed to the door, then cursed when he heard footsteps, and a woman's voice, 'So that's where you're skulking, you varmints. No good waiting for the master in there, he won't be home tonight. Best you go to the kitchen for your dinners before cook's cat eats it.'

The door was thrust open, the dogs waddled off through it, still giving rusting barks.

In the grey evening light the maid caught sight of him and Stephen hastily pulled up the kerchief when she squawked, 'Oh, my gawd, who're you?' Her eyes widened as she opened her mouth to scream.

One punch in the stomach robbed her of the breath required to carry out the threat, another to the head snapped it back and rendered her unconscious. The dogs had stopped their noise and padded off, more concerned about their dinner than seeing off the intruders. He dragged the maid into the study, allowing her to drop to the floor with a soft thud before creeping out through the hall. Closing the front door quietly

behind him he scurried off through the shrubbery to where Patrick stood waiting with the
horses.

'Let's get out of here, fast,' he said.

Emma stopped in the middle of a sentence when
a carriage was heard. She ran to the window,
where the smile on her face widened. 'How
wonderful, it's my father and mother's carriage –
they must have come to introduce themselves to
you. And behind them is a phaeton with two
men, who look rather serious and official. Goodness, what on earth is going on? I must admit, life
has been rather exciting since Benedict brought
you here, Amber.'

She turned, her eyes sparkling. 'You'd better
hide up in your room while I find out what's
going on, dear. I think the men are with my
parents, and if they are I will send for you.
Otherwise I'll deny that you're a guest here, if
asked.'

As Amber hurried up the stairs Emma flew into
the hall and out through the front door. She exchanged hugs and kisses with her parents. 'Mama,
Papa, what a pleasant surprise. And you bring
visitors with you, do you not?'

Her father smiled at her obvious caution.
'They've come to see Miss Hartford.'

'But Benedict said–'

'Both are lawyers, my dear. This is Mr Thomas
Dunstan from London, who handled the estate of
the late Lord Hartford. And this is Mr Alfredo
Dominico, who has come all the way from Turin

140

in Italy with urgent news for her. I will vouch for them both. Gentlemen, this is my daughter, Lady Stratton.'

Both gentlemen bowed over her hand, and the Italian gave a broad smile as he said gallantly, 'The earl is lucky to have such exquisite ladies littering his 'ousehold.'

She exchanged an amused glance with her mother, then said, 'Goodness, how intriguing it all is. Would you like to wait in the morning room, gentlemen? You can talk to Miss Hartford there in private.' She beckoned to a hovering maid. 'Show the gentlemen to the morning room and make sure they have some refreshment.' The lawyers were the recipient of a dazzling smile. 'Miss Hartford will be with you shortly.'

She sent another maid up for Amber and they waited at the bottom for the stairs as she came down, a neat figure in a pale blue morning gown, its high neckline trimmed modestly with a lace. She wore a shy smile on her face.

Amber's heart was thumping as the earl came up to meet her, taking her hand in his to assist her down the last few steps in a gentlemanly manner. Benedict resembled him. He stopped in front of his wife. 'Here she is, Imogene ... Miss Amber Hartford. She's a lovely sprite, is she not? No wonder Bennet decided to carry her off.'

Amber curtseyed. 'It was more by accident than design, My Lord. Your son was in the position of little choice. I'm so pleased to make your acquaintance, My lady.'

'And I you.' Benedict's quietly elegant mother

141

kissed her on both cheeks and smiled. 'Welcome to the family, my dear.'

'Thank you. Benedict walks in the earl's image. I have never seen a son so like his father.'

'Yes ... they are alike, even in their ways. He is a good son.'

'He has his mother's beautiful eyes, though,' the earl murmured, grinning when he earned himself a reproving smile.

There was no sign of the two men who had come with them, though Amber heard the murmur of voices in the morning room.

'We have brought two lawyers to see you,' the earl said.

'Two!' Alarm filled her. 'Am I to be handed over to my cousin's care, then, after all?'

Emma slid an arm round her. 'Rest assured, I will not allow that to happen. One of your visitors is Thomas Dunstan, the lawyer.'

'I know of him, though we haven't met. He handled my grandfather's estate.'

'That is so. The other gentleman is an Italian called Alfredo Dominico. Also a lawyer.'

'My mother was Italian,' Amber said, and excitement nudged at her. 'Do my Italian aunts wish to meet me? It's something I've always hoped for.'

The earl shook his head. 'Unfortunately, your aunts are no more. Mr Dominico is handling the estate of the Contessa Consulata Puzo, who has recently died. You are the chief beneficiary in her last will and testament, my dear. The gentlemen are waiting for you in the morning room.'

Her aunt? It was unbelievable that one of the

142

women who had disowned her and left her to be brought up in a convent had made her a beneficiary in her will. Despite her curiosity Amber felt a thrust of anger that she'd been cast aside as though she were nothing of importance. 'Must I see them? I've never known my mother's family and cannot help but think it's all a mistake.'

The earl smiled. 'It's not a mistake, and you will have to see the lawyers sometime. They've come a long way, my dear. It's best that the business be conducted now, then you'll know where you stand. Would you like me to stay with you and advise you? I'm sure Emma and her mother will find plenty to talk about in our absence.'

She smiled and nodded with relief.

The two men stood when she entered, and after introductions were made the earl withdrew to lean on the mantelpiece. The Italian gentleman lifted her hand to his mouth and whispered, 'Enchanted, my dear. How like your mother you are.'

'You knew her?'

'*Si*, we were children together.' He drew a miniature from his pocket and handed it to her. 'This is Lucia, your mother. She was the youngest daughter. Next came Orsola, then Consulata, who asked me to present this to you straight away.'

The woman in the portrait was about the same age as Amber was now. She could have been looking at herself in the mirror. Dark hair framed pale, translucent skin. Her eyes had a greenish hue.

'That was painted on the birthday before...' He shrugged. 'But we will not talk of that time,

143

it is too sad. The sight of you brings me 'appiness for you are so much like her. Lucia was a sweet young woman, filled with a joy for living, and she loved your father with a true 'eart. She will be smiling down from heaven at this very moment. You will look for her out of your window tonight, Ambra Rosa. Lucia will be the brightest star in the heavens. How proud she will be to see what a lovely young woman her *bambino* has become.'

His words were as sincere as his voice, and they filled her with an indescribable longing. Amber's eyes filled with tears as her hand closed around the brooch. Her mother would have spoken in the same accented way, and it was not the way Amber had imagined as a child, but a voice that carried the words in a more melodic fashion. They rolled like warm honey from his tongue and made her think of sunshine, blue skies and a bright ocean of clear, blue water. She liked this Italian lawyer.

She took the handkerchief the earl offered and dabbed at her tears, saying in a choked voice, 'Thank you for bringing me this, Mr Dominico. It was very kind of you. You cannot know what it means for me to have a likeness of her after all these years.'

His smile was wide. 'I didn't mean to make you sad. But now I 'ave I will get down to business while you compose yourself, and soon you will be very 'appy instead.'

It was a stunned Amber who gazed at him a few moments later. She was now the possessor of a fortune. 'Did my grandfather know about this legacy, Mr Dominico?'

'He had hopes on your behalf, but died before they came to fruition. There was correspondence between Lord Hartford and your aunt over the years. I have brought your grandfather's letters to you. It was the contessa's wish that someone be appointed to advise you, and Mr Dunstan had indicated his willingness to do so, should you so approve.'

'If my grandfather trusted Mr Dunstan with his business, then I see no reason why I shouldn't.'

'Thank you, Miss Hartford. I will leave you with a suitable allowance, and if there is anything you want.'

'There is something I want very much to purchase if you can obtain it for me.'

'I will try ... what is it?'

'Hartford House was my grandfather's home. I believe Patrick will sell it eventually. When he does I would like to buy it.' Worried, she said, 'I can afford it, can I not?'

Now it was Thomas Dunstan's turn to smile. 'Without a doubt, and you're quite correct. Your cousin does wish to sell it, and I'm sure your grandfather would have been heartened to know that his home will remain in your care. I'll negotiate on your behalf. I understand your cousin wishes to travel abroad, so expect a quick sale.'

'You had better keep the name of the buyer a secret, then. For if my cousin learns of my legacy he will want more than the property is worth. I will be glad when Patrick has gone, so I don't have to keep looking over my shoulder. I do wish matters between us could have been better, since he's my only kin.'

Four days later when Emma was in the kitchen supervising meals for the week and Amber was enjoying a few moments of solitude, a maid handed her a letter from Mr Dunstan, along with a package.

'Thank you, Annie.' Her heart fluttered as she wondered if the package was from Benedict, but then Thomas Dunstan came to mind. It was probably another set of legal papers to read and sign, she thought, groaning inwardly as she unwrapped it.

There was a note attached to the papers that read simply, *It might be in your best interests to see this before your marriage rather than after it, Miss Hartford.* It was signed, *A concerned friend.*

It was the marriage contract agreed to between her own grandfather and Benedict's. But it wasn't signed, and she didn't recognize the handwriting. It certainly wasn't Mr Dunstan's, nor that of her grandfather.

Two sheets of paper were attached. She started to read, then when she'd finished she read it all over again. The details hadn't changed the second time. Her grandfather had loaned money to Reverend Andrews to build Brierly House. The place was her dowry, money her grandfather hadn't wanted Patrick to lay his hands on. He had set out to buy her an advantageous marriage. If the marriage didn't go ahead the principal sum of the loan, plus any difference in value, plus interest on said loan must be paid to her.

'So that's what my grandfather meant when he

said my future was taken care of,' she murmured. She felt betrayed by him ... and by Benedict, who must have been motivated by the contract when he'd proposed.

It had been fortuitous that Benedict had been in time to rescue her from Patrick and his friends, and she was grateful for that. But he'd omitted to tell her she was needed to consolidate his property. Instead, he'd offered her marriage on the premise that he'd compromised her.

And now...? Because she'd fallen in love with him she was rushing into marriage because she'd had nowhere else to go.

His father and mother must have been aware of this, and his family. Dear God ... had they all conspired to deceive her? Hurt growing inside her, Amber didn't know what to do about it, and even while she understood the predicament Benedict had found himself in, he'd plunged in her estimation.

To take her mind off the problem she opened the letter from Thomas Dunstan. It was almost an anticlimax to read that her cousin had agreed to the offer she'd made for the purchase of Hartford House and its contents. Thomas Dunstan informed her that he was preparing the papers. He asked her to call in the next time she was in London where they'd be ready for signature. Otherwise, he would send his clerk.

How ironic that she'd wanted her former home for Benedict, as a wedding present. She might forget marriage, move back in and live there by herself. After spending twenty years there she knew how to run the small estate in a manner

147

that would bring in an income – not that she needed one now. And she'd be able to send Jake to school nearby.

As for Brierly House, she'd forfeit the loan. It would not be fair to make Benedict liable for his grandfather's debt. And it wouldn't be acceptable to her to allow him to honour the debt through marriage. Oh ... she felt so mixed up inside. She had wanted so much to become Benedict's wife.

Emma had dressmakers working full time making her a gown for the event. It was beautiful, high-waisted made of cream silk, with a brocade pelisse. Already Emma had sent out invitations to friends and family members. Amber groaned and placed her head in her hands. She had a feeling that events were about to overtake her.

'Miss, are you all right?' Annie said.

'I have the beginnings of a headache that's all. I think I'll go and lie down for a little while.' What she wanted was a little solitude, where she could think things over in a rational manner and come to a definite conclusion.

But even that was denied her when Emma bustled into the room and said, 'Annie tells me you're unwell.'

'It's just a little headache. Hardly anything, Emma.'

'Thank goodness. You're moping because you haven't seen Bennet, aren't you? You mustn't worry about him, you know. He has a strong constitution and will be well in no time.'

'I'm sure he will.'

'Can you ride? We'll take the horses and visit

148

Laconbridge House, that will blow the cobwebs away. You haven't seen it yet, have you? I'm sure you'll be impressed. We can call in on Caro on the way back.'

She set Annie scuttling off to rouse the stable hands. 'I'll go and prise Archie out of his den. He and the groom can accompany us.'

'But what if your husband is busy?'

'Oh, he'll soon unbusy himself if I ask him; Archie is entirely accommodating like that. He's an absolute angel and I just adore him.'

'Were you in love with Archie when you married him, Emma?'

'Oh yes, and Caroline fell in love with Kitt as soon as she met him. He was Archie's best friend, which was very convenient. We had a double wedding in the church at Minstead.'

Where Benedict intended to marry her.

'Our parents set us a good example, you see, though I imagine they'd have kicked up a fuss if we'd fallen in love with unsuitable men. They also fell in love as soon as they met, but mama was promised to another. Papa took her from under her father's nose. He persuaded her to run off with him one Sunday after the church service and married her himself. That's why we're so pleased that Benedict has fallen in love. He's following in the family tradition.'

'But how do you know a man truly loves you, and it's not just ... *manly desire?* What if he knew something that his intended didn't ... that he had to marry her to save his estate from ruin, and he pretended to love her, when really he only desired her.'

Emma grinned at her. 'Don't let this recent legacy bother you, my dear. You didn't have any estate when my brother met you, so you know his proposal wasn't mercenary. Bennett is wealthy in his own right, and his horse stud brings in good returns. Believe me, he would have no trouble attracting a wealthy heiress if he'd let it be known he was on the marriage market. Come, come, Amber ... all brides have these misgivings. I have absolutely no doubt that my brother adores you.'

Emma's manner was so open, it occurred to Amber that she must not be aware of the agreement, or of the motivation behind a marriage between them.

Amber had not been on a horse for a while. The one chosen for her was a sturdy chestnut mare with white legs. Her name was Merry. Amber enjoyed the ride through the forest, the adjoining heath and the lanes winding through the gentle green countryside.

'You have a good seat,' Archie told her as he helped her to dismount.

She gazed at the house with the ivy climbing the walls, and its stone facade warmed by the sun. One day Benedict would inherit, and if she married him, she would live here in these splendid surrounds.

She remembered Archie. 'The horse is so well-behaved.'

'She's a safe mount for a lady to ride. One from Bennet's stud. Merry was bred from his favourite mare. She's sound of wind and has a neat gait, so she offers a comfortable ride.'

They found the Laconbridge household subdued.

'What is it, mama?' Emma asked her.

'A stranger entered our home when we last
visited you. They found the key to the strongbox,
stole money and the gold and enamel snuff box
from your father's desk.'

'Oh, how dreadful,' Amber gasped.

'What else, mother? I can see from your eyes
that you're upset. Bennet hasn't taken a turn for
the worst, has he?'

'One of the maids surprised the thief. The poor
girl was attacked by the felon.'

'How badly is she hurt?'

'Her stomach and face are bruised and swollen.
He hit the young woman so hard that she was
knocked unconscious and the doctor feared for
her life. Now she jumps at the sight of her own
shadow.'

Something Amber had experienced herself.
'Did she get a good look at the thief?'

'It was dusk. He pulled a kerchief over the
lower part of his face when he saw her. She
thought he was tall, and she said that something
about him smelled peculiar.'

'How?' Emma asked her.

'She couldn't explain. She thought he might
have been chewing the wild mint that grows in
these parts.'

Although she couldn't say why, Stephen Gould
came to Amber's mind.

While Archie went in search of the earl the
women moved into the morning room.

The countess appeared agitated. 'This is the

151

first time we've been robbed in this manner. The worst aspect of it is knowing that a stranger has been in my home, and probably there were two of them watching us from the shrubbery, for they found the imprint of both horses and riders. Your father is going to have the lilacs removed and flower beds put there instead. He thinks it was probably an opportunist, but it makes me feel so vulnerable. Only God knows what the poor maid is going through. She's a nice girl and a good worker. Her family lives in Christchurch. I was thinking of asking your father to compensate her and send her home for a week or so to rest. What do you think, Emma?'

'She seems to have suffered badly, so some time off will help her to heal and get over her fright, I should imagine.'

What a wonderful gesture, Amber thought, as a maid brought them in refreshment. How could such nice people set out to rob her of her dowry. But perhaps the papers she'd received had been written simply to cause mischief. Patrick came into her mind, but it hadn't been his writing, which was badly formed.

She needed advice, but who could she trust? Mr Dunstan came into mind.

# TEN

After three days of arguing with herself Amber decided it was time she took her life into her own hands. First, she needed to sort out the question of the marriage agreement.

'I'm going to London to see Mr Dunstan,' she told her hosts over breakfast. 'I believe there's a coach from Lyndhurst.'

'What nonsense is this?' Emma exclaimed. 'You know very well that Bennet has placed you in our care. If he was well enough he'd absolutely forbid it.'

Amber's chin came up as she said quietly, 'I can't think of any reason why he should forbid me to see my legal representative, can you?'

Archie gazed sharply at her then averted his gaze. He knows, she thought sadly, and pushed a little harder to see what his reaction would be.

'Let me just make one thing clear. Benedict may have rescued me when I was in need of it, and I regard him with the greatest respect. However, he holds no authority over me whatsoever.' Except for the fact he was the keeper of her heart, she thought ruefully.

'You have promised yourself to him, and in two weeks you are to be married. Out of respect for him can this matter not rest until after the event. Is it anything to do with the package and letter that arrived for you? If so, Archie might be able to help you with anything legal it contained.'

She would not satisfy Emma's curiosity on this occasion. 'I imagine he could, but it's not really necessary since I'm quite conversant with the contents,' she said, and he looked slightly uncomfortable.

'It can't be that important after all, then. Now, let's hear no more of this and eat our breakfasts.'

Emma seemed miffed so Amber sought to mollify her. 'Don't think I'm not grateful for your hospitality, Emma but are my own feelings and wishes to be held to no account?'

'Oh, damn it, Amber, do be quiet,' Emma said crossly. 'I don't want you to be grateful and you're making me feel like the nagging, controlling creature I am.'

Archie nearly choked on his coffee.

'I'm sorry,' she stuttered, slightly taken aback.

'You're using Mr Dunstan as an excuse, when really you want to go to London to spend some of that money you inherited.'

She was about to deny it when Emma continued, 'And why not? You're sadly in need of a new wardrobe, so a week in London will be quite the thing.' She brightened. 'Hmmm, I imagine Caro will want to come as well so we'll advise you.'

She bowed to the inevitable. 'That's kind of you.'

Emma's voice bubbled with enthusiasm. 'I'll send a servant with a message and we'll take the family coach, Caro's as well, since it will be much more convenient than the stage and we can put all the packages in one. We'll take Annie with us. She'll maid for all of us, and she'll be able to fit

154

in a visit to her family while she's there. Oh what fun it will be! The exercise will take your mind off of Bennet's illness altogether.'

Archie twisted his wife a rueful smile and growled, 'I'll accompany you, so I can keep my hand on your purse strings. I'll drop in on Caroline while I'm on my way over to see Bennet. I want to see how he's faring.'

Emma gazed at him. 'Why didn't you tell me you were going to see Bennet? We could have written him a letter wishing him a speedy recovery.'

'I've just remembered it. Don't worry. I'll tell him the pair of you still love him.' Amber found herself the recipient of a probing glance. 'That would be the truth, wouldn't it, Amber?'

Did she love him? As if he was part of her heart, her mind and her soul. How could any woman not love him? But she couldn't bare her heart for all to see. She was not used to being part of a family, to sharing her hopes and her fears – feelings that were most tender and private to her. And she wondered why a straight-forward yes was so difficult to say to Archie when if Benedict had asked her the same question she could have told him the truth. As she struggled to form an answer in her mind Emma laughed at her husband.

'Stop teasing Archie, you've made her blush. Of course she loves him. You're an absolute hero for dropping in on Caro, my love. I don't deserve you.'

Both women laughed when he gave a long suffering sigh and murmured, 'You certainly don't. I told you that when we first married.'

So much for taking control of her own life, Amber thought ruefully as Emma began to enthuse over what they'd do in London. The visit didn't seem to include Thomas Dunstan.

She managed to intercept Archie just as he was leaving, to hand him a note she'd hastily scribbled. 'If Benedict is well enough would you please give him this. It's to wish him a speedy recovery. And there's something I'd like to ask you, Archie.'

His eyes took on a guarded expression. 'What is is, Amber?'

She couldn't tell him not to discuss her business with Benedict. 'I need to see my lawyer when I'm in London, so would you accompany me to his office?'

'Of course. Is it for a specific reason?'

'Well, yes,' and guilt tore through her for sidetracking him. 'Mr Dunstan has negotiated with my cousin for me to buy my former home. I'd rather Benedict didn't know I've bought it ... you see, it's to be a surprise.'

'I'd hazard a guess and say it's a gift for Bennet, since he told me how much he liked the place. He thought he might buy it himself if it came onto the market. I do think that cousin of yours is a complete fool to liquidate his assets.'

'Patrick never had much of a life. He was brought up without parental love and guidance from an early age. His father was a ne're-do-well, you see, and my grandfather favoured me. Patrick resented me for it, so I can't really blame him for feeling that way.'

'My dear, you must not make excuses for him. His bad relationship with your grandfather is not your fault. His behaviour left much to be desired. Remember, while you remain unmarried Lord Hartford is your heir. Do be careful that news of your good fortune doesn't reach his ears. Many men would kill to get their hands on such a large sum.'

Her blood ran cold. Surely not! 'I will be careful, Archie, and your warning is noted.' She held out an arm. 'Look, you're making me come out in goose bumps. If you'd rather we didn't go to London I'll understand.'

'It's too late now Emma has arranged it all in her mind.' His smile lit up his face. 'You must find it tiresome coming into a family where everyone knows your business, and we all insist on offering you the benefit of our advice.'

'It's difficult to keep up, for I'm used to peace and quiet all around me. There seems to be a tide carrying me along here, but it runs so fast that sometimes I'd like to be in calmer water, where I could think things through and determine my own course.'

'That quiet strength you have will stand you in good stead. When you're wed you'll find contentment in the home you make with Bennet and in the children you share. You have the same sense of serenity about you that his mother has. You're a perfect match for him, and he knows it.'

She smiled at the picture he'd conjured up. 'There's so much affection between you as a family that I find quite appealing. I often wondered what belonging to a family would be like. I'm afraid you must find me very dull and countrified.'

'Not at all.' He kissed her cheek. 'Don't worry, my dear, your secret is safe with me,' he said, then strode off.

Benedict ignored George's protests and sent him off to get some coffee.

Pulling his robe around him, and noting that his head throbbed a little less miserably than it had the day before and his fever had abated slightly, he took a chair by one of the open windows, allowing Archie to do the same.

'What does the note say Archie?' he croaked.

*Dear Benedict,*
*Pleased be assured that I'm well looked after by Lord and lady Stratton, and yes, I'm being vigilant.*
*Even the footmen go armed when we are in the open air, so I feel very safe.*

'How on earth did she know that?' Archie said.
'She's got eyes in her head, hasn't she?'
'Very pretty eyes they are, too.'
'A sort of a greenish grey with dark eyelashes.'
Archie grinned. 'I thought they were greyish green, but no matter.'

*I do hope your condition is improving. Archie will inform you of my recent good fortune, no doubt. I have no time to go into it all now, because we travel to London tomorrow.*
*All good wishes. I will pray for a rapid improvement*

*in your health,*
   *Amber Rose Hartford.*


Benedict gazed at his brother-in-law through bleary eyes. 'She's going to London. Is that wise?'

'We are all going to London. Emma has decided on a shopping spree, and where Emma goes, Caro goes. They have set their minds on assisting Amber to buy all the lacy fripperies and delights that wives like to tempt their husbands with.'

Benedict managed a grin at the thought, but it felt as lukewarm as he did. 'Keep Amber and her fripperies safe for me. If she needs any cash I'll reimburse you when you return.'

'Don't worry, Kitt and I will look after Amber. And she's observant – my footmen do go armed. There's even more reason to now. That good fortune Amber mentioned … she's become the sole legatee of her Italian aunt's fortune. You will be marrying a very wealthy young woman, Bennet.'

Although happy for her, Benedict's heart sank. 'Has the news got out yet?'

'No … but we both know it won't take long. Are you sure this marriage is what you want?'

'I've never been so sure of anything in my life.' He moved his arm aside when George came back in with the coffee, making room for him. 'Why do you ask?'

'Forgive me for saying so but Amber has struck me as being uncertain. She says she's being carried along on a wave of everyone else's enthusiasm. Emma and Caroline have taken her over completely, your mother and father adore her–'

'And so do I. Damn it, Archie, I should be there to romance her and protect her, so she doesn't have time to question her reactions ... but I feel as weak as a newly born kitten.'

His man tutt-tutted as he poured coffee for them, then said in a rather regal manner, 'I'll go downstairs and wait for the physician to arrive. No doubt he will be unhappy to know his instructions have been ignored and will insist that you go back to bed.'

'No doubt he will. Do you intend to strong-arm me George?'

George sniffed. 'Certainly not, but if sir is not recovered enough to take his wedding vows on the appointed day I trust–'

'If you censure me one more time, George, I'll throw you out of the window by the scruff of your neck. Not only does it put me in a bad humour, it makes my head ache. Do you understand?'

'Yes, sir. I'll tidy up your bed before I go so it's neat when you decide to get back into it, shall I?' He plumped the pillows and straightened the covers so not a crease shadowed the surface, while Benedict drummed his fingers on the arm of his chair and swore under his breath.

As soon as George left, Benedict said, 'What else has happened, Archie?'

'Somebody sneaked into your father's study and robbed him.'

Alarm surged through him. 'Was my father hurt?'

'Luckily he and your mother were visiting us at

160

the time. One of the maids was knocked unconscious, but she'll survive her ordeal.'

'Good grief! Have they any idea of who the culprit might be?'

'I can't help thinking that it's somehow connected to Amber, though I have no proof. You know, I suspect she's learned about her connection to this place, and that was why she wants to see the lawyer. When I quizzed her she said it was about her inheritance. Dunstan has been appointed her advisor, you know.'

'Which might make matters awkward for him since he's been advising me and my father on the matter of Brierly House.'

'I imagine Dunstan didn't see a conflict of interest because the marriage is so close. He'll relinquish the task to you once you're wed.'

The more Benedict thought about the marriage agreement the more the matter pricked on his conscience. He must talk to Amber, tell her about the agreement as soon as he was better. Hell, he could give Brierly House to her as a wedding present. It would be a sign of his good faith. But Amber was no fool. She'd see through it, since everything she owned would become his after marriage.

'Have you thought that it might be Amber's damnable cousin and his friends causing mischief?'

'Could be. There were signs that two men had been watching the place from the shrubbery. They stole a purse and a gold and enamel snuff box. Your father is going to replace the shrubbery with a flower bed. You might like to consider arming a couple of your servants until the felons are apprehended.'

'Thank you, I will, though I doubt if I'm in any danger.'

'Quite so. It was probably a couple of opportunists. I shouldn't have worried you with it,' Archie said.

Benedict drank his coffee, his hands cupped around the bowl to stop them from trembling. His face began to flush.

Archie gazed at him with some concern. 'My visit has overtaxed you, Bennet. You'd better get back into bed, since I hear the doctor's carriage coming up the drive. Here, take my arm.'

As Benedict sank wearily back into his pillows, he said, 'Give my lady a red rose from my garden. Tell her I think of her constantly.'

Archie chuckled. 'That must be rather uncomfortable.' Benedict managed a faint smile. 'It is rather, but the anticipation is pleasant nevertheless.'


## ELEVEN

The journey to London was tedious, but was made without incident. The roads grew busier as they reached the outskirts of the capital.

Emma and Caroline chattered like a couple of magpies and never seemed to run out of subjects to keep them all amused. The earl's London residence in St James' square was always available for the family visits. The spacious square was teeming with vendors as well as horses and carriages, and it was littered with horse dung. The staff didn't seem surprised by the unexpected arrival of so many, and bustled in and out with luggage.

'We will need a room for Miss Hartford,' Caroline told the housekeeper, without explaining exactly where Miss Hartford fitted into the scheme of things.

Emma added, 'Use the viscount's room, since it has a nice outlook over the garden.'

The housekeeper must have picked up the undercurrents in her voice for she smiled. 'Yes, My Lady. May I enquire as to the length of the visit so cook can cater for meals?'

'No more than a week. We are to do some last minute shopping before...'

Emma caught her breath when Caroline poked her in the ribs and ended hurriedly with, '...before we're obliged to return to the country. Now, Amber, my dear. Archie tells me you're to see your advisor. It would be convenient if you conducted your business in the morning first thing, then we can start on the real reason we're here, and without interruption. One of the footmen will take a note to his establishment telling him what time to expect you.'

As was usual, Emma's arrangements ran on well-greased wheels. Later, Amber was glad of the peace and quiet as she rested before dinner. She suspected that Emma had sensed her reticence about the wedding.

The walls of Bennet's room – and yes, she was

163

beginning to think of him as such – were lined in grey watered taffeta. There was a gentleman's chest of polished wood with ornate handles. She pulled open the little drawers to be confronted with small items, including a silver watch with Reverend Andrew Brierly inscribed on it. She connected it with Brierly House. It must be the grandfather who had made the agreement with her own grandfather. Odd to think they had known each other, possibly been friends.

There were several letters in one drawer. As she lifted a paper it released a faint perfume. Resisting the temptation to read it she opened another drawer containing a lace handkerchief and a garter of pink satin with black lace. Giving a faint grin, she thought: How deliciously sinful the forbidden must be. She intended to be twice as sinful once Benedict had shown her how.

His wardrobe held few garments – a robe, two suits, one a dress suit with buckled breeches, the other black dittos. Extra linens, hose, cravats and shirts were neatly folded in the drawers. A pair of shoes and a pair of boots were lined up on shelf. There was a sailing ship on the dresser, hair brushes, scissors, razor and strop in a gentleman's cabinet. Everything needed for a hurried visit, in fact.

The bed was high and inviting, the air a lavender-scented drift through the open window from the garden. There was a slight stench as well – like a distant ferment of rotting vegetables. Probably it was coming from the Thames river, she'd heard it was dirty. But then, the streets of London and the square itself was not very clean.

Amber's body ached from the long journey and her eyes would hardly stay open. Stripping down to her chemise she slipped under the covers and into a cloud of soft feathers that filled the mattress. The pillow her head nestled into smelled like Benedict and she smiled, wondering if her imagination had stretched so far that she could recognize him from smell alone. She doubted it.

Closing her eyes she imagined herself lying in this bed with him. Man and wife! She'd accepted his proposal now, and she would honour it. But her grandfather had taught her to be honest. Benedict now knew of her good fortune. It was obvious that he didn't need her wealth, so why hadn't he been able to tell her about Brierly House?

The matter of the agreement would need to be discussed as soon as he was well enough. She didn't want to start married life with a lie between them.

Benedict recovered quickly. It seemed as though his affliction couldn't wait to depart from his body. Within two days he was out of bed, despite the doctor's protests, his cough almost non-existent. Within three he was astride his horse getting a little exercise. The next day he was on his way to London with the gloomy prognosis of his man, George Fildew ringing in his ears.

He arrived at St James's Square in the middle of the afternoon, to find that everyone was out. A stable lad took Juniper to be fed and rested.

'Where did they go?' he asked the butler.

'Shopping, my Lord.'

'Even Miss Hartford?'

The butler smiled. The upcoming nuptials were now an extremely strong rumour, since one of the maids had recognized the ring the young lady was wearing as one belonging to the viscount. 'Miss Hartford is shopping, Lady Stratton and Mrs Foster, accompanied by the gentlemen, are advising her, My Lord. I do believe they are all paying a visit to Lady Varden afterwards.'

'Ah ... I see. I think I'll give that one a miss.' He grinned and headed for the stairs two at a time, turning at the top to say, 'I'll rest until they return. Have someone send up some warm water so I can wash at that time.'

'Yes, My Lord.' The sleeping arrangements occurred to the butler a little later and he grinned. No doubt his lordship would sort that out for himself, since two of the guest rooms were always kept in readiness. The viscount was not the type of gentleman to insist that a guest must be moved to cater to his own comfort.

The ride had sapped some of Benedict's newly discovered energy. Even so he leaned back against the door panel with a smile on his face as his glance ran over the boxes, most with their contents spilling out. Gowns of different hues lay over the back of the chair, along with silky chemises. Dozens of stocking were neatly folded in a box. On top, several pairs of garters resided. He picked up one fashioned from white lace with a red satin heart embroidered on the side, and chuckled. His sisters were proving to be a bad influence on his country mouse.

So, Amber and her new wardrobe was using his room, he thought. He picked up a gauzy sash, holding the softness of it against his cheek and smelling the faint perfume of her skin. He didn't mind the feminine clutter. Clearing a space on the bed he sat on the side, pulled off his boots and rolled into the middle where he fell instantly asleep.

Shopping had been fun. Lady Varden had been difficult. She was Archie's great aunt, and very deaf, so everyone was obliged to shout. The visit didn't last long, but now Amber was exhausted. She was tempted to withdraw from the party and return to the house in St James's Square to rest. If she did the others would follow suit, and she would spoil it for them.

'The Baron is a charming man, and such a wit. But beware, Amber, he's very fond of women.'

He was a rake, not a wit, she thought when he kissed her hand, using his tongue to tickle her palm. He was too old for such behaviour. His pale eyes had a reptilian look to them and he flicked a glance at her breasts as he straightened. 'What a charming young lady,' he whispered, then looked at the twins. 'Tell me about her if you please.'

'Miss Hartford is the granddaughter of the late Lord Hartford, and is my guest,' Emma said.

'Ah, I do believe I've met your cousin, Patrick Hartford. He had expectations there, I believe.'

Alarmed as she made the connection, Amber stepped back. She had no wish to discuss Patrick. But the Baron had turned to Emma. 'I'd heard you had a young woman staying with you, Lady Stratton. Why did you not visit me sooner?'

Caroline said, 'We're in London to shop, Lord Carlton, this is the first time we've had to socialize. You were first on our list, after my husband's relative, Lady Varden.'

'Ah yes, the sprightly Eugenia. We had a falling out, and have not spoken in years ... how is she?'

'Still sprightly.'

He smiled at her, saying softly, 'I've heard that Miss Hartford comes with considerable wealth – a legacy from an Italian aunt.'

'Oh, Lord,' Caroline muttered, 'Can nothing remain secret?'

Amber gazed at him with barely concealed irritation. 'My financial position is none of your business, Lord Carlton, and I'd be obliged if you would refrain from speaking about me to others, as if I were not present.'

His eyebrows arched. 'Ah ... the girl is outspoken. A pity. Jonas, stop lurking in the window seat and show yourself. I've been told that you've met with this young woman before, and your behaviour left much to be desired. Why did you not acquaint me with that fact?'

It was a cruel trick to play on her, and Amber gasped when when Jonas Carlton came out from behind a screen. His face was as embarrassed as she felt, and she could only say accusingly, 'You!'

'Miss Hartford.' He took her hand in his, said stiffly, 'I'm so sorry for my behaviour when we first met. Can you ever forgive me?'

'After the way you treated me. How dare you

even think I could pardon your behaviour, you disgusting creature ... you worthless guttersnipe.'

Emma and Caroline gasped.

'We were drunk ... things went too far. I didn't intend to hurt you.' There was a plea in his voice. 'For God's sake, Miss Hartford, at least give me the chance to speak to you and settle this matter in private.'

'What's this ... what's this, Jonas?' Lord Carlton said, his voice pitched high, his voice avid. 'Look at the young woman, she's trembling. Is there more I should know?'

Her companions gazed at each other, Emma and Caroline looking mystified. When Archie gazed at her with an apology in his eyes she felt no need to explain. He knew what had happened to her. Benedict had told him. Mortified, she snatched her hand away and cracked Jonas across the face with it before pushing past him. She hurried towards the door.

It was Kitt who caught up with her first, with Caroline and Emma in tow. He ushered them all into the carriage, sending them on their way with orders to the driver and a whispered, 'Archie and I will deal with this.'

Emma and Caroline gazed at her, then at each other in consternation. Caroline gave a nervous giggle. 'Oh, Lord, this will be all over London tomorrow. You were wonderful, Amber.'

'I don't feel wonderful. Just setting eyes on him made me feel ... soiled.'

'But all the same ... a *worthless guttersnipe*. How brave and awe inspiring you are. I'd never have dared to say such a thing to him.' Emma leaned forward and took her hands. Her eyes were filled with curiosity. 'We have wondered, Caro and I ... and I saw your bruises. Could you bring yourself to tell us how badly he treated you?'

'Jonas Carlton led me around on a rein on my hands and knees at the behest of his companions, and he kept jerking on it to choke me, and made inappropriate suggestions.'

'He said he'd been imbibing too much liquor.'

'All three of them had.'

'There were three of them?' the twins said together in horror.

'The worst was Stephen Gould. I believe he had his mind set on...' She watched the twins eyes widen in horror and added hastily, 'But he didn't have his way. The third was my cousin, Patrick Hartford.'

'And your cousin allowed this to happen?' Emma said fiercely. 'If I'm ever introduced to him I shall cut him dead.'

'And I shall go further and cut his throat until he bleeds to death.' Caroline kissed her cheek, then hugged her tight. 'You must rest when we get home. You poor dear, you must have been absolutely terrified with nobody to help you.'

'I did have Jake. I hid him in a cupboard and he escaped and went to find help. He was very brave for a small boy.'

'No wonder you are so attached to the lad, when he showed such courage.'

Tears came to Amber's eyes, for the caring nature of the sisters had warmed her. She couldn't remember anyone who'd ever troubled themselves with how she'd felt, not even her grandfather. It had made her insular.

'Thank you both for your sympathy, but don't be too kind-hearted lest I start feeling sorry for myself. Thank goodness Jake found Benedict in time to warn him of what to expect.'

'It was preordained by fate,' Emma declared, and turned enthusiastically towards her sister. 'We must take Amber to see that fortune teller we consulted last year, mustn't we Caro.'

'Gypsy Florence, the one who told us that three sons would be born into the family on the same day next spring? That means one of us will give birth to twins. Oh, what fun that would be.'

'Archie would like to have another son, and so would I. It's quite nice having Jake in the nursery now he's settled down. The girls dote on him, though I daresay they would treat a baby brother like a doll, like we did with Bennet. He was so sweet with his blue eyes. Do you remember how he used to laugh when we tickled his stomach...'

Amber smiled as she listened to the talk about Benedict, who seemed to be the twins' favourite subject, but the thought of tickling his stomach was slightly, and deliciously ... *wicked*.

As if talking about him had made him appear, there he was when they returned home, sprawled on his ticklish stomach in the middle of her bed, his head reclined to one side and resting on his hand.

She took a seat on the edge of the bed and gazed down at him, needing a little time to contemplate this man she intended to marry. Long, taut thighs columned up to a neat, but manly backside. His

171

back was broad and muscled, powerful-looking.

How vulnerable he looked in sleep, his hair tousled, his eyelashes a dark sweep. Inside her desire flamed. She wanted to touch those muscled thighs, to cup him gently in her hands and feel him firm against her palms. She dare think no further, instead placing a chaste kiss against his dark hairline.

Benedict rolled over on his back, flinging his arm out. His eyes fluttered open and he stared at her. 'My beautiful Amaryllis. How I've missed you.' His voice was a whisper of silk, his smile like cream as he slipped his arm around her waist and pulled her down against him. His welcome kiss rendered her breathless.

When she caught her breath she discovered they'd sunk into the soft mattress with herself on top of him. Every man part of him was corresponding with every womanly part of her. Her legs had parted over his thighs and he was growing hard against her. Lord, how big he was, and how languid and accessible she felt as she murmured half-heartedly, 'Benedict Costain, allow me to escape from the liberties you are contemplating. We are not married yet.'

'Shush. I've just woken up from a dream of seduction, so let me love you a little,' he said, kissing each tender nub of her breasts until they pushed hard against her bodice like ripe acorns waiting to fall from their cups.

She pushed her hand through his hair and pulled his head back, her fingers grasping a bunch of its springy length. 'Will only a little be enough?'

He laughed. 'I doubt it. I'm only human, and so are you.'

'Then why torture each other?'

'Because that's the nature of men and woman.'

'Then love me more than a little when the time comes. But that time is not now, my Benedict. There's something you should know.'

Her eyes sought his and his smile faded. 'Now you have a fortune you've decided not to wed me after all. Is that it?'

Scrambling from his side she put some distance between them. 'No, that is not it. I'll honour the agreement our grandfathers made, and the promise I made to you. There is another matter – one you may not like.'

'Which from your expression is also less than palatable to you. You have all my attention.'

'Today I visited Lord Carlton with your family. Jonas Carlton was there. It was such a shock. He tried to apologize, but my heart refused to accept it, and I threw it back at him.'

He nodded. 'It's natural to be passionate when you're angry.'

'There is more. I hit him in front of everyone, and I called him names.' Tears pricked at her her eyes. 'I acted like a fishwife and have embarrassed everybody in your family, as well as myself.'

He came up off the bed in one fluid motion and slid into his jacket, the joys of the flesh forgotten. 'Where's Kitt and Archie?'

'Still at the Baron's house, trying to sort it out.'

'How many other guests were there?'

'None ... just us.'

'That's good.' He came to stand tall before her, his eyes a blaze of blue as they gazed into hers. 'It sounds as though the baron has heard of his heir's exploits and set a trap to confront him with you. The baron is a philanderer, but he's a charitable man with a reputation for fairness. A public dressing down of his heir in his own home would have affronted and humiliated him. It would be better to have accepted Carlton's apology. I may be able to save the situation if you're prepared to help yourself.'

Mentally, she stamped her foot. 'I do not feel the need to apologise. He deserved it.'

'No doubt, Amber. But one word from Lord Carlton and your reputation will be gone in a puff of wind.'

Her blood ran cold. 'You mean he'd lie about me?'

'He wouldn't have to lie, just indicate he'd been slandered. London operates on rumour and gossip. You're new to society, so will be fresh meat for the buzzards. They'll crucify you given half the chance.'

She shivered, then said fiercely, 'So I must swallow my pride and accept his apology, even though he's the one at fault. I certainly will not.'

'Is your pride so important to you that it can disregard an attempt to put matters right and stand up to public scrutiny? Trading insult for insult is not a good way to settle a dispute.'

What had happened to her former quiet life? 'Is there an alternative?'

'Yes ... marry me. Now. As my wife your rep-utation will be untouchable, unless someone cares to answer to me. I'll accept Jonas Carlton's apology on your behalf.'

Alarmed, she stared at him. 'You don't intend to challenge him to a duel?'

'The Code Duello forbids it, since Carlton has no rank. If I'm challenged, either the baron would stand in for his heir – and he used to be an extremely good shot. Or somebody would have to stand in for me. Kitt would probably volunteer to defend your honour.'

'He cannot do that. He might be killed, then his wife and children...' Her eyes widened in surprise. 'Did you say, marry you now?'

'I did. Then I can indicate to the Baron that an apology in writing for the insult previously paid to my wife would be acceptable to me.'

'This very minute ... in secret?'

'Without even thinking about it.' He laughed. 'Don't look so surprised. I could probably persuade a clergy do the deed at short notice.'

'But Emma and Caroline are making the arrangements for our wedding.'

'Oh, we can be married a second time, just to satisfy them.'

A smile touched her mouth and a reckless excitement overtook her. 'I'll wear my new bonnet.'

Benedict left instructions with a footman as they sneaked out, knowing they would never get away with this if Emma or Caroline saw them. Luckily, the sisters were too busy gossiping about what had taken place to notice their guest leave with their brother.

The pair took a hired carriage to the venue. The church was a dusty cavern in a narrow street, the door was open and the clergy was nowhere to be found.

He gazed at her in consternation. 'We cannot be married legally without clergy, but will you exchange vows with me now here, in front of the altar.'

When she nodded he took both her hands in his and she gazed into his eyes.

'I, Benedict Costain, pledge myself to you in marriage this day, Amber Rose. I will guard you in honour, care for you always and hold you close to my heart, and as long as we both live.'

She hoped that would be a long time, and smiled. 'I, Amber Rose Hartford, take you, Benedict Costain, to be my husband. I promise to respect you, to be true to you always and keep you in my affection.'

'There, it is done, Amber,' and he stooped to gently kissed her.

Benedict dropped a generous amount of money into the poor box as they left the church hand in hand.

She gave him a sideways glance and grinned. Even though legally dubious, it had been a romantic gesture, a few moments of closeness that had bound them together. 'I don't feel very married yet.'

'You will soon, my love.' He handed her up into the carriage. 'Let's go home. I'll leave you there while I go straight on to Carlton's house. You'd better advise my sisters of the vows we exchanged. I'm just glad I won't be there to witness their reaction; they hate not knowing what's going on around them. You might have to stamp your foot, and you have my permission to pull rank.'

Before she headed into the house, she said. 'I'd forgotten to enquire about your illness. Are you sure you're recovered?'

'That was quite a wifely remark.' Leaning out of the carriage window he kissed her long and hard. She was grinning when the carriage moved off.

She'd hardly got inside when Caroline and Emma came clattering down the stairs with a barrage of questions.

'Where have you been?'

'Was that Bennet, kissing you in public? How absolutely wicked of him. Is he better?'

'He must be if he was kissing her. Why didn't he come inside, Amber?'

Then together. 'Oh ... we so hate so much being kept in the dark.'

'I've been to the church. Yes it was Benedict, yes he was kissing me, and yes ... he appears to have recovered. He didn't come inside because he's gone to Carlton House.'

Emma came closer to gaze at her. 'You look rather odd. Come over here. Caroline, does Amber look odd to you?'

Caroline peered at her. 'Her face is flushed ... and her smile is rather peculiar and dazed–'

'I have just exchanged vows with Benedict,' she said.

'...she has tears in her eyes. My dear, you're not sickening for anything, are you? Do you have any pain?'

'Will the pair of you never stop talking long enough to actually listen. I have just told you that

I've exchanged vows with your brother,' she said more loudly.

They fell quiet and gazed at her.

'I've been Benedict's wife for exactly fifteen minutes.'

Emma said faintly, 'Good...'

'....gracious,' finished Caroline.

They sank on to a velvet sofa together like a pair of pale blue swans, gazing at each other, rendered mute with surprise.

Expecting a tirade, Amber said carefully, 'Please do not be vexed. It happened so quickly. Benedict was lying on the bed asleep when I went upstairs, and he woke. I told him what had happened at the Baron's House and I cried, so he comforted me. And then ... we just got carried away. It was Benedict's idea to exchange vows now, so I put on my new bonnet and we went to the church.' She flopped into the chair opposite them. 'Good Lord, this is extremely disturbing. I don't know what came over me.'

'Bennet can be very persuasive,' Caroline offered. Emma raised an eyebrow. 'You mentioned you got carried away. May I enquire–'

Amber blushed at the misunderstanding and reminded them, 'Your brother is a gentleman.'

'So was Archie.'

'And Kitt. Being gentlemanly doesn't stop men from being ... *men.*'

Voices restored, the sisters exchanged a grin. Emma said, 'But of course Bennet is perfect, so above such impulsive behaviour. He was nearly persuaded to become a clergy by our grandfather. For a while he walked around with his hands pressed together in prayer. You could almost see his halo shining.'

Amber frowned. 'I beg to differ. He's hardly perfect, is completely impulsive, and is not in the least bit angelic now.'

'Oh, he was only six then, and had learned he'd been named after a saint, which was rather a handicap to begin with. He was praying that father would buy him a proper horse for his seventh birthday. He lost his faith when it didn't eventuate. It was rather a relief at the time, wasn't it Caro?'

'At least he stopped blessing everyone in sight.'

Amber gazed from one sister to the other, both bright-eyed with laughter. 'The pair of you are incorrigible.'

'And you, dearest sister-in-law are gullible. Now, what are we to do about the wedding we were arranging. It would be inconvenient to cancel the arrangements when the invitations have already been sent and the earl's staff instructed.'

'Oh, the marriage must go ahead as planned, since today's ceremony was hurried ... and there was nobody there in the church. It wasn't a proper marriage and I really don't feel married yet. I doubt if Benedict does, either. You're right, Caroline. Benedict really is persuasive. It was such a romantic gesture.'

Emma and Caroline exchanged a glance.

# TWELVE

The baron was apologetic, but his eyes were troubled. 'Miss Hartford was perfectly within her rights to be angry, My Lord. My only regret about the incident was that it occurred in public, when my nephew asked to talk to her in private. It was embarrassing for all concerned, but especially for the young lady. I'll apologize in writing on behalf of my nephew, with suitable reparation.'

'I would prefer the apology to come directly from your nephew.'

'So would I. Alas, he absented himself before your hot-headed friend over there could challenge him to a duel on your behalf. Jonas is, no doubt, licking his wounds. If he was not my only relative I'd disinherit him over this episode. But he's still young and needs to sow his oats, as do we all, I suppose.'

'You know I cannot accept that as an excuse.'

'No, no, of course not. It was not offered as one, but was merely the idle musings of an old man. Nevertheless, the apology was sincerely and spontaneously offered and it should not have been rejected out of hand. The young lady was passionate, a quality which should be reserved for the bedchamber, where it can be fully exploited. Her Italian blood, I imagine. To which of you does she belong?'

'Miss Hartford is my ... *wife*,' Benedict said rather self-consciously, and his brothers-in-law gazed at each other and grinned.

'Your wife!' The baron gazed at him with some perplexity. 'Miss Hartford is rather an odd way to refer to her then, is it not. Without offence, may I enquire is young lady is aware of the fact that she's married to you?'

'I rather doubt it. We only exchanged vows an hour ago, without clergy, and I'm just getting used to it myself,' he said drily.

'Ah yes ... I see. I do recall that chivalry runs strongly in your family. You've taken the insult upon yourself in the name of love. I find that truly touching. You should be servicing the wench, not fronting up to an old trout like me.'

Benedict's lips twitched as he struggled not to laugh. The wily rogue was right. 'Miss Hartford was brought up in the country and was unaware of the protocols surrounding this affair.'

'At least you did not call me out, for which I'm grateful, My Lord. I'm pleased you've turned up since your companions were becoming rather a nuisance. In actual fact my hand shakes too much to aim a pistol now.' He grinned round at them. 'The ladies don't seem to mind it too much, though.'

Archie and Kitt chuckled.

The baron sobered. 'My nephew starts at Cambridge before too long. Between now and then I'll cut off his allowance; that will bring him to heel. No doubt he'll return home when he's hungry, at which time I'll make him aware of his shortcomings. In the meantime, my sincere apologies. Now gentlemen, may I offer you a brandy while we wait for my secretary to draft the letter?'

The paper was duly brought to him to sign, then folded and sealed. A small box was laid on top. 'A flower for the young woman, with my compliments,' he said. 'Such passion in her. You're a lucky man, Lord Costain.'

Lucky man indeed, Benedict thought as Archie and Kitt bore him off to celebrate his dubious nuptials. He was glad he'd put them straight about the nature of it though, then wondered with an anticipation bordering on the indecent if Amber would regard the vows they'd exchanged as binding. It would be interesting to find out!

Emma and Caroline had worked fast. By the time their husbands and brother arrived home, the carriages were almost packed and the horses being saddled.

The two men exchanged a glance of tacit agreement when told they were shortly to take to the road. If Amber hadn't made clear to their wives about the nature of the promises made between herself and the viscount, it was nothing to do with them.

Bennet would take advantage of the situation presented to him, Archie thought. There was no doubt that he needed to reel Amber Hartford in fast, and taking her to bed would secure that.

Kitt put up a token resistance, as was expected of him. 'We won't be home before dark,' he grumbled, watching Caroline with interest as she began to disrobe before changing into her travelling clothes

'We'll spend the night at that inn we used before.'

'I don't see why we can't stay the night here and leave early in the morning?'

'Because it's Amber and Benedict's wedding night. Don't grumble, my darling Kitt, they should be alone.'

He grinned as he wished Bennet luck with his bride.

'You're leering at me,' she said.

'I don't leer. How can they be alone when there's a house full of servants?'

'Servants are different. They don't nudge each other and give each knowing looks in the morning. At least not in front of their employers.'

'Actually, Bennet's not that well. We've put him in the spare bedroom.'

Caroline narrowed her eyes. Taking her husband by the lapels she brought his face down to hers to smell his breath. 'You've been drinking, you lout, and you were definitely leering at me.'

He grinned, then kissed her. 'You're right, and I hadn't drunk enough to render me incapable. I feel rather amorous, as it happens.'

'As it happens, so do I.'

Archie had been having a similar conversation with Emma.

Unlike Kitt, he didn't argue. He just heaved an exaggerated sigh of resignation and said, 'I'll be glad to be alone with you again, my love. Having guests is always a strain. You have to walk around with all your buttons done up. Can you loosen my

183

cravat a little. It's strangling me.'

His arms came round her when she complied. Tucking one hand under each of her buttocks he drew her closer. 'There, that's better.'

Throwing the cravat aside, she placed a kiss at the hollow of his throat and murmured, 'You taste salty.'

'I feel salty. Now, put your hands down between us and unfasten my buttons.'

'But, Archie, your breeches will fall down.'

He chuckled. 'I sincerely hope so.'

Oblivious to what was going on around her Amber was soaking in the bathtub.

Two hours later, rested, perfumed and arrayed in a new cream gown trimmed with pink rosebuds and lace, she made her way downstairs.

The butler gave her a small bow, said tentatively, 'My Lady.'

So, word had got around. The house seemed awfully quiet. 'Where's Lady Stratton and Mrs Foster?'

'They departed for Hampshire with their husbands, not more than two hours ago.'

'They decided to return home without me?' For a moment Amber felt hurt, and wondered if she'd been forgotten, then Benedict's face rushed into her mind. She was his responsibility now. Turning pink she enquired, 'Is Lord Costain at home?'

'The viscount has been resting and is now dressing for dinner. May I offer my sincere congratulations on your marriage, My Lady. So romantic. We knew something was in the air,

184

especially when the viscount rose from his sick bed to follow you to London.'

Sick bed! Benedict had appeared to be a fine and healthy man to her, and she smiled. She opened her mouth to explain the situation to him, then decided the truth might embarrass him, so she merely said, 'Thank you.'

Benedict joined her ten minutes later, his glance going over her. 'You look exquisite.'

'It's all down to the maid. I might try and steal Annie away from Emma. She's wasted in the laundry.'

'I'll arrange it for you.' He handed her the note of apology and a small box containing a brooch. 'It's a gift from the baron, reparation for any embarrassment you may have suffered. All settled without a shot being fired, thank God.' The box contained a brooch set with diamonds, fashioned in the shape of a flower. Benedict took the jewel from her fingers and pinned it to her bodice.

She couldn't help but admire it, despite what it signified. 'How pretty it is, but I'd rather not accept this. It will always be a reminder.'

He sighed. 'To return it would be the ultimate insult for the baron.'

She removed it from her bodice and placed it back in the box. 'I have no intention of insulting him further, but I'm not obliged to wear it. Thank you for defending me.'

'Don't be so stiff, Amber Rose.' He grinned. 'What was it you called his nephew ... a worthless guttersnipe?'

Now her temper had subsided it sounded

dreadful indeed, but her ire was easily roused again when thinking of Jonas Carlton and she didn't have to work very hard to retrieve it. Her hands went to her hips. 'I do not intend to take back one word I uttered.'

He chuckled. 'Perhaps a birthday gift from your husband will remove the scowl from your face.'

How kind of him, but how had he known it was her birthday?

The pendant he gave her contained a flawless emerald surrounded by small diamonds, and there was a ring to match. It replaced the signet ring she wore, which he slipped back on his little finger. She shivered when he fastened it around her neck. Tears gathered on her lashes as the emerald fell like a green raindrop to her breast-bone, where it nestled.

'Thank you, Benedict ... it's so pretty.'

Impulsively, she hugged him tight.

She realized that the gown she was wearing was rather low cut, and the lace at the neckline barely covered the rise of her breasts. The silk chemise she wore underneath slid cool and seductive against her skin. White garters decorated with ribbons and rosebuds hugged her hose against her thighs. She had dressed as a bride for him, for she was under no illusions that he intended to seduce her later.

A kiss brushed the hollow behind her ear, so the hairs at the nape of her neck reacted with little prickles. She wondered if his kiss would draw the same shivering reaction from other part of her body, and she squirmed with pleasure at the thought, her body alive to the possibilities and the need to be exploited by him.

'Kiss me?' he said, his voice soft.

Everything was bubbling inside her and she felt like laughing. She couldn't meet his eyes and her face was warm. 'I can't believe that I just ran off and promised myself to you in that dusty old church, and without really knowing you.' She lifted her face to his and brushed her mouth against his lips. 'There's your kiss.'

A grin slid across his face. 'That was a kiss a child would bestow on her uncle. Would you like to try it for a second time?'

She blushed, gazing up at him through her lashes, knowing she was being provocative when she laughed and suggested, 'I think you might have to help me?'

He took her face in his palms and brought his mouth to within a heartbeat of hers. She waited, her eyes closed, her breath held in and her senses filled with anticipation as his breath trembled against hers. Then Amber remembered she was supposed to be kissing him.

She reached out with the tip of her tongue to touch against his lips. But she touched against his tongue instead, and slid into his mouth, where tongues entwined together in a slow, moist dance. Sensation danced through her, leaving her moist and dazed, so she felt she might burst from it.

Even Benedict looked shaken when they finally pulled apart to gaze at one other.

'Was that better?' she said, knowing just how much better it had seemed to her.

'Perfect.' He gathered her against his chest and

held her there, kissing the top of her head. Then he let her go and slid his hand around hers, entwining their fingers. 'Let's go in for dinner.'

Amber couldn't remember what they'd eaten afterwards, but it had been a simple meal. There had been a confection that tasted of almonds afterwards.

When dusk set in Benedict led her upstairs. Several candles were burning in their holders, and a small table was set with champagne, two glasses and a bowl of strawberries dipped in chocolate and coated in sugar.

'If I'm to be rejected as a lover tonight, let this be the moment,' he said with a smile.

'I'm nervous, and curious and...' Her laughter had a husky undertone, 'seething with anticipation, I think you will not be rejected.'

'Just as a bride should be.'

He must have arranged this earlier, she thought as he seated her on the sofa. He removed his jacket before he took a seat next to her. Light sparked fire from the crystal as he filled the glasses with fizzing wine. He dipped a strawberry into the chocolate and sugar, then fed it to her. It was delicious. Even more delicious was when he licked the remnants of chocolate and sugar from her mouth. That was followed by a few sips of the wine.

There couldn't be a sweeter seduction, she thought, her voice full of laughter when she said after the second glass, 'Enough! I'm not used to it and it's going to my head.'

'It's supposed to.' He emptied his own glass, loosened his cravat and tossed it aside, then pulled her to her feet.

'What now, my Benedict?'

'Turn around.'

When she did he unfastened her bodice and her gown pooled around her ankles. Slightly dizzy, she drew in a deep breath. When she expelled it each breast was supported by pair of waiting hands that cupped around them gently. His thumbs caressed each centre into hardness. 'A perfect handful,' he purred against her ear.

She leant back into his body, full of need, his kisses bringing her to life, and she felt his hardness spring against her buttocks, and his thighs muscular against her chemise. His hands moved over her, down over her stomach to explore the shape of her through the silk.

'Mmmm,' she sighed and he edged the flimsy garment she wore up over her knees, then inch by inch over her thighs until his hands could reach underneath the bunched up froth of silk to touch and caress the prize he was seeking. A delicious thrill shocked through her when his gentle exploratory touches brought a rush of moist heat to her loins. When she thought she couldn't stand any more he turned her around to face him then fell to his knees and kissed her there.

She gave a small cry of pleasure and her fingers twisted in his hair when his tongue slipped inside her with a flickering motion. Never in her wildest dreams had she imagined that such pleasure existed. He seemed to sense the moment when she trembled on the brink, for he moved away and the moment slipped by, leaving an ache behind as he loosened the ribbons on her chemise and allowed it to slip to the floor.

Now she was naked except for her stockings, her garters and her jewellery. Suddenly shy, she formed her hands into a vee to cover herself.

'Your body is exquisite, Amber Rose,' he purred. 'Remove your hands so I can look at you properly.'

She teased him with her laughter and shook her head, 'Not while you're still fully clothed. I feel like a hussy standing here naked.'

His chuckle shivered against her ear. 'You're welcome to be a hussy, especially in the privacy of our bedroom. I'll join you if it will make you feel better. Have you ever seen a man naked?'

'Of course not.'

His breeches and shirt were quickly discarded. She daren't look at him, though she had an impression of a lean body with broad shoulders and a flat stomach. He stepped closer, reached out to pluck the pins from her hair and watched it tumble to her waist. He leaned forward and inhaled the perfume it released.

He smiled, then taking her hands, placed them around the rampant maleness of him. His skin was like taut satin. Curiosity sent her hands exploring the ridged surface, and he grew even more. He throbbed against her palms as he kissed her mouth. Suddenly she was swept into his arms and carried to the bed, where they fell together into its softness.

The candle light flickered and danced as his fingers and tongue caressed her. Amber succumbed to the erotic urges of her own body. He took what he wanted from her, and made her crave for more. She became oblivious to anything

190

but the sensation of his touch and her own, and she grew moist with cravings inside her.

Eventually, he crouched over her, spread her wide and gazed down at her. She was splayed, his hands pinning hers to the bed above her head as she gazed up at him through the dark tumble of her hair.

There was a look on his face, almost predatory, and his eyes were dark and unseeing with passion. For a moment his smile was full of his need and she closed her eyes, abandoning herself to that need. His mouth closed over hers and his tongue slid slowly into her. Then his body lowered against hers and he entered her, thrusting through the initial barrier with a purposeful stroke, her surprised cry captured by his mouth.

Body and soul he took his fill of her, and somewhere in the midst of it she lost her mind, and the woman took over and rose to meet the erotic, thrusting powerful frenzy of him. She wanted to scream her own needs out to him, but her mouth was filled with her lover's tongue and her fingernails dug into his flesh. He seemed to sense her climax, for he fed it with his own. She gave a prolonged groan at the intensity of it as they reached some sort of peak and spiralled downwards into the calm.

They were damp with perspiration, and her heart was pounding in her chest. Benedict's breath was harsh, like a wounded animal. She remembered he'd been ill and held him against her, smoothing his hair while he quieted.

Then he chuckled, a slow satisfied rumble that made her grin.

'I hope I didn't hurt you?'

'I didn't mind that you were a little forceful. I have to admit that I enjoyed your attention,' she confessed. 'But now it is over and we must sleep.'

'You were a wicked kitten, all purrs and claws.'

'And you were a lion,' she said, and gently bit him on the shoulder.

He growled menacingly at her, then his tongue curled about the nub of her breasts and with a shock of pleasure, she realized that is wasn't over at all. In fact, they'd only just begun.

## THIRTEEN

Two days later a disgruntled Jonas Carlton joined his former companions at Hartford House, where he unsaddled his horse in the stable, thankful there was feed for him. He didn't imagine they'd be staying long in the house that Patrick despised.

The garden was waist high in weeds. He pounded at the front door until he was allowed in. The interior was almost as neglected as the garden. But the dust sheets had been taken off the downstairs furniture and the smashed wine bottles had been cleared away. As usual, his companions were inebriated.

'My uncle has cut off my allowance,' he grumbled after washing the dust of the journey from his throat with a glass of burgundy. 'It's your cousin's fault, Patrick. The baron had got wind of what happened here. I was all set to apologize to save face, but she took to me in front of her companions like a banshee from hell. She slapped my face into the bargain.'

Stephen laughed, 'I like a woman with spirit.'

'Spirit, or spite? After she was bundled out by Lord Stratton I got a dreadful quizzing from my uncle. I left him to handle things, then when I returned he promptly cut off my allowance and sent me to my room, like a schoolboy. He said I'd spoiled my chances for a good marriage with her. I got out of there before he placed the ball and chain around my leg. I had no idea a union with your cousin would have entered his mind.'

Patrick laughed. 'Marriage? Good Lord. Her only asset is her looks–'

'And a strong claim to Brierly House,' Stephen cut in. 'But even that has the encumbrance of Costain and his family. They won't give the property up without a fight, especially to a second party. Marriage? Hah! I'd rather consider an exchange of cash for a night with the girl than marry her.'

Patrick surprised himself by defending Amber Rose. 'My cousin is not a whore.'

'Didn't you say her mother was? Like mother, like daughter. When she has no means of support she'll willingly lift her skirt and sell her remaining asset.'

Jonas grinned as he told them, 'It seems that your cousin does have means. Rumours abound that she's come into a fortune from the Italian side of her family, at least one hundred thousand guineas. Is it any wonder that the viscount's family is guarding her.'

'And she's supposed to wed him in a week or so.' Patrick gazed at his two companions with an aggrieved eye. 'Perhaps I'll wed her myself. I could leave her here and set myself up in London.'

Stephen's eyes narrowed. 'Why wed her? If she met with an accident the fortune would be yours? Besides, we'd agreed to go to abroad together.'

Patrick stared uneasily at Stephen. 'My cousin has done nothing to deserve such a fate. I don't like her but I wouldn't kill her in cold blood, not even for a fortune. Besides, as soon as the house sells I'll have some cash of my own.'

'Most of which you'll owe to me,' Stephen said drily. 'Be sensible, Patrick. It would take just a moment or two to ambush her.'

'We haven't been able to get near her so far.'

'We managed to get in and out of the earl's house unobserved, so there's no reason why we shouldn't achieve the same thing at the Stratton residence. We'll watch the place and wait till everyone is asleep. Three armed men with their faces covered wouldn't be recognized. A pillow over her face and she wouldn't stand a chance.'

'Count me out,' Jonas said, wishing he'd stayed in London. 'I don't mind a bit of sport, but I draw the line at killing a woman in her sleep.'

Finding courage in Jonas's words, Patrick nodded. 'I agree. I'd be the first person the authorities would come after.'

'We could abduct her and hold her for ransom instead. Once we've got the money we could leave a note saying where she can be found.'

The three of them exchanged a glance, then

194

Jonas murmured, 'Where would we hide her?'

'There's an abandoned hut in the forest. Maisie at the inn told me it used to be the dwelling of a charcoal burner. I went to have a look at it out of curiosity. It's well-hidden, and we could leave your cousin there.'

'We'd have to be careful she didn't recognize us.'

'We'll tie her up and blindfold her. Then we can remove our disguises. Once we've collected the cash we'll split up and go our separate ways. You can go on ahead, Patrick. We can rendezvous abroad with the money at a later date. Jonas can follow after. We'll ask for a thousand guineas to guarantee her safety.'

Patrick's gasp matched that of Jonas at the thought of asking for such a sum.

Stephen smiled, as if knowing he had them hooked. 'She's worth much more. If you had the guts to brazen it out you could inherit the entire Italian fortune, Patrick.'

A sudden knock at the door put paid to the conversation. It was a messenger. Patrick signed for the note and ran his thumb under the seal. He smiled with satisfaction when he read it. 'Hartford House has been sold, and for the sum I specified. I'm going into Poole to sign some papers with Dunstan's agent, then I can collect the bank draft. I'm to meet the agent at the King George. We will need to vacate Hartford House within two weeks. He can have the place now, as long as he pays me.'

'I'll accompany you to Poole so you can honour your debt to me, then,' Stephen murmured, taking a dagger from his boot and toying with it. 'What about you, Jonas, are you coming with us?'

He should have kept the news of the girl's fortune to himself, Jonas thought, and knew he'd never forgive himself if anything happened to her.

'I'll accompany you as far as Poole, stay the night there then return to London. I must make peace with my uncle. I intend to have my allowance restored before I take up my place at Cambridge, and I'll have to convince him that I'm a reformed character.'

And judging by the way Stephen was looking at him, Jonas knew he'd have to watch his back from now on.

The inn was crowded and noisy. Jonas yawned. His companions with their carousing and womanising had lost their power to attract him. They lived life too fast and were always surrounded by tension. Stephen Gould in particular was a bad lot, as his uncle, the baron, had frequently pointed out to him. Patrick was normally good company, but he changed when in company with Stephen, who was a bad influence.

That was something he'd been guilty of himself up till now, Jonas admitted. He knew right from wrong and he'd deserved the punishment the girl had dished out. She'd made him face his own shame.

The trio made Poole within the hour. They found lodgings not far from the harbour, began drinking and then became involved in a game of cards with some seamen. As was usual, Patrick began to lose to Stephen.

Jonas backed away from the game and declined Stephen's offer of an IOU. He didn't want to place himself in the same position as Patrick. Hugging a pot of ale and watching the game, he thought he saw Stephen palm a card. But it had been quick, and he didn't have the courage to challenge him.

When Patrick went out to relieve himself. Jonas excused himself, saying, 'I have the need on me for a woman.'

Stephen stood too. Slipping a peppermint lozenge into his mouth he sucked on it, saying casually, 'I know a place where they're young and clean.'

'No need. There's a woman I always visit when I'm in Poole.' It was a lie, but Jonas didn't trust Stephen, and he was relieved when the man sank back into his chair. Stephen had been watching him all evening, as if he knew Jonas had made up his mind to head for Hampshire and warn Lord Costain of the plot being hatched. He hoped the action would go a little way into redeeming him in everyone's eyes, including his own. If it didn't, at least the young woman could be kept out of harm's way.

He left the warm fug of the inn, which smelled of tobacco, sweat and spilled ale, passing Patrick who was coming back in. 'I'm off after a woman,' he said. 'A word to the wise, Patrick. You're already up to your ears in debt to Gould and I think I saw him palm a card, so stop gambling. Also, I advise you not to allow yourself to be drawn into a scheme to abduct your cousin. It could get you killed.'

'Devil take him,' Patrick muttered, a scowl settling on his face.

Jonas placed a hand on his arm. 'Don't rejoin Stephen. Come with me to London. We'll warn Costain of what's afoot, on the way.'

'Not until after I've won my money back from him.' Shaking his arm off, Patrick lurched through the door.

He'd done his best. A light drizzle was falling outside and the sky was overcast. The air felt clean and fresh as Jonas sucked it into his lungs. Loosening the fall of his breeches he stood by a bollard on the quay and sighed with pleasure as he relieved himself into the water.

There was a noise behind him. He twisted, automatically putting an arm up in defence of himself. Before he could fully turn something hit him hard across the head and part of his shoulder. He caught a whiff of peppermint before his body toppled into the dark, cold water between two fishing boats that rubbed gently but relentlessly together.

Now Amber Rose had been initiated into the delights of the flesh she'd become a willing partner to Benedict. She cared not that the marriage wasn't a legal one, that would follow. She enjoyed the extra excitement of Benedict's being her lover. The uncertain experience of becoming a wife in the flesh was now over with, the void now occupied by imaginings of pleasure, or indeed, learning the various ways one could practise the pleasures of love.

She'd already discovered that to breathe gently into Benedict's ear, or gently nip the curve of his jaw would make him shiver. She smiled as she gazed at him. She intended to learn all the ways of pleasing him, allow him any liberty he desired.

As if he'd read her thoughts he turned, his eyes narrowed and offered a little knowing little smile. When colour crept into her cheeks he chuckled, which made her blush even more.

It was early morning. The grey smudged sky was streaked pale yellow on the horizon and the ghostly remains of last night's moon hugged the last blink of a star. London was barely awake, for Benedict had wanted an early start.

He'd said, 'If possible I'd like to get clear of the city before the streets get too crowded, and arrive home before dark.'

The transport he'd utilized to carry them back to Hampshire was the London carriage with the family crest. It was luxurious and pulled by a team of four matching greys that had been bred and trained at the Brierly stud. As well as the coachman there was an under-coachman accompanying them, and a stable hand acting as an outrider. She noticed that all the men were armed to the teeth. They'd be well protected from any felons that might chance their luck during the daylight hours.

Annie, Amber and the luggage took up much of the carriage interior. The trunk was for Jake, for they'd visited the school his father had once once attended, and had discovered some belongings stored there that had once belonged to his parents.

The school had not been a good one, but an institution that catered for male children born on the wrong side of the blanket to the mistresses of the merchant classes. There they were educated, in the hope they would become useful citizens. When Benedict had suggested to the headmaster that the contents of the trunk were rather sparse for the lifetime of a man and his family, the school's owner managed to find a silver watch and a chess set with ivory pieces in his cupboard.

'We sold the clothing and a silver brooch to cover his father's debts, My Lord,' he'd said. 'The boy should have taken his family's effects with him.'

'How would he carry such a load, when you threw the boy out to fend for himself?'

The man had shrugged. 'This is a school not a home for impoverished children. We have to be businesslike. If the student fees cannot be paid then we must give a place to a child who has a sponsor. As I recall, Jake Selby had a good brain. He could have easily found employment and earned enough to keep himself after he left us. He was one of our better students.'

'Due, no doubt to his father's influence.'

'As you say, My Lord. Mr Selby was a fine teacher. Master Selby is quite welcome to return to the school, should he acquire a benefactor to sponsor him.'

'He was lucky enough to find a sponsor in my wife before he starved to death. But I doubt if she'll wish Jake to return to your establishment.' He smiled at her. 'What are your feelings on this, my dear? We can find somewhere better, I suspect.'

She shook her head. 'I'd rather Jake didn't return here. I'm sure he'll be pleased to have something to remind him of his parents though. He held them in great esteem.'

'I'll send a cart to pick up the trunk. If you discover anything else that should have been legated to Master Selby, no doubt he'd be happy to accept what is his rightful due.'

But there was precious little added. His mother's sewing box with its coloured cottons, a little bag covered in beads and a pair of magnifying spectacles. It had been a family that existed rather than lived well. Amber couldn't wait to get away from the awful place, and was determined that Jake would do better than that for himself in the future.

Benedict had stated his intention to act as one of the outriders. His parting kiss was firm rather than sensual, his mind now on the journey ahead and far removed from the previous night, which they'd spent in sensual abandonment.

When she yawned behind her hand he gently touched her face. 'Try and get some rest, my love. I'll wake you when we reach the inn in time for breakfast. I'll take you to my sister's residence, after which I'll visit my parents and tell them the truth of what has happened between us.'

'Not everything. Just that our marriage needs to be legalized,' he assured her with a grin, when the alarm she felt filled her eyes. He whispered in her ear, 'I wouldn't like them to be embarrassed by somebody else telling them.'

'Of course. What about my embarrassment?'

'I love your blushes.' He kissed her again and helped her into the carriage before mounting his own horse and saying, 'Annie, make sure your mistress gets some rest.'

They set out with a jerk, then the horses settled into their stride. A grinning Annie placed a cushion under her head. Amber kicked off her shoes and curled onto the seat with a rug over her. Gradually, the noise of the horses, the wheels rattling over the cobbles and the creaking of harness leathers merged into one.

Waking for a breakfast of eggs, a thick slice of smoked bacon and fried bread washed down by tea, they then set off again. The journey was uneventful, and they reached the Strattons' residence just before dusk.

'The family is visiting the earl and the countess to finalize plans for the wedding. They won't be home before morning, My Lord,' the butler said, and sent the servants scurrying for the luggage. 'I believe they were expecting you to arrive tomorrow.'

'I see.' He smiled at her. 'Don't worry, Amber, I won't leave you alone.'

'It's all right, you go and join them.'

'Come with me.'

'I don't feel like travelling any further. I'm sure I'll be safe in a house full of servants, and I'll have Jake for company. I haven't seen much of him lately and this will provide me with an opportunity to talk to him about his future.' She feigned a yawn. 'I'm desperately in need of a good night's sleep.'

The butler had discreetly removed himself from the immediacy of their conversation and with sharp eyes was watching the servants bring in her packages.

Benedict's eyes crinkled with amusement and his voice dropped in pitch, 'Are you telling me you haven't been sleeping well at night?'

'I've slept deeply, but not for long enough.' She giggled. 'Kiss me goodbye and depart, Benedict. I know you have things to do. I'll be perfectly all right. I won't go out of the house and I'll lock my door when I go to bed.'

There was a show of reluctance as he parted with her, leaving instructions with the butler about locking the house up securely, and making sure the footmen were vigilant. 'Station an armed man at each end of the corridor tonight, when Miss Hartford retires.'

'Yes, I will, sir. The downstairs windows are already closed and locked and the servants will be instructed to keep a sharp eye out.'

Amber walked with Benedict to his horse.

'Promise me you'll take care,' he said, and she could see the concern in his eyes.

She kissed the hand he gently squeezed hers with. 'I promise. You take care as well.'

'I'll see you at the altar the day after tomorrow.'

She watched him ride away, the carriage following, for the horses would need to be rested overnight at Laconbridge. She blew him a kiss when he turned to wave at her. When he was out of sight she felt lonely, and set apart from the closely knit family she was to marry into. She wished she'd gone with him, but it was too late now.

The butler gently coughed after Benedict disappeared from sight. 'Miss Hartford?'

Obviously Emma hadn't informed her servants of Amber's private marriage to Benedict. For that she was grateful, for the illegality of it bothered her a little. The butler politely stood to one side while she entered the house, closed the doors behind him and secured them with bolts. 'Will you be taking dinner in the dining hall, Miss Hartford?'

'I'm going up to fetch Jake. Have my dinner sent up on a tray to my room, and with something extra for Jake. Some soup and a pudding perhaps.'

'Master Selby had his tea earlier,' he reminded her.

'He's a boy. I'm sure Jake can find room in his stomach for an extra helping of food.'

The butler smiled at her. 'I'm sure he can, Miss Hartford.'

The nursery maid didn't like her routine being upset. 'Master Selby is ready for bed, Miss Hartford.'

'He can sleep in my room. There are plenty of sheets and blankets. I'll make up the truckle bed.'

'But, miss...'

'No arguments,' she told her firmly. 'I haven't seen Jake for days. I imagine you can find plenty to do without him being underfoot.' She took Jake's hand. 'Come along, Jake.'

Jake was grinning from ear to ear. She laughed

and picked up speed. Soon they were racing each other along the corridor to her room, there they flung themselves into the middle of the bed, out of breath.

'You look as though you've just escaped from prison,' she said.

'I have. The nursery is full of rules, Miss Amber. Even the windows have bars on them in case the children climb on the window sills and fall out. Charlotte and Susannah are nice, but they're always telling me what to do. And they said their brother is bigger than me, and he'll beat me up when he comes home from school.'

Amber grinned, the girls were just like their mother and aunt. 'I shouldn't think so, Jake. They're teasing you. Besides, I doubt if you'll be here when he comes home.'

'I hope not. I don't want to fight anyone. And we don't get enough to eat. The nursery maid said we'll get nightmares if we eat too much before going to bed. But sometimes I wake up in the middle of the night and I'm hungry enough to steal a chicken from its coop and cook it.'

She laughed at the reminder. 'As long as it's not cooked on a shovel used for dung.'

'I'm too old to be in a nursery and wear silly frilled blouses and skeleton suits,' he said morosely, 'And they keep washing my face and hands.'

She managed to keep a straight face. 'That must be dreadful. See those packages over there? It's a whole new wardrobe for you. Most of the garments were selected by myself, with some advice from Lord Costain. He thought that pantaloons under Russian tunics with plain collars and jackets were more suitable for you. There's everything you need, including a cap to wear and a new pair of boots.'

'I don't know how to thank you, Miss Amber,' he said. 'You're kind, and so is Lord Costain.'

'If you grow into a decent, well-educated and polite young man who can earn a decent living for himself, that will be thanks enough. And as you won't be in the nursery for much longer I want you to remember that our hosts, their children and their staff have been exceedingly kind to us. It would be a nice gesture for you to pen a letter in your best writing, thanking Lord and Lady Stratton for their hospitality. And also to thank the maids.'

When she rose from the bed and straightened her skirts, Jake stood too. He looked around him. 'This is a grand room.'

'It's the one Lord Costain uses when he stays here. I'm to marry him the day after tomorrow, you know.'

Jake nodded, 'The nursery maids talk of nothing else.' He thought for a moment before gazing at her. 'Things will change when you're married, I reckon. I wasn't born into the upper crust, so what will happen to me, Miss?'

'We'll discuss that a little later, but I still intend that you should go to school and make something of yourself. Lord Costain agrees with me. I imagine he will go to a lawyer and make application to become your legal guardian. I do hope you intend to take up the opportunity being offered.'

'Yes, Miss Amber.'

'Since you're my best friend until you make new ones at school, I shall take you into my confidence on certain matters. I have purchased Hartford House, and I'm giving it to Lord Costain as a surprise gift when we wed. I believe he thought it would make a good horse stud when he first saw it, so I do hope we can go back there to live.' She put her hand in her pocket. 'In the meantime I've got something for you. Open your hand.' When he did she placed the silver watch in his palm.

Jake gazed down at it for a moment, then he flipped open the lid and looked inside. Tears filled his eyes. His lips were trembling as he gazed up at her questioningly. 'This belonged to my father.'

'Yes ... I know, dear. Now it's yours, Jake, as is your right. Lord Costain took me to the school in London where your father taught, and we made inquiries on your behalf. We've brought back a trunk filled with your parents' belongings. They were left behind at the school and stored there.'

'I could only carry one bag and I put clothes and food in it, and some money. It was stolen by some bigger boys while I was travelling.'

'The clothing that belonged to your family has been disposed of, we understand, and probably other personal items too. I believe it was to pay a debt your father owed. Mostly there were books in the trunk, but the headmaster returned a lovely chess set he'd stored in a cupboard, as well as a few other things. We thought you'd like to have them.'

'My father was teaching me to play the game.'

To her consternation Jake burst into tears. Usually, the lad was self-contained and grown up in his ways and thinking. But he was only a little boy after all, and a brave one at that. Now he needed mothering a little, she thought. Gently she gathered the boy into her arms and held him close while he grieved for the family he'd loved and lost.

## FOURTEEN

Matt Striker gazed at the man lying on the bed. 'Will he live, doctor?'

'Likely he will. It depends if his lungs become infected. Half the harbour was inside him. The broken ribs and leg should heal if he doesn't move around too much, but that knock on his head might give him trouble if his skull is cracked. Do you know who he is?'

'His watch is inscribed, Jonas Carlton. I've seen him before, in Bridport with a couple of companions. He was with the same two earlier tonight, I believe.'

Jonas clutched his side and groaned as he heaved, and spat more water from his mouth. His eyes fluttered open. 'Where am I?' His groan became an agonized scream as he tried to sit up. He flopped back on his pillow, made fully conscious by the pain.

'I fished you out of the harbour,' Matt told him. 'You had some coins in your pocket, enough to pay for the doctor.'

'I hurt like hell. How badly am I injured?'

'Cracked ribs and you've broken a bone in your lower leg. There's a lump the size of an apple on your head. You damn near drowned into the bargain.'

'Someone hit me from behind.'

'Something surely did, and it wasn't a low flying gull. I've splinted the leg and bound the ribs. I can't do much about the head except dose you up with some laudanum for the pain. If you get a fever most likely it'll kill you, so you'll be going into the infirmary as soon as there's a bed available.'

'Damn it to hell, man, I'm not going into any infirmary.' Jonas's eyes expressed the urgency in him. 'I need to get to Hampshire as quickly as I can. Will you fetch my horse? It's a chestnut with a white blaze on his nose. I left it at the inn on the quayside opposite the fishing boats.'

The doctor cackled with laughter. 'If you think you can ride a horse, go ahead.'

Matt grinned as the fool tried to sit up again, then the pain became too much for him. His eyes rolled up in his head and he subsided on to the pillow in a faint.

The doctor cackled. 'Some fools never learn. I'll send the infirmary cart over for him as soon as there's a bed to spare, Matt.' He pulled the door behind him as he left.

Matt gazed at his brother-in-law and shrugged. 'I have a few days' leave left, Tom, so can look after him. We'd best put his nag in your stable. If we leave it where it is it'll be dished up on somebody's dinner plate come Sunday.'

Tom grinned. 'I'll fetch the beast.'

'No, you keep an eye on him while I collect it. I know what his two companions look like, they might still be around. They must have missed him by now. I'll need to know who to inform if he dies. I'll be back in half an hour, then you can get home to Meg and the kids. She'll be wondering where you are.'

Matt found the horse still patiently standing where it had been tethered. The inn was almost empty except for a couple of drunks hunched over a brandy bottle in the corner. Of the two men there was no sign. 'They left an hour ago,' the publican told him. 'The shorter of the pair, ran out of money. He was in a sour mood.'

'What about the third man? Did you see him leave?'

'No. The other one asked everyone in the bar if they'd seen their companion. No one had. Then he said the fellow must had gone looking for a woman, and he hoped everyone had their wives locked up. That made them laugh, I can tell you, since the few left in the bar were mostly seaman, and we all know they have wives and daughters in every port.'

When he burst into raucous laughter Matt joined in.

'He left a large tip for the serving maid, bought everyone a pot of ale and said to tell their companion they'd gone back to Bridport if he turned up. He wasn't exactly a friendly chap before, so it seemed like an odd thing for him to do.' He jerked his thumb towards the door. 'His

210

companion's horse is still tied up outside so he must be making a night of it with Sally Bowers' girls.'

'Their companion turned up in the harbour,' Matt said. 'He's got broken bones but should survive. I was hoping to find out something about him, in case I have to inform his next of kin.'

The publican swiped a cloth through a puddle of spilled ale. 'It wouldn't be the first time someone fell into the harbour.' The cloth suddenly stopped its movement and his eyes sharpened. 'One of the men said he was Lord Hartford. Not that he acted like a lord, but then we don't get many gentlemen in here to compare him to.'

*Hartford?* As he left the inn Matt remembered a young woman with large eyes and many bruises, and he doubted if the name was a coincidence. He might drop in on Hartford House and see if he could sniff out what was going on.

The young man's horse was a handsome gelding who behaved perfectly, even with a stranger riding on his back. 'You ride him home,' he said to Tom. 'I reckon I'll be going to Bridport in the morning to look for the acquaintances of our invalid, and to let them know he's all right. Ask Meg to come over and keep an eye on Carlton in case the infirmary cart turns up.'

But there was more to this affair, Matt felt it in his bones. He set out early next morning, but when he reached Hartford House there was no sign of the men. His rap at the door was answered by a middle-aged woman who said she was Mrs Phelps, the housekeeper.

211

'I haven't seen hide nor hair of Lord Hartford and his two friends since yesterday. The reverend's wife dropped in this morning. She reckons that Hartford house has been sold, and she wondered if I knew who'd bought it. She said I'll lose my position, and that Lord Hartford has run up bills everywhere. I don't know whether to come in every morning to housekeep, or not.'

'I shouldn't worry too much, Mrs Phelps. I expect the new owner will be here soon. He'll need staff, and you'll be in a good position to be employed. I don't suppose you know where Lord Hartford has gone?'

'He said something about going to a wedding, then the two of them exchanged a laugh as though it was funny. The third man didn't seem too happy about it. You could see it in his eyes.' She ventured to say, 'I thought perhaps it was his wedding, one of those hurried affairs. But he wasn't dressed for a wedding. Fact be, he was dusty from the road and they went out shortly afterwards. Haven't seen them since.'

After further questioning, and on being satisfied he'd learned all she knew, Matt bid her good day and headed back towards Poole, mulling over all the bits of information accumulating in his head.

He kept thinking of the girl. Unease filled him as the pieces of the puzzle began to fall into place, in a very disturbing manner.

Meg was sitting at the kitchen table when Matt got home.

'Is everything all right?'

'Aye. Yon Jonas Carlton asked for some paper and ink. He wrote a letter and then asked for some wax to seal it with. He wants it sent as soon as possible ... said the person it was sent to would pay the messenger if it was presented with his watch.'

Curious, Matt went through to the bedroom. The young man looked agitated when he saw him with the letter. 'It's imperative that gets to my uncle today.'

'I'll send it off with the normal messenger, but it won't get to London today, Mr Carlton.' He glanced down at the letter. 'Is this Baron a relative of yours?'

'My uncle. I'm his heir.'

'I see.' He smiled gently at the man. 'There's skulduggery afoot. I think you'd better tell me what's going on. If it's what I think it is there will be heavy penalties to pay if that young woman, Miss Hartford is harmed in any way.'

'I know,' Jonas said, his frustration showing in his face. 'I was going to try and put a stop to it but he ... Stephen Gould began to suspect–'

'And he banged you over the head and threw you into the harbour to drown.' That's why the man had made a show of concern for his friend in the inn. It had been a ruse to disassociate himself from the crime if Carlton's body was discovered.

'I think it was him. I remember smelling the peppermint he sucks.'

'And Hartford ... is he in on it?'

'I doubt if Patrick would be a party to killing me, though he might have been talked into taking part in the abduction, especially if he lost money gambling. Stephen has a plausible tongue, and

213

Patrick owes him a lot of money.'

Matt's eyes sharpened. 'What abduction is that you're referring too?'

'Miss Hartford's. She's come into a fortune. At first Stephen wanted to kill her so Patrick would inherit. Then when Patrick refused, Stephen came up with the idea of holding her to ransom. That's why I left the inn early. I'd intended to travel to Hampshire to warn the Earl of Laconbridge, for his son, Lord Costain is to wed Miss Hartford tomorrow.'

Matt glanced at his watch and stood. Already it was gone noon. 'I must go and warn them. Meg will look after you until the infirmary sends the cart. I'll make sure your letter to your uncle gets to its destination. There a bag of official mail going to London by boat. He should get it early next morning.'

'Will I get into trouble?'

'If anything happens to Miss Hartford and the matter goes before a magistrate you'll be expected to appear as a witness. Then it will depend on your credibility. Gould may have done you a favour by pushing you into the harbour. I hope I can get to the young lady in time.'

'Take my horse, he's fast and sound of wind,' Jonas said, wincing with pain as he tried turn over.

'Thank you, I will. Be polite to my sister, Meg, or it'll be the worst for you.'

'Yes, sir. I'm appreciative of her care, and mindful of her sharp tongue.'

Matt grinned. When he reached the door he tapped the letter against his hand. 'Do you think this relative will come to your aid?'

'I hope so, but I wouldn't blame him if he turned his back on me.'

'If I wrote a letter to try to convince him that you're a reformed character, would that be the truth, then?'

Jonas nodded. 'I can safely say I've learned my lesson, sir.'

Matt smiled. He had no time for lawbreakers, and there was none more upright than a man who'd learned from his mistakes.

A couple of hours later Matthew realized that the young man had been right. His horse was fast. It covered the ground in a long-legged canter that not only looked graceful, but gave him a smooth ride. Used to the sturdy mounts provided for the revenue, Matt felt like a prince astride this thoroughbred.

It was a fair day with the smell of early autumn in the air, as though a faint disturbed decay of leaves was released as the horse stirred up the undergrowth. Matt kept a lookout for Lord Hartford and Stephen Gould, but the road was light of other travellers.

'Have two strangers been through here today?' he asked the keeper of the inn, and described them.

'Not today, sir. It's been quiet. Yesterday people were coming and going all day ... most of them strangers.'

'What about last night, late?'

'The doors are locked from midnight, and the guests were in bed. There were a couple of merchants travelling with a cart from Southampton.

They hired a room. It's not safe to travel at night without outriders. Did you want something to eat, sir? Our Maisie has just cooked a batch of lamb pies and they go down well with a pot of ale.'

Matt nodded as his stomach growled. He'd been a long time without food.

'Maisie!' the innkeeper yelled a couple of times.

Eventually a plump woman put in an appearance, her arms full of bedding. 'What are you yelling about?'

'Where's Maisie?'

'She went off on the back of the donkey a few minutes since. I reckon she's gone off to meet that sweetheart of hers. You should keep a better eye on that daughter of yours. She's only sixteen and is already too free with the men who come in here. I told her it was no way to catch a husband, and I reckon that puss will get herself into trouble one of these days.'

'Damned girl, I'll smack her arse for her when she comes back,' he grumbled. 'Bring the gentleman a couple of pies, please Aggie. Is there anything else you'd like, sir?'

'Yes, directions to the Earl of Laconbridge's residence.'

'Here for the wedding, are you, sir? I hear that the earl is going to escort the bride to the church personally.'

'No ... I have other business.' Biting into the pie Matt sighed with bliss as the rich gravy flavours burst against his tongue. 'Your daughter's a good cook.'

'That she is, sir. But she's a wild one. Aggie's

right, she'll get herself into trouble one of these days. Now, as for Laconbridge House, I reckon the shortest way is across the heath and the track through the forest.'

Matt enjoyed his meal then set out on his way again. To his left the heathlands were a blaze of purple heather, beyond was the dense, dark line of the forest, faintly intimidating because the shadows were lengthening.

As he neared the tree line he passed a girl astride a pony. She was coming in from the opposite direction. She was a pretty thing who smiled at him and said, 'Good afternoon, sir.'

'Good day, Maisie?' he said.

Her smile widened. 'How did you know my name, sir?'

'I've just eaten a couple of your pies, they were very good.'

She slanted her eyes at him. 'My pies always be good. You can eat them any time, as long as you pay well for them.'

She was too pert for one so young. 'Best you watch your mouth, girl, lest you give a man the wrong idea. Get off home, your pa's looking for you.'

She went bright red and muttered, 'A lot you know about anything, mister.' Then she dug her heels into her donkey's rump and picked up speed.

The forest was quiet, dim and cool. It had a relaxing effect on Matt, who was beginning to feel less alert this late into the day.

To his right a twig cracked. He brought the horse to a halt and listened. All was silent expect the flutter of leaves in the breeze and the beat of a pulse inside his ear.

He started off again at a faster pace, then heard a horse behind him. He was reaching for his pistol when the ball hit him in the back a moment before he heard the report of it. He slid from the horse's back and rolled down a slope into a ditch, landing in a patch of mud.

Footsteps followed him down and he tried not to go tense or scream out when a brown-booted foot struck him in the side. It hurt like hell, especially when he tried not to breathe in case the movement of his chest gave him away.

'Straight through the heart by the look of that hole in his jacket. I think he's dead,' a man's voice said in satisfaction.

'I wonder what he was doing on Jonas's horse?'

'The last time I saw the nag it was tied up outside the inn at Poole. I imagine he did Jonas in and stole it.'

'But Maisie said he was looking for us, so he might be someone in authority.'

'All the more reason to get rid of him.'

'You shouldn't have shot him in the back Stephen, he didn't have a chance to defend himself.'

'For God's sake stop whining. He didn't ask for us by name, and it could have been anyone from the description. Go through his pockets. The horse ran off but he wouldn't have gone far. Put a bullet through his head to make sure.'

'I won't shoot a man in cold blood.'

'He's already dead. Stop arguing and do it,' he said. 'I'll go and see if I can find Jonas's horse.'

'Shit! I can't do him in,' the man muttered, rummaging in Matt's pockets. He took the few shillings, gazed at it and muttered, 'Poor bugger, you haven't got much.' He remembered the money he'd wasted gambling, and Jonas urging him to walk away from Stephen.

Matt couldn't hold his breath any longer and it left his body in a rush.

Patrick jumped and his voice was jittery. 'You're alive, thank God. What shall I do? They'll hang me.'

'I'm not badly hurt. Pretend to shoot me and leave the money,' Matt whispered. 'They can't hang you if I'm not dead, but they can for highway robbery. You won't regret it.'

'Hurry up, will you,' Stephen shouted

Matt's money was dropped into the mud, Patrick Hartford's voice was thin and high-pitched with panic. 'I've got to go. If he finds out you're alive he'll shoot you himself.' Metal clicked against metal as the hammer was pulled back. As Matt braced himself there was a shot. His body jerked, then he sagged into the earth as leaf litter spouted up in front of him.

Patrick Hartford went behind a tree and began to heave.

Laughter came from the top of the slope. 'You've never killed a man before, have you? Kick some leaves over him so he won't be seen.'

Wiping his mouth, Matt's unlikely saviour did what he was told, then walked back up the slope, saying casually, 'I didn't kill him, he was already dead.'

'I was lying. I thought it was time you were

blooded. The next time you have to kill someone it will be easier.'

'You bastard!' To Matt's relief and to Lord Hartford's credit, the man managed a shaky laugh and refrained from looking back at him as he said, 'Come on, let's go back to the cottage. Where's the horse?'

'He was spooked and took off. We'll never catch him. Maisie has left us some food at the cottage. You can stay there while I spy out the land. I might go and see Maisie afterwards, so don't wait up.'

When the sound of the horses faded, Matt managed to stagger to his feet. He'd lost some blood, but by some miracle the bullet had travelled along his shoulder blade and had lodged just under the skin, near where the arm fitted into its socket. The area was beginning to swell. It needed cutting out, but although he had a knife in his boot he couldn't see the area, and his hands were trembling too much to safely attempt the job. He'd have to leave the ball in place, and hope he found help before poisoning set in.

Stuffing his cravat under his waistcoat to staunch the blood was the best he could do. And he could walk with the aid of a stout stick he found in the undergrowth.

Soon, the light began to be swallowed by the dusk, and the trail became more difficult. He just hoped he was still on the right path.

# FIFTEEN

At the Stratton house Amber, Emma and Caroline were playing a lively game of cricket on the lawn with the children.

'Well done,' Emma shrieked when Jake hit the ball into the shadows under an oak. 'That's a win for Susannah's team. Time we went inside now, the light's going and nurse will want to ready you for bed.'

'I don't want to go to bed,' Susannah grumbled, and that started the other girls off.

'Neither do I. Can I wear my blue dress and my new bonnet tomorrow, mama?'

'I want to wear my yellow one.'

'You're both wearing pink,' Emma said firmly.

'I'm glad I'm not a girl,' William said loftily, and exchanged a grin with Jake. The pair walked off towards the house, jostling each other.

'I'll get the ball,' Amber said, while the children were ushered towards the house, but nobody heard her because the adults' eyes, ears and hands were occupied with tired and grumbling children.

There was a dark patch under the oak where the sunlight didn't reach. The leafy branches swept down to the ground in a graceful sweep. The light inside was a quiet hush of jade. Someone had thought to place a wooden seat there. Acorn pipes littered the ground and crunched beneath her feet. Emma had told her that one of the Stratton family had planted the tree one hundred and twenty years previously.

She ran a finger over a heart pierced with an arrow carved in the seat and smiled when she saw Emma and Archie's initials. Archie had proposed marriage to Emma here. What a wonderfully romantic place.

Benedict had rather taken their marriage for granted, and she'd gone along with it because she'd fallen in love with him. It had all been too fast. Love had happened before she'd had time to think, and she'd been swept away by it. Did Benedict feel the same?

Picking up the ball Amber took in a few seconds to enjoy the moment of quiet. Then her spine began to prickle with unease, for she had a sense of being watched.

But there had been no sign of her cousin, and Jonas Carlton was in London. She experienced a faint sense of loss, for Patrick was her only relative and she wished things had been different for them. He was ruining his life, and she wondered if she might be able to talk some sense into him if Stephen Gould's influence was removed.

Nervously she gazed around her, but saw nothing. She chided herself for being silly, but nearly jumped out of her skin when the curtain of leaves was swept aside. At the same time a squirrel streaked up the trunk chattering with alarm. Halfway up it turned and streaked down just as fast. Leaping to the ground it and ran jerkily towards a stand of silver birches.

'Odd behaviour for a squirrel,' Kitt rumbled.

Her hand had flown to her chest. 'Between you and the squirrel you've given me such a fright! I came to find the ball. It was so peaceful here I just wanted to stay for a while and think.'

'It's no good trying to hide from us, Amber, dear. Come on, take my arm. I'm under orders to bring you in. Emma and Caro want to decide on a hairstyle for you before dinner. They'll be busy getting themselves ready in the morning and won't have time.'

'I thought we'd already decided on one.'

He chuckled. 'Obviously not. We'll be leaving for the church at eleven to stand up with Bennet, and the earl will be coming to collect you half an hour later in the family carriage.' He chuckled. 'That half hour by yourself is the only peace you'll get tomorrow. Try and get a good night's sleep. Are you comfortable in the room you're occupying?'

'It has a lovely view over the garden, and yes, the bed is as soft as a cloud. You know, Kitt,' she said as they strolled back towards the house. 'I couldn't wish for a better family, even though I'm not used to having so many people looking after me.'

'Having us all telling you what to do and how to do it, d'you mean?' he said, and began to laugh.

'Now you're making me feel ungrateful. Emma and Caroline have hearts of gold, and their intentions are good.'

'Which is just as well because as a pair they're a force to be reckoned with. You shouldn't feel guilty for wanting to escape from them now and again. Bennet will be easier to live with, I promise.'

Safely hidden amongst the leafy branches of the tree Stephen Gould smiled. He could have taken her in the last few minutes, but with one of the men in close proximity, he wouldn't have got very far. Tomorrow he'd have half an hour before she was collected. That wasn't enough time to get clean away.

He stared at the house. It was risky, but he'd have to fall back on his second plan – the one he'd prepared for during the afternoon. He'd take her tonight when the household was asleep. They wouldn't expect someone to walk into the house and snatch her from her bed.

He climbed down from the tree when it grew dark and stared towards the house. At least he knew that she slept in one of the front rooms.

Patiently, he kept watch. Just after eleven a light appeared in an upstairs window. For a moment he saw the curve of her bosom outlined against the light, and her hair was a dark halo with the light shining through. He could make out the white column of her throat. She seemed to be looking up at the moon, and was probably dreaming romantic dreams about the viscount. His grin tightened. Romantic dreams or not, he was going to have her first.

Pulling out his pistol he held it at arm's length. He could have killed her now, but it would have been too easy. He imagined the ball tearing into the soft skin of her throat, and the blood gushing warmly through the vale of her breasts while she struggled to find the air to call for help. He'd never killed a woman.

But he didn't want the lady dead ... at least, not yet. He wanted to play with her, abuse her, so he could watch the disdain she'd expressed in her eyes to turn to fear before she begged him for mercy. When he had the ransom money safely in his hands, he'd be gone, and she'd be left to die alone in the dark.

As for Patrick. A man who wasn't prepared to shoulder any of the risk couldn't be trusted. Like Jonas, Patrick was turning soft. Stephen strode off, his plan formulating in his head. He just hoped Maisie would do exactly as he'd told her.

'Promise you'll take me with you, Stephen,' she said a little later, as they kept watch from under the oak tree.

'Of course I will,' he lied. 'As soon as you bring me the ransom. We can't go without that. You know what you've got to do and where I'll be.'

'The plan won't work without your help. It's not as if you haven't done it before with him. You did leave him the note?'

'Yes ... do we have to keep going over it? I'm not stupid.'

'You won't live long if you double-cross me,' he warned, with enough purpose in his voice to make her shiver. 'Besides, nothing will turn you into a lady. But who wants one. I love you just as you are. Just keep that footman occupied for half an hour or so, like I told you.'

'Must I?' she whined.

He wanted to throttle her. 'I'll buy you that red gown you want, and we'll get married the day after tomorrow, I promise. Now get into position inside the arbor.'

A smile spread across her face and she kissed him before she scurried off towards the arbor of roses with its stone bench.

Now Stephen sat alone under the oak and watched the Stratton household settle for the night. Soon there was just a faint light left glowing from a night lantern.

Just after one o'clock a scrawny young man came creeping through the shadows, whistling quietly to himself.

Stephen stepped behind the trunk of the oak tree and patted his waistcoat, where several lengths of thin cord, a linen bag and a kerchief was hidden.

'Maisie,' the footman whispered a few moments later. 'I got your note, so here I am.'

'Over here, my big man,' she said from the direction of the arbor, then, 'You took your time. 'Ere ... keep your hands to yourself, and don't be so flaming eager. I'm not lying on my back on this hard bench. Let's make ourselves comfortable in the pavilion, first.'

'I can't stay long. If I'm missed there'll be hell to pay. I'm supposed to be guarding the hall...'

'Why, is the hall going to escape if you're not there? Ooh! What's that wriggling in your breeches, a puppy dog?' Maisie giggled, and even Stephen smiled at that when the pair hurried towards the little pavilion. She was a born whore.

Stephen headed for the house at a run, found the unlocked door and let himself in. The danger of entering a house full of people who might wake at any moment and challenge him was exhilarating. But he'd taken his bearings earlier, and knew exactly where he was going.

The corridors and stairs were thickly carpeted, so his feet made no sound, but he was cautious, and took care.

He found his prey easily. Amber Rose was lying in the bed, breathing softly, her hair spread across the pillows. He didn't have time to admire her. Springing on to her chest so she couldn't take a breath, he stuffed a kerchief in her mouth when she opened it, pulled a linen bag down over her head and tied a cord around her mouth, the knot over the gag.

It was all over in seconds. She woke from sleep, struggling. A swift punch and her head rolled to one side. Pulling the covers back he tied her hands and feet then heaved her over his shoulder. He breathed a sigh of relief at her light weight. Throwing the ransom note on to her bed he silently made his way down the stairs and out of the house.

It was all over in minutes.

Across the road in a secluded spot there was a carriage and pair he'd hired. His horse was tied to the back. He'd be at Hartford House before the occupants of the house woke and got the note.

The woman began to come round when he reached the vehicle. She made muted protests, high pitched with panic. 'Be quiet, else I'll kill you,' he growled against her ear before he threw her into the carriage.

She began to make little sniffling noises. It gave him satisfaction to think she was crying. He tied her legs to her hands at the back, drew the curtains across and rolled a blanket tightly round her body, tying it with a cord in case she tried to escape.

She was trussed up like a pig now, and would be going nowhere. Climbing onto the coachman's seat he set the carriage in motion. In case he was intercepted he placed a loaded blunderbuss within reach, a weapon which would kill or disable up to three people within the spread of its shot.

Amber's pain increased with every jolt, though the carriage was being driven at a slow steady speed. So the driver wouldn't draw attention to himself, she thought.

They'd been on the road for at least an hour. It had taken some time for her panic to subside. At first she thought she'd choke to death on the gag but she'd forced herself to take long, even breaths through her nose, something that had calmed her and allowed her to think more rationally. She could breathe through the fabric enclosing her head, so she wouldn't die through lack of air.

Her legs and arms were another matter. There was very little leeway in the binding, but she was able to move her feet within her tight wrapping and she used the motion to exercise them, so to avoid the cramp that would inevitably attack her calves if she didn't. It was no use struggling. She used what ingenuity she possessed to provide for her own comfort and suffered the rest – the itches she couldn't scratch, the gag that effectively drew the moisture from her mouth and tongue, the need to relieve herself and the slow burn of the anger restrained inside her.

Amber's self-control had never been put to such a test. Her body was so tense she thought it might explode and fly off in all directions once her bindings were released.

To keep herself occupied she began to compose music in her mind, in time to the rhythm of the wheels and the thud of horses hooves. After a while the noise faded into the background and lulled her into a fitful sort of sleep.

When she woke she had no idea of how much time had passed, but they were travelling over gravel. The carriage came to a halt and a couple of moment's later the door was flung open. She was dragged out of the carriage, hoisted over her abductor's shoulder and carried inside. The pain in her body was excruciating, but she only had the energy to whimper. Down some steps they went and she was dropped onto a mattress in a manner that knocked the wind from her body. Blessedly, the binds around her hands were loosened. There was the sound of someone walking away, a door was closed and a key turned in the lock.

Carefully, she began to work on further loosening her bonds. It was agony as the life returned to her neglected limbs. The place where she was held prisoner had a dank smell, and when she pulled the hood from her eyes it was to encounter only pitch darkness.

Discarding the gag she opened her mouth wide and drew in the deepest breath, then ran her tongue over her teeth and lips to moisten them as much as she could. When she felt stronger she massaged her legs then climbed unsteadily to her feet. Her body was attacked by pins and needles as the life came back into them. Cool flagstones were a balm against the soles of her bare feet. She reached out with her hands and touched something cold and smooth. 'A bottle,' she whispered, then felt another and another. 'I'm in a wine cellar.'

Taking a bottle from its rack she groped around to find something to open it with. Her hand fell on an iron ladle. Resting the handle against the cork, a few thumps from the heel of her hand sent it down into the bottle. She raised the bottle to her lips. Wine gushed into her mouth, over her chin and soaked into her nightgown as she gulped some of it down, grimacing at the sharp taste. If nothing else, it was wet.

'Not too much,' she cautioned herself.

The direction the man had taken to the door was clear in her mind and she cautiously headed in the same direction, her arms held out in front of her. She stubbed her toes against some steps then went up them, counting as she went. The door she encountered was secure. An eye against the keyhole showed a faint lifting of the darkness, nothing more, and even that might be her imagination. Pressing her ear against the panel she listened for any sound to break the silence. She was about to feel her way down again when a clock began a deep chime.

Six chimes later and she began to laugh. She knew that sound. She'd lived with it all her life. It was the long clock in the hall and she was in the cellar of Hartford House! She went back down the steps with much more confidence that when she'd gone up them. It wouldn't take Benedict long to realize where she was. He would look for her here eventually. With him would come his brothers-in-law, and they would skin alive the person who'd abducted her.

It had to be Patrick and Stephen, though she'd formed an impression that only one man had been involved. She remembered a faint smell of peppermint and connected it to the robbery at the earl's house. Stephen Gould used peppermint lozenges. He must have learned of her legacy and abducted her for ransom.

The thought that she'd brought trouble down on the earl's house made her feel sad, and although she'd rather not believe that her cousin would commit such a crime against her, she had no choice.

Stephen had forgotten about the woman Patrick had hired until she accosted him in the hall and said, 'Is Lord Hartford with you, sir?'

'Uh ... no, he's not. How long have you been here?'

'Just a minute or so. I usually come in at six and the clock was chiming as I arrived, though it sounded odd.'

'Odd?'

231

'I daresay you'll think I'm silly, but it was as if it were ... laughing. It shouldn't be run down since I only wound it yesterday. Could be the weather caused it, mayhap there's rain on the way.'

So, the Hartford bitch had been laughing. Not that she had anything to laugh about, and that would change when she'd been on her own for a day of two. He forced himself to smile at the woman's fancy. 'It does that when rain's on the way. The metal expands, I believe.'

'That's likely the explanation, though I'd heard that the house is haunted. Not that I've heard anything untoward myself, but sometimes I feel as though someone's watching me from up on the landing there, where the portrait of the gentleman is. He has right wicked eyes.'

The hair stood up on the back of Stephen's neck as his glance followed hers to the portrait. There was a family resemblance to Patrick, though the portrait had eyes that seemed to glare straight into his. It was probably Patrick's great-grandfather.

The woman shivered, gazed nervously around her and brought her arms across her chest. 'I'd heard the house had been sold. Lord Hartford hasn't paid my wages and I wondered if you could advance me them, seeing as how you're a friend of his. Do you know who the new owner is?'

Stephen thought quickly. This woman could quite easily queer things for him if she got an inkling of what was going on. But ridding himself of her would cause more problems than it was worth. Someone would look for her.

'I've bought the place,' he lied. Fishing in his pocket he brought forth a couple of coins as he searched his memory for her name. 'Mrs Phelps, isn't it? I won't need your services. I'm going abroad for several months and have just come to make sure everything is still secure. Will this cover what's owed to you?'

'Yes, sir.' She pocketed the money. 'Perhaps you'll be in need of a housekeeper when you return, sir?'

'Yes, I imagine I will.' He couldn't leave her here. 'I'm going into Poole shortly to deliver the carriage to the livery stable. You can ride in it if you wish.'

'That's right kind of you, sir, but I'm going in the opposite direction, sir. It's only a short walk.' She curtseyed and walked towards the door.

Stephen doubted if she'd be back; the locals were a superstitious lot.

But Mrs Phelps did go back, and as soon as Stephen had gone. Rather than leave the hens to be killed by foxes she'd decided to take them to her sister's cottage. Just as she was about to shove the first bird into a sack she heard a high-pitched sobbing wail coming from inside the house.

Dropping the sack, she picked up her skirts and ran.

# SIXTEEN

Shaken from sleep by his man when it was barely light, Benedict's bleary gaze encountered Archie and Kitt, who were standing behind George. He came wide awake to gazed sharply from one to another. 'Something's happened to Amber, hasn't it?'

'She's gone, Bennet. Someone gained access into the house during the night and abducted her from under our noses. I haven't had time to question the staff properly yet, but it seems that someone was less than vigilant. I'm so sorry.'

'It's not your fault, Archie, so don't feel guilty.'

'They left this on her bed. It's addressed to you, but we opened it,' Archie said, and threw down a piece of paper.

Benedict quickly read it. 'They want one thousand guineas in exchange for her safe return.'

*One person must deliver it. Place it at the base of the twisted oak at seven-thirty a.m., then ride away. You'll be watched. A note will be delivered by hand to Laconbridge House informing you of the whereabouts of Miss Hartford two hours after the ransom has been delivered. Any attempt at trickery and Miss Hartford will be killed.*

'Damn! It's open ground all the way back to the forest from that oak. They'll have the shelter of

234

the copse behind them and will be able to pick us off. There will be nowhere to take shelter.' He looked up at them. The money and his own safety was of less importance to him than the welfare of Amber Rose. 'Can we raise that much between us? I have approximately two hundred and fifty guineas in my strong box.'

Kitt nodded. 'We have the rest. We stopped off at my residence and have brought with us everything we have available. It will just about cover the ransom.'

Taking a key from his bedside table Benedict threw it to Kitt. 'You know where my strong box is.' He swung his legs over the side of bed and suffered George's attempts to dress him with impatience. Thrusting him aside he pulled on his breeches and riding boots, then he snatched up his jacket. 'Does my father know, Archie?'

'We came here first.'

'Then we'll go straight there after I've delivered the ransom. We haven't got much time.'

'What about the wedding?'

He shrugged. 'There won't be one, unless I get the bride back. We'll deal with that problem when the time comes. George, tell the staff what's going on. I imagine we'll have to postpone things.'

'Yes, sir. I hope the young lady is safely found.'

Benedict allowed his fear to surface for a moment. 'So do I, George. If Miss Hartford is not found safe and well I'll follow the perpetrators of this crime into hell to take my revenge. They'll die slowly, believe me.'

An hour later the three men rode out. It was a pretty morning, a mist drifted waist high above the dewy grass and hung like pearl drops from the spiders webs. It wasn't dense enough to hide them, or the oak tree with its twisted, trunk, which had been distorted by a lightning strike several summers ago.

'Stay here,' he told his companions. 'I don't want Amber's safety compromised. We can look for her abductors afterwards. I think we know who they are.' He rode off towards the oak.

As instructed, Benedict dropped the four leather satchels to the far side of the oak trunk.

'If you hurt her I'll see you rot in hell,' he said out loud, then turned and rode away without looking back.

It wasn't until the men had gone from sight that Maisie dared creep out of her hiding place. Her heart had never pounded quite so loudly before. Lord Costain had appeared so stern and unforgiving that she'd been scared he might strangle her if he decided to search the copse and found her.

Picking the satchels up one by one she placed them in the sack tied to the donkey's back, distributing the weight evenly. She hadn't expected it to be quite so heavy. 'How the devil am I going to carry four of them by myself?' she whispered.

No one will suspect a girl, Stephen had said, but he'd forgotten that girls weren't as muscular or as strong as men. It would be obvious to anyone that she was carrying something heavy, if she could carry it at all.

She had no intention of leaving the gold behind

though, and remembered her father's handcart. She would have to steal it. And she must hurry, because she had to get over to the harbour at Lymington. The fishing boat Stephen had arranged, wouldn't wait.

She smiled happily when she remembered the red dress he'd promised to buy her when they were married.

Amber had shouted out and banged on the cellar door intermittently, but to no avail. After a while it became obvious she was alone in the house. The darkness in the cellar was dense and only the chime of the clock helped her to keep count of the passing hours.

The temperature plummeted. Her only warmth was the blanket. Using the handle of the iron ladle, she managed to make a hole in it big enough for her head to slip though. She pulled it over her nightgown despite the horsey smell it gave off, tying it around her waist with one of the cords. At least it didn't keep slipping off now, and it left her arms free.

She began to feel hungry. About this time Annie usually brought her tea on a tray, then water to wash in. Then she'd go downstairs and be served breakfast of her choice from the many dishes set out. At least she had wine to drink, but it made her head spin if she drank too much at once, and it created a sour taste in her mouth and caused the pit of her stomach to ache.

She heard a series of creaks as though there were footsteps overhead, and she rushed to the door, yelling, 'Help me!'

Nobody answered.

Perhaps it was her grandfather, letting her know he was watching over her. The thought gave her comfort. 'Why is Patrick doing this to me, Grandfather?' she said. 'I would have helped him. He only had to ask.'

*Are you sure it's Patrick?*

Was she? She doubted it was Jonas Carlton after their confrontation at his uncle's house. He would be the first they'd suspect if she disappeared. But Patrick? He wouldn't have been able to resist goading her, and he wasn't past bullying her, especially when he had too much drink inside him. But the thought of him abducting her and demanding a ransom was somehow alien.

She didn't have to think very hard to find an alternative. She shuddered at the thought of Stephen Gould's sadistic eyes. He wouldn't care if he hurt her. He'd enjoy it.

*What if Gould came back? What if he violated her, then killed her?*

The colour ebbed from her face. Now she was aware of what took place she knew the strength of a man when he was aroused, and the control needed. She doubted if she'd enjoy the attention of one ruthless enough to use the intimate act in anger to punish and humiliate.

She had no weapon to fight him off with. Her fingers touched the cord around her waist and her eyes widened as her mind began to consider the possibilities. She knew the layout of the cellar and where certain objects were usually kept. And yes ... she did have weapons.

Over the next hour she began to prepare to defend herself, because she wasn't going to succumb without a fight. Gradually, she dragged a small, but heavy table across to the right of the stairs. On it she placed the iron ladle. Now it was close at hand if she needed it.

As a line of first defence she lay bottles of wine on the steps. They would roll under foot and make it hard for anyone to keep their balance.

Her fingers closed around a broom and were hastily withdrawn when she encountered a thick sticky material and remembered the spiders. She left it propped against a wall, where it would act as a last resort.

Gathering together the cords that had bound her, she tightly knotted them together. One end she tied to a wine rack, the other was stretched across the stairs and secured to the leg of the table.

Satisfied she'd done all she could, she sank on to her mattress and scowled into the darkness until boredom overtook her and she fell asleep.

Patrick had been looking for the wounded man for half the night and had slept fitfully. When he woke it was later than he'd expected. He was still alone. Jonas's horse had found his, and the pair nuzzled each other like the old friends they were.

Instantly, he was aware that Stephen had run out on him. He was relieved, for it left him with a clear conscience. But conscience couldn't be cleared that easily, he thought, when he remembered the man in the forest.

He set out again, going back to the spot where the man had been shot. After a while he came across some spots of blood and began to follow them. It was an hour before he found him. The man had gone round in a circle, and was seated against a tree trunk, grey-faced and with his eyes closed.

He opened them when he heard the horse and said tiredly, 'I hoped you would look for me. I might as well tell you. I was on my way to the Earl of Laconbridge's estate with a message from your friend Jonas Carlton. I was to tell him of the plot afoot to abduct a young woman who was about to marry into his family.'

Patrick nodded. 'The girl is my cousin, but Stephen has gone, so it's no longer urgent.'

'You were part of the plot?'

'Much to my shame. I owed Stephen money but the plan to abduct Amber was not to my liking. Can you ride?'

'As long as we go slowly. I'm in a great deal of pain now.'

Patrick administered brandy from his flask and helped the man on to the horse. 'Tell me if you feel faint.'

'Is Gould capable of carrying out an abduction single-handed?' Matt suddenly said.

Fear leaped into Patrick's breast. 'It's possible … yes.'

'Then let's make all haste. If the girl has gone and if she dies at Gould's hands you'll be equally guilty, since you conspired with him.'

'I didn't conspire to kill her,' Patrick said. 'We were going to hold her in the charcoal burner's cottage and claim a ransom for her return.'

'For your sake, I hope nothing has happened to her.'

Two miles away, in the luxurious comfort of his drawing room, the earl was saying to his agent, 'There will be no wedding today. Go to the church with a notice to that effect. The reverend can place it on the door.'

'Yes, My Lord.'

When he'd gone the earl turned to his family, who were now gathered together in the one spot. Their faces were glum. The company was subdued, since the time had long passed when a messenger should have informed them of Amber's whereabouts.

The earl stated the obvious. 'The delay has bought her abductors time. They already have the ransom money and could be anywhere by now. We must hope that Miss Hartford is still alive, and must find her as soon as possible.' He was interrupted by a knock at the door. 'I told you not to disturb us unless there was sufficient reason?' he growled when the butler entered.

'Begging your pardon, My Lord, I believe there is sufficient reason. There are two strangers at the gate requesting admittance. One states that he's Lord Hartford. He's leading a wounded man on another horse who said he's acquainted with Viscount Costain. His name is Matt Striker.'

'Matt Striker?' Benedict's brow cleared. 'Yes, I know Matt. He helped me rescue Amber Rose from her cousin and is in the revenue service.

241

Lord Hartford is with him, you say? Does this mean he had nothing to do with the abduction?'

'There's only one way to find out,' the earl said and turned to the butler. 'Tell the gatekeeper to relieve them of any weapons they may be carrying. Bring them to my study. We'll interrogate them there.'

'Yes, My Lord.'

The countess smiled at her husband. 'Not too rigorously, I hope, James. One of the men is wounded, after all. And didn't Bennet say he knew him?'

'I do, and will vouch for his integrity. I can't say the same for Patrick Hartford though. The man's a disgrace.'

'Do you know what's wrong with this wounded man?' his father said to the butler.

'I believe he's been shot, Sir.'

'It would be better to lay the wounded man out on the table in the laundry room if he's bleeding. Has anyone got the stomach to remove a ball?'

'I'll have a look at it,' Archie offered. 'If it's too deep he'll need a surgeon.'

Kitt offered to help, in case the patient needed holding down.

'We'll prepare something to cleanse the wound with in case it becomes infected, and a herbal pack and bandages to aid healing,' the countess said, and she motioned to her daughters who followed her out with a show of reluctance.

Emma was disappointed at not being part of the interrogation. 'Why do men always get to do the exciting stuff,' she cried out as soon as the drawing room door closed behind them.

'If you think digging a bullet out of a man is exciting I'll ask your father to allow you to assist your husband,' her mother told her.

'You know very well that Emma meant the interrogation, Mamma,' Caroline said in her sister's defence.

'And you know very well that men have to be allowed to take the lead in such matters. We can only advise them of the way to go about it in a more gentle fashion. Don't worry, my dears. No doubt we'll be allowed to apply our healing lotions and bandages once the poor man has been butchered by your husbands.'

When her daughters pulled a wry face, Imogene's smile faded. 'I cannot imagine what that poor girl has been going through, and feel that Bennet will be quite ruthless in his pursuit of her abductors.'

'Bennet might kill them out of hand,' Emma said with a touch of relish as they reached the still room.

Imogene looked worried. 'I do hope my son has more restraint than that. I must ask your father to advise him.'

'Oh, Mama. You know very well that papa has so much passion in him that he'd throttle anyone who laid a finger on you, or us, and without asking them questions first. So how can he advise Bennet? Papa wouldn't stop to think, and since Bennet is cut in his mould, neither will he.'

'I imagine Bennet will challenge that awful cousin of Amber's to a duel,' then Caroline added, clearly aghast, 'What if Amber is ... *ruined?*'

The three women stared at each other for a few seconds, then Imogene murmured, 'For her sake we will not consider that a catastrophe of that nature will occur. If it does then Bennet will search his soul and follow his heart, and we will accept the decision he makes as the right one. After that it will be never mentioned again.'

Emma giggled. 'I pray Bennet doesn't go all holy on us again.'

'So do I.' Imogene's eyes began to sparkle when she laughed. 'Knowing his father, I'm not such a fool to imagine his son is less than manly when he's with Amber, any more than I imagined you to be reticent with your prospective husbands. In fact, I'm certain none of you were in the least bit shy since God designed men and women to enjoy each other, and the attraction is hard to resist when the affections are involved.'

'*Mamma!*' they both exclaimed going rather pink in the face.

Imogene grinned as she set a mortar and pestle on the marble table. 'Being regarded as a saint by one's children is annoying. Kindly remember that you were created in exactly the same manner as you created my grandchildren.'

Emma said, 'When I was a child I asked the reverend why Caroline and I were exactly the same. The reverend said you were doubly blessed.'

After the three stopped laughing, Imogene said, 'Pass that St John's Wort, would you dear? We'll mix it with some aloe so it doesn't burn the skin. Caroline, you can collect the aloe from the garden while Emma prepares the bandages.'

Pink-faced, but grinning at each other, Imogene's two daughters began to scurry to her bidding.

From a high shelf she took down a wooden box containing scissors, knives, and odds and ends, such as needles and strong thread. She handed it to one of the kitchen servants who was standing by. It hadn't been used very often.

'Make sure these implements are washed and dried, and the razor honed. Place them on a clean tray and take them through to the laundry maid. Tell her to spread a clean and folded sheet on the laundry table. Set out some clean cloths, towels and a bowl with soap and warm water. And tell cook to keep a kettle boiling on the hob in case it's needed. We're expecting a wounded man.'

While Matt was stoically being doctored, Benedict and his father were questioning Patrick Hartford in the study. His father's agent was also in attendance.

'So, with Stephen Gould you were a party to the plot to abduct your cousin.'

Unhappily, Patrick nodded.

'You're a coward, sir,' the earl told him. 'Would you have gone ahead with the plan if Stephen Gould hadn't double-crossed you?'

Patrick shrugged. 'At the time I hadn't heard that he'd tried to kill Jonas. Then Matt Striker appeared riding Jonas's horse. Stephen shot him, and then insisted that I administer a *coup-de-gras*.'

'You attempted to kill a wounded man?'

245

'No, My Lord. I saw he was alive and pretended to shoot him, then I went back to the charcoal burner's cottage to wait. Stephen was supposed to bring my cousin to the cottage.'

'You're a disgrace, Sir.'

'I'm aware of that, My Lord, but you telling me so doesn't make me any more of a disgrace, and neither does it help to find my cousin.'

The acerbic answer Patrick Hartford had aimed at the earl surprised and impressed Benedict. When his back was against the wall Hartford had guts of a sort, after all.

'I did try and find the wounded man, but it was too dark. I discovered him this morning and learned he was on his way here with a message. That's when I discovered that Stephen cracked Jonas over the head and pushed him in the harbour. He must have suspected he would warn someone. He was near death when Matt Striker pulled him out, and is suffering from broken bones.'

Benedict shuffled from one foot to the other. The man may have acted like a rogue, but he was trying to put things right. Patrick could have left Matt to fend for himself and taken off like a cowardly cur. All the same, he was responsible for the plight Amber now found herself in, he reminded himself.

Patrick said, 'I'm worried Stephen may have killed Amber, as was his original plan. He'd have nothing to gain except the ransom and the thrill of doing it.'

Straightening up, Benedict said quietly, 'You'd have something to gain. Her fortune.'

'I rather thought that you were after it, Costain.'

The earl managed to prevent his son from hitting Hartford. 'You should have stopped Gould.'

'He watched my every move. He knew I'd never killed a man, which is why he wanted me to shoot Matt in cold blood – so I'd be involved in the crime. I've got no stomach for killing. I think he may have changed his plan at the last minute, when he realized I wasn't going to go along with it.'

Benedict wondered how far this changed attitude would last if Hartford was pushed to the limit. 'Take notice. Whatever the outcome of this affair for Amber, I intend to call you out when it's all over – and I will kill you.'

Patrick paled, but said nothing.

'Was it you who collected the ransom?'

'No. It would have been Maisie from the inn, I imagine. She's young and impressionable.'

'Try and find her.' The earl nodded to his agent who swiftly left the room and headed for the stable.

'Think, man. Do you have any idea where he may have taken your cousin.'

'He'd planned to use the cottage, but I haven't seen him since yesterday. He may have taken her to Hartford House. He knows where the key is, and it's empty and isolated. It's been sold, but the new owner doesn't take up residence until next week.'

'Is there anywhere she can hide if she escapes him?'

'I've only visited the house a few times. There are cellars and attics, and there was talk of a secret passage by the servants. There often is in old houses, though.'

Jake came into Benedict's mind. Amber was close enough to him to have told him her secrets. Leaving his father to handle the rest of the interrogation he went upstairs, taking them two at a time. Apart from Jake, the children were unaware of what had taken place.

The boy gazed anxiously at him when he took him aside. 'Is there any news, sir?'

'Not yet, Jake. You might be able to help though. Can you remember Miss Amber talking about a secret passage?'

'Yes, Sir. She took me through it. It starts in the hallway. There's a cupboard under the stairs, for boots and capes and stuff. At the high end is a wooden door that can be slid to one side. It looks like a panel and has a hole in so you can put your finger through to lift the latch. There's some stairs going down, then a longer passage, and some stairs going up.'

'Where does the tunnel come out?'

'In the tack room in the stable. There's a big iron trap door in the floor that lifts up, 'cepting we couldn't go up through it because Miss Amber wasn't strong enough to lift it by herself, and it wouldn't budge. She said that one of her ancestors was a smuggler, and he used the tunnel to hide goods in. She said her grandfather was going to have it filled in because rats use it to gain access to the house now and again. But he died before he could.'

The tunnel seemed to have made a great impression on the boy. 'Thank you, Jake. I'll go and look for her at Hartford House. I'll let you know that she's safe as soon as I can.'

'Miss Amber will be all right, Sir, won't she?'

He took the boy's hands in his. 'I won't be less than honest with you, Jake. She's in grave danger, but I'll do my best to rescue her.'

'Be careful in the tunnel, sir,' Jake said in a trembling voice. 'You're tall and the roof in the tunnel is low. We had to use a lantern to find our way. And even though it's built of brick, here and there one or two had fallen into the tunnel and water had leaked through.' He shuddered. 'It smelled.'

'You've remembered the directions accurately, I hope, Jake, since I won't have a lantern.'

'Yes, sir. I didn't like the place because it pressed in. I was scared that the roof might cave in and we'd be buried, or the candle might go out and I'd be lost. Miss Amber said we couldn't get lost because there was only one beginning and one end to the tunnel. And she promised me that it wouldn't cave in since it had been there for a hundred years or more.'

Benedict didn't feel reassured by the boy's words. A hundred years of the earth pressing down on the bricks would only weaken the structure. 'I'll be careful.'

The smiling faces of his nieces and nephews had reminded him that he'd involved his brothers-in-law enough. Downstairs, he said to his father. 'I'm going to leave straight away, before Kitt and Archie get wind of it. Delay them as long as you can, this isn't their fight.'

When father and son exchanged an embrace there was no need for words.

'Allow me to accompany you,' Patrick said when Benedict turned away. 'I could be of some help, or at least prove a distraction.'

A laugh grated from him. 'I want the man to know why he's dying.'

'And I want to redeem myself in my cousin's eyes before I die,' Patrick said in a low voice. 'Don't deny me that. Besides, you cannot challenge him. He has no rank.'

'I can,' Kitt said strolling into the room with Archie behind him. 'You weren't considering leaving us behind, were you, Bennet.'

'I don't want my sisters to be widowed, gentlemen.'

Archie laughed. 'Neither do we, so we'll be careful. Now, let's not waste time arguing but get on our way before the women get wind of it.'

'What about me?' Patrick said.

Benedict was inclined to trust Patrick at this time. The man had no stomach for killing in cold blood, so at the very least he wouldn't have to watch his own back. Even so, Benedict took him by his lapels and engaged his eyes. 'As long as you're aware it will make no difference to the outcome for you. If any harm has befallen Amber I'll follow you to the ends of the earth to avenge her. D'you understand?'

Patrick gave a small sigh of resignation and nodded.

# SEVENTEEN

Stephen smiled with relief when Maisie stepped ashore on the quay at Poole.

She was wind-blown, pale-faced, out of temper and clutching her stomach. 'I felt sick all the way, and thought I'd never reach dry land,' she grumbled.

The fisherman dropped her bags on to the quayside. 'Here she is, sir, safe and sound. God knows what she's got in those two bags, but they be so heavy she can hardly lift them.'

'It ain't none of your business what a lady keeps in her bags,' Maisie said peevishly.

Stephen managed a laugh as he threw a guinea to the man, though he felt like slapping her. She'd worn a garish green gown that matched the oversized bow on her bonnet. It drew attention. 'You know what women are like, they can't leave anything behind.'

'What's wrong with it,' she snapped, when he mentioned the colour of her dress. 'Those satchels were so heavy I had to leave everything I had behind, so I wore my best one. And look at it, all wet from salt water and smelling of fish. It will be covered in stains when it dries. You'll have to buy me something new ... that nice red one you promised me.'

Stephen could barely hide his shudder. She was strident, but it didn't matter. She wouldn't be with him for much longer. He took her to a room at a boarding house, took advantage of her body which helped improve her mood, and his, then left her with ten guineas to spend on herself. Her eyes lit up at the sight of it. 'That be a fortune.'

'Buy your red gown. I'll be back for you tomorrow afternoon and we can go on board then,' he lied.

'Aye, but you said we were getting married.'

'We are, it's arranged. The captain will marry us as soon as the ship puts out to sea.'

She moved to the window and gazed out over the harbour. 'Which ship are we going on, Stephen?'

He waved a hand towards a tangle of masts swaying back and forth with the motion of the water. 'It's over there, you can't see it from here.' He kissed the back of her neck. 'I'd better go before the landlady comes up to see what we're up to.'

'That sour old cat would only be jealous.'

Although she didn't know it, Maisie was referring to Sally Bowers, who ran the local whorehouse as well as the boarding house. Usually the place was occupied by passengers waiting to board their ships. She'd soon provide Maisie with a job when she ran out of money.

'The High Street is in that direction if you need the shops.' He gave her an extra guinea. 'Buy yourself something sensible to wear on board, as well. I don't want the seamen leering at you.'

A coquettish look came his way. 'You do love me, don't you?'

'Would I be going to all this trouble if I didn't?' Shrugging into his coat he gave her a quick hug, picked up the money satchels and left her, feeling pleased with the way things were working out. Maisie had been worth every penny of the money he'd given her, but she was already fading from his mind as he headed out of town.

Sally Bowers watched him go. Then she saw the girl come out of the boarding house to strut confidently towards the shops in her bright dress, smiling boldly at the men who glanced at her.

Sally assessed her. She was young and good-looking with a fine pair of breasts, a strong back and well-muscled flanks that would hold her in good stead. Her flirtatious and knowing manner told Sally her virginity was long dispensed with.

A smile sped across her face. She must make the girl's acquaintance for she'd need some help and advice in a day or so, especially when her man didn't come back to pay the rent.

Jonas Carlton was on the cart being taken to the infirmary when he saw Maisie. Telling the driver to stop he called out her name.

She came to the cart and laughed as she looked down on him. 'You look as though you've been in the wars, Jonas. Stephen is in town.'

'Then for God's sake don't tell him you've seen me. He thinks I'm dead.'

Maisie's smiled faltered. 'Why would he think that?'

'Because he hit me over the head and pushed me into the harbour.'

She tossed her head. 'It must have been someone else. If I tell Stephen what you've said about him, he *will* kill you then.'

'And you, most likely, for knowing too much. Beware of him, Maisie. I'm advising you for your own good. Has he involved you in that scheme with Lord Hartford to kidnap his cousin?'

Her eyes narrowed. 'I don't know what you're talking about. Lord Hartford isn't with him. Stephen's going to marry me as soon as we get on board–' She clapped a hand over her mouth, then giggled. 'I'm supposed to keep it a secret.'

He felt sorry for her. 'For pity's sake, Maisie, Stephen's using you. He's ruthless. He won't marry you, and by now the Costain family will be after him because I sent someone to warn them yesterday.'

'Then why didn't they come after me when I collected the ransom?'

Why indeed? Matt Springer had given himself plenty of time. Jonas hoped that the revenue man hadn't come to any harm. And if Patrick wasn't with Stephen, it was quite possible he'd killed them both... Amber Hartford as well.

'Leave town,' he warned. 'Go back to where you belong before it's too late.'

'I'm never going back, and you're a liar. Stephen loves me and we're going to be wed.'

'Don't say you haven't been warned, Maisie.'

She gazed at him for a moment, uncertain. Then money jingled as she put her hand in her pocket. She brought out a gold coin and smiled as she tossed it. The coin glinted in the sun as it spun. Deftly she caught in and slipped it back into her pocket.

'Silly girl,' he murmured as she stuck her nose in the air and walked off. 'You're going to have to learn from experience, the same as I did.'

Amber's moods alternated between anger, boredom and despair.

At the moment she was feeling sorry for herself. She was ravenously hungry. Her stomach rattled and gurgled in protest. The ache in her head had grown with each gulp of wine, her mouth was dry and stale ... and tears trickled down her cheeks.

The bout of self-pity made her hate herself. 'Go on, cry,' she flung into the darkness. 'A lot of good that will do you.'

Anger filled her body and she screamed out with the energy of her hate, 'Let me out, you coward, while I've got strength left to kill you.'

She smiled at the thought, imagining Stephen losing his footing on the bottles, tumbling head-over-heels down the stairs then tripping over the cord. If that didn't kill him she'd hit him over the head with the iron ladle.

She began to tremble as her anger evaporated leaving her weak. She huddled into the mattress, the dirty blanket clutched against her body, her knees drawn up against her stomach to try and warm her feet. Chills ran through her body, and the air she breathed smelled of mould.

What if she'd been left here to die ... what if nobody thought to look for her here before it was too late? Her heart began to thump erratically, until the noise filled her chest and rose into her ears. She pinched her wrist hard to quell her rising panic and took long deep breaths to calm herself. Into the calm came the sound of the clock, modulated and stately. *Bong... Bong... Bong.* But was it three in the morning or the afternoon?

In sudden confusion she tried to count backwards. Being brought here seemed such a long time ago. She was trapped like a rat in a hole. Her small surge of energy fled. She lay there, apathetic and disorientated, gazing into the darkness before sleep provided her with an escape from her fears.

She jerked suddenly awake. There had been a noise – not a squeak, a chime or a creak, but a proper noise. The sound another person might make. There was a scuff of footsteps that stopped outside the cellar door. She could almost smell someone.

'Who is it?' she whispered, then came upright and said louder. 'Who is it? I'm down here in the cellar.'

'I know you are, my dear. I put you there.'

Hairs prickled along her neck as she recognized the voice and she said in despair. 'Is my cousin with you, Stephen? I want to talk to him.'

He chuckled. 'Patrick lost his nerve for the game. I never realized he was so weak in the stomach until it was nearly too late.'

'He's twice the man you are. Let me out. I'll pay you.'

'Oh, I've already been paid. Lord Costain handed over one thousand guineas for your safe return.'

'So you're going to let me out.'

'Of course I am.' Her mood lightened then was crashed down again when he said. 'But only to keep me entertained this evening. Costain won't want you after that, anyway.'

Benedict wouldn't want her? Her face paled as the meaning became clear. 'You have the ransom. Why don't you allow me to go?'

'Because you know who I am.'

'I'll double the ransom if you release me unharmed.'

He chuckled. 'You're not such a fool, and neither am I.'

'Do you think Lord Costain won't guess where I'm being kept and come looking for me.'

'He might, but guessing it and proving it is two different things. It's *my* guess that they'll have Patrick in custody for murder by now.'

Wide-eyed, she stared into the darkness. 'Patrick has killed someone?'

'Your cousin is too cowardly to kill a mouse.'

Her flare of relief was short-lived.

'The evidence will point to him, though. I imagine he'll be questioned rigorously. They'll want to know what happened to his friend, Jonas, as well as to you.'

'Jonas Carlton? But he's in London. I saw him barely a week ago at the home of his uncle.'

'Ah yes ... Jonas told me that you took him to task. You'll be pleased to hear that you had a profound effect on him. He flatly refused to take part in this affair. He decided to go home to his uncle, present himself as a reformed character and then beg his forgiveness. I stopped him.'

She didn't bother ask him how, she didn't want the details. She was just sorry she hadn't allowed Jonas to apologize. If she had he'd still be alive. 'Patrick will tell them I'm here.'

Stephen laughed. 'But he doesn't know you're here. He might think of it, of course, but by the time they arrive I'll be long gone and you'll be dead.'

'You're going to kill me?' Terror raced through her. 'How?'

'Oh, I won't do anything nasty to you, unless you provoke me beyond endurance. I'll just leave you in the cellar so you can starve to death. I daresay the new owner will get a bit of a fright when he finds your body. They might think it was a tragic accident, that you accidentally locked yourself in. Most likely they'll blame it on Patrick. After all, he is your beneficiary and you've inherited a sizeable fortune to leave him. In the years to come your ghost can have some fun haunting this place.'

Amber bit down on her tongue. He'd gloat if he knew that she'd purchased Hartford House. 'May I have a candle for light and some water to drink,' she said in a low voice.

There was a clunk of a key in the lock and the door was swung open. She shielded her eyes from the sudden glare of lantern light with her arm. When her eyes adjusted she gazed up at his tall figure, though his face was too shadowed to see it.

Behind him was escape, the passage that led to the hall, to the front door or to the stairs to the upper regions of the house. There she could think of half a dozen places to hide.

When he dipped a foot on to the first stair she tensed and held her breath. He drew his foot back, picked up a bottle, looked at the label and stood it upright, saying, 'Your grandfather's brandy is too good to waste.' To her dismay he laughed as he began to kick the rest of the bottles from the step. 'I'm not such a fool as you imagine, Amber. Dismantle your man traps then you can come up.'

Doing as she was told she went up towards the light. Stephen tied her hands behind her back, hobbled her ankles so she couldn't run, then slipped the leading rein around her neck again. He looked her up and down then laughed. 'Oh dear, what a filthy, raggle-taggle creature you are. Still pretty though. I'm sure I'll find a use for you later.' He stooped to pick up the bottle, then kissed her on the mouth.

Amber determined to put up with the grinding wetness of it, but then she nearly gagged. She couldn't kick or hit him, so she sank her teeth into his bottom lip.

'You bitch!' He backhanded her across the face so hard that she cried out with the pain of it. His eyes were like angry wasps as he gazed into hers. 'No matter. I like a little resistance. There's nothing quite so exciting as an unwilling woman.'

Pressing a handkerchief against the welling blood he jerked on the rein, dragging her, almost choking, along the passage behind him to the dining room. The silver had gone from the table and sideboard, the solid silver candlesticks and trays were no longer in their usual places. The windows were still shuttered. The gaps in the boards showed it was early evening and the gloaming light was faintly purple.

There was some bread, ham and cheese on the table ... a bowl of apples from the orchard. Stephen pushed her into a chair, opened the bottle and looked for some glasses, kicking the doors to the sideboard shut when he couldn't see them. She could have told him where they were but was disinclined to be helpful.

Eventually, he found them in the cupboard set into the wall, which had been fitted out with wine and glass racks so to act as a dispensary for the convenience of the servants. He threw her a dark look when she smiled.

'You'll have to untie my hands so I can eat and drink.'

'Will I?' He poured the brandy into a glass, almost filling it, then held it to her mouth. 'Drink it.'

She turned her head aside. 'I don't want brandy. I'd like some water.'

Stephen didn't argue. He held her nose until she opened her mouth then poured the brandy inside. Some spilled over her chin and down her front. Coughing and spluttering she gulped down the rest. Fire spread from her stomach into her limbs.

When he ate a chunk of bread piled high with ham and cheese, her mouth watered. He followed it with an apple so juicy that when crunched between his teeth the juice spurted down his chin. His glance never left her as he savoured each bite. Eventually there was nothing left but a few crumbs.

She hoped the bread was full of insects, and imagined him writhing of the ground screaming in agony while they gnawed their way out.

Lethargy began to creep though her. When her head nodded forward he made her drink another glass of brandy. A few minutes later and everything had slowed down.

Stephen smiled. 'You're drunk, Amber Rose.'

'I'm aware of that.' Struggling to keep hold of her senses, her words seemed to stretch and blur when she said, 'You're scum ... a worm of the first order.'

Rising, he came round to where she sat and, taking her by the hair he jerked her to her feet. His smile had an edge of nastiness to it when he said, 'I could kill you in a second.'

She drew in a sharp breath when he took a dagger from his belt and held the cold metal surface against her neck. He drew it gently across without breaking the skin. Then he stooped to slash through her leg bindings, followed by the cords at her wrists.

'You're letting me go?' she said with faint hope.

'Certainly not. We're going to play a little game, my dear. You have ten minutes in which to hide upstairs. Then I'll come looking for you. If you can hide from me for ten minutes more, I'll let you live ... for a price.'

Alarm sent goose bumps racing through her body. 'What price?'

He whispered something foully suggestive in her ear.

'I'd sooner die,' she spat out.

'Then you shall.' She cringed when a knife blade flashed and the hair in his grip parted from her head. He dropped the cut locks at her feet, took out his watch and said affably. 'I'll have you first and you don't have to be willing.'

'Are you insane?' she whispered.

The eyes that came up to hers seemed perfectly sane, but something was lacking in their expression. Pity or conscience ... perhaps both.

The secret tunnel that led to the stables came into her mind, but she had no chance to get to it unseen, for he pushed her out of the dining room and into the hall. There, the clock relentlessly ticked away the seconds of her life in the dimming light.

'Time starts now.' He took a seat on the bottom stair and began to prepare the flint box to light a candle from. Amber had no choice to go anywhere but up the wide staircase. She thought she could feel his glance on her as she went.

Where could she hide? she thought, when she got to the first landing, and out of his sight. It was not a huge or pretentious house, but a home of comfortable proportions that was easy to run and maintain, her grandfather had said of it, which was one of the reasons he'd loved it so much.

There were only two corridors, one to the left and one to right, with rooms either side. They would not take long to search. The staircase went on upwards to the servants' rooms and nursery, then to the attics above.

Amber hesitated for a few seconds, trying to gather her wits together. It might have been better if she'd asked for more brandy, enough so she could lose her senses altogether and pass into a drunken stupor. At least she wouldn't have been aware of any horrible event that might overtake her this night. *She also wouldn't have been able to fight back!*

She thought of her grandfather again, and she smiled as she took the corridor to the left.

The four men left their horses in the copse and made their way across Hartford House meadows. All was quiet except for the wind sighing in the trees and the soft thud of footfalls in the grass.

The air had an early autumn dampness to it. The house was a solid shadow, the evening star shining brightly above a dark shape of a chimney that thrust into the sky.

Benedict shivered as an owl hooted.

'The house doesn't look occupied,' Kitt whispered. His words were instantly disproved when there came the quiet snicker of a horse. And as they reached the stable they saw the solitary flicker of a lantern behind the shutters, and a prick of light between the boards nailed across the house windows.

'The horse belongs to Stephen and it's saddled. It looks as though he intends to use it before too long,' Patrick whispered. He pulled the saddle bags from the horse. There was chink of coin as he dropped them to the floor and shoved them under a pile of straw with the toe of his boot.

'Your ransom, gentlemen.'

Thinking of what Amber must be suffering at the hands of Gould, Benedict felt sick.

The trapdoor was easily found, but it was padlocked. No wonder Amber hadn't been able to open it. The key hung on a hook in the wall. The trapdoor squeaked as they pulled it open.

He took the lantern with him. 'I'll go down first. Watch your heads,' he said, and felt for the top step with his foot. When he reached the bottom he held out his arms and touched the tunnel of either side. It was wide enough to be comfortable, but he had to bend almost double to move along it.

Being enclosed affected them all as they carefully shuffled along the length of the tunnel. Breathing was heavy, but nobody spoke or voiced any fear. All of them swore as they tripped over a fallen brick. Finally, Benedict stubbed a foot against a barrier.

'I think we've come to the steps,' he whispered. 'Be quiet now. I'll go up, see if I can find the catch and open the panel. I understand it slides aside.'

His fingers found the mechanism, his mind pictured it and he pushed against a lever with his thumb. There was a loud, metallic click. He froze.

About to climb the stair, Stephen had frozen too. What the hell was that? He listened. As if listening encouraged noise the clock seemed to tick louder, floorboards creaked overhead and the chandelier tinkled as a draught played with it.

After a while he relaxed. Lighting a couple of lanterns from the candle, he positioned one at the bottom of the staircase.

A door stealthily closed upstairs. Stephen smiled as he brought his mind back to the game. She was a plucky piece of goods who would try to outwit him. He was going to enjoy the sport, and the eventual outcome after the chase.

'I'm coming to look for you, Amber Rose,' he called out softly, and picked up the second lantern and moved swiftly up the stairs.

When time brought no reaction to the click, Benedict carefully moved the panel to one side and stepped through into a cupboard full of outdoor garments. Reaching out for the door into the house he turned the handle, then quietly swore. It was locked, something he hadn't taken into consideration.

Turning, he whispered down the stairs, 'If I can't pick the lock I'm going to have to try and kick the door into the house down.'

There was a whispered conference then Kitt said quietly. 'Hartford has suggested that you may be able to lever the hinges off with a blade.'

'I haven't got one.'

A dagger was passed up to him and he started work on the top hinge. It was manufactured from thick metal.

# EIGHTEEN

Amber had been tempted to hide in her own wardrobe, but she suspected that would be the bolt hole Stephen would expect her to use.

She used her few spare minutes as wisely as possible, opening windows in as many rooms as she could, then leaving the doors ajar, so the doors would move and creak in the cross draughts, even slam shut if the wind came up. If it hadn't been such a long way down she would have jumped from the window.

She froze when she heard the loud click. It panicked her a little. Thinking it was Stephen she ran to her grandfather's room, where she'd decided to hide earlier. She transferred the key from the inside of the door to the outside. If she managed to escape she would lock him inside.

There was only one place she could hide where Stephen might not think to look. The cupboards and linen box were too enclosed, and there was no room under the bed. As with the other rooms she opened the window, which framed a shining moon that inconveniently illuminated everything with a soft silver glow. Damn! It was too late to find another hiding place. Just above the window was a decorative ledge under the corner of the roof, with a gargoyle to carry away rain water from the gutter.

Ripping a piece from her nightie she threw it up

towards the gargoyle, where it hung from its fearful, snarling snout, caught on its teeth as if the beast had just ripped it from her.

Shedding the clumsy blanket she threw it out of the window, then climbed on to the end of the bed. Quickly, she pulled herself up one of the carved poles and lay on her stomach on the canopy of the four-poster bed.

The last time she'd been up here she'd been young, and hiding from her governess. Now the ceiling seemed lower, and the fabric of the canopy sagged beneath her increased weight. It also smelled of dust. She gripped the wooden frame with her fingers, trying to keep her weight off the material. It was hard work which taxed her muscles. Her pursuer would shoot her through the fabric if he saw her outlined there she thought despairingly. But she had nowhere else to run, now.

In the distance she heard a horse snicker, and another animal answer. It sounded as though it was coming from the copse. Her spirits rose. Perhaps Benedict had come looking for her. She took a deep breath to calm her jittery nerves.

Outside in the corridor a door slammed, then another. 'Clever ruse with the doors and windows, Amber Rose,' Stephen shouted out, 'I'm enjoying your little game ... but I'll find you eventually.'

It took him but a few minutes to search each room, then the door to the room she was in creaked open. He went straight to the window and looked out, then up to where the strip of fabric hung. He chuckled and gently closed the window. 'I can't believe my little vixen jumped out or climbed up on to the roof. I wonder where she can be. In the linen box perhaps?' He threw open the lid then slammed it shut again.

The disturbance in the air sent the dust swirling. Her nose and throat began to itch.

Her pursuer disappeared into the manservant's room, but was back in seconds to throw open the door of the mahogany wardrobe. Satisfied it was empty he turned and sniffed at the air. The light cast by the lantern didn't reach her shadowed position. 'The big bad wolf can smell you, my tender little lamb,' he cooed.

He was trying to break her nerve, but he wouldn't succeed, she thought fiercely, trying not to betray her position, though she longed to clear her throat.

Dust tickled her nose. *Oh no ... a sneeze!* Desperately she pinched her nose end between her finger and thumb. Her body jerked violently with the muffled sneeze she gave.

'Oh, there you are, just where I want you,' he said, as the canopy tore open and gave way under her weight. She dropped through to bounce on to the mattress below. Placing the lantern on the dresser Stephen joined her, pinned her to the bed and kissed her.

She pushed him away, screaming and struggling as he began to paw her.

Benedict had managed to remove the top hinge, but as soon as he heard Amber scream he threw caution to the winds. He used the heel of his foot as a battering ram. The door tore from its hinges under the force behind it, and they were through to the house.

Stephen Gould must have heard the noise for Amber went quiet, except for the odd whimper, which tore his heart out.

'Let me go up there first,' Patrick whispered. 'He's more likely to trust me and I might be able to flush him out.'

Benedict nodded. 'I'll be right behind you, so no tricks.'

He positioned Archie and Kitt beyond the circle of light cast by the lantern in the hall and followed Patrick up the stairs to the first landing. Mindful that Patrick knew the layout of the house better than he did, Benedict stayed a few paces behind and to the side of him.

When they got to the landing, Patrick called out. 'Stephen, it's me, Patrick. Where's my cousin?'

There came a small whimpering noise from the left, one that was cut suddenly short. Benedict saw a faint glow under one of the doors. He restrained the urge that told him to go barging up there, but quietly directed Patrick's attention to it.

'You have her in my grandfather's room. I'm going to come along the corridor. I'm not armed, and I'm alone.'

The door opened, spilling light into the corridor. 'You're too cowardly to come here alone, Patrick. Take one step and I'll shoot you down.'

'Who else would I bring, especially when there's when a thousand guineas at stake? I want my share, Stephen. I have to get away. They'll be after me for the murder of that man in the forest

269

if they find his body. Is my cousin all right?'

'Why do you care?'

'I don't care. I was thinking that while she's still alive she might want to compensate us for leaving her that way. All it will take is a letter of credit to the bank signed by Amber and Thomas Dunstan. I can easily copy his signature. Where's Maisie? I thought she was with you?'

'I left the slut in Sally Bowers's boarding house.'

'After she helped you?'

'Maisie will fit in well there. Stop being such a saint.'

Benedict brought up his pistol when a figure stepped out into the light. No, not one figure, but two. Stephen had Amber in front of him in a choke-hold, using her as a shield. He tightened his grip when she gave a frustrated squeak and tried to heel him in the shin.

*The man's insane, don't inflame him,* Benedict prayed as she clawed at his arm in a futile quest to loosen his grip.

'Lift your arms and turn around,' Stephen ordered.

Patrick did as he was told.

Seemingly satisfied that his former friend was unarmed, Stephen laughed and pushed Amber to the floor. Planting a foot in her stomach, he placed his pistol against her temple. 'You're a fool to think I'm going to be taken in by you, Patrick. You're too cowardly to face me, with or without your weapons. You're playing for time. Who have you told?'

'Nobody, d'you think I want to end up in prison. All I want is my cousin left unharmed.

270

Look at her, she's terrified.'

'That's part of the entertainment. There's nothing to stop me from shooting both of you, right here and now. My ship leaves in an hour so I really must be going soon.' The hammer clicked.

Amber obviously didn't intend to be shot out of hand. Suddenly, she wrapped her arms around Stephen's leg and rolled away from him. Thrown off balance, his arms flailed and the gun discharged. Plaster fell from the ceiling. He grabbed a second pistol from his waist, cocking it, his eyes on Amber.

Benedict instinctively fired his own pistol. Stephen's reflex shot was almost point blank, yet as he dropped, by some miracle it missed Amber by a hair's breadth and thudded into the floor beside her.

Amber scuttled away. Gasping for breath, her eyes wide with terror she huddled in a corner. Tremors rippled through her as she gazed at Stephen. When Benedict tried to help her up, she pushed his hand away and hissed. 'Don't touch me.'

His heart went out to her. Softly he said, 'It's me, Benedict. Stephen can't hurt you now, my love. He's dead.'

Indeed, it had been a merciful, clean kill, straight through the heart. More than the man had deserved.

Kitt and Archie had come running, pistols drawn. They summed up the situation and smiled at each other.

'Good shot, Bennet,' Kitt said.

271

Amber made a distressed sound in her throat.

Archie went into the nearest room, coming back with a blanket to wrap the body in. He emptied the man's pockets first. Coins, a key, a handkerchief and an enamelled gold snuff box.

Benedict picked up the snuff box, turning it over in his hand before he slipped it into his pocket. 'This belongs to my father. It must have been Gould who robbed Laconbridge and attacked the maid. Were you a party to that, Hartford?'

'I didn't know he'd robbed the place. We went in to look for the agreement made between our grandfathers. Stephen thought I might have a claim to your property. He copied it and sent it to my cousin.'

So Amber had known about the loan for some time. Feeling uncomfortable, Benedict's glance went to her, but she showed no sign of having heard Patrick. She was staring wide-eyed at Gould's body, her expression terrified. He moved to hide it from her line of sight as his brothers-in-law began to wrap the blanket round the corpse.

'We'll put his body in one of the rooms in the other wing until morning, then contact the authorities in Bridport. No doubt the magistrate will want statements from us all.'

He stooped to where Amber was huddled in her dirty, ripped nightgown. Her hair was a dark tangle, her exposed skin was bruised and her neck chaffed. She had a remote air about her and jerked her head away when he reached out to touch her face.

'Will you be able to tell them what happened here tonight, Amber?'

The gesture had wounded him, and he could have wept when she turned her head away from him. She needed a woman to help her through this, he thought.

Kitt said awkwardly. 'We'll collect our horses from the copse and bring them round to the stables after we've dealt with Gould's body.'

'The magistrate can wait until morning. Make all haste to Laconbridge House and rouse my father and mother if you will. Ask my mother to come as soon as possible. Tell her Amber is in need of her counsel. Tell her...' He shrugged. 'Well, you know what to tell her.'

'We'll escort them back.' His brothers-in-law carried the corpse away, blood seeping into the blanket.

Patrick was pale-faced.

Benedict didn't know how to approach Amber. He enlisted Patrick's help. 'See if you can help your cousin.'

But as soon as Patrick reached out a hand she leapt to her feet and cried out, 'Leave me alone!' and bolted like a rabbit into one of the rooms. The door slammed behind her and the key turned in the lock.

'That's her room,' Patrick said ineffectively when Benedict put his ear against the panel and gently called out her name. 'Her clothes have been thrown everywhere.'

A storm of weeping reached his ears, great gulping sobs. Benedict felt helpless in the face of Amber's melancholy mood, and wretched. God only knew what the girl had been through, which was something he didn't really want to dwell on either. 'My mother will know what to do.'

'I'll fetch Mrs Phelps from the village. She was my housekeeper. At least she'll be able to boil some water.'

'Boil water! For what reason?'

Patrick shrugged vaguely. 'Perhaps some tea will settle her nerves. Or perhaps she might like to wash.'

For a moment or two Benedict wondered if she needed to wash. Even if she did, he knew it wouldn't make her appear any the less in his eyes.

Then, as Patrick walked away he remembered the gold in the stable. Patrick could help himself and never return if he was of a mind.

He found that he didn't care. At this moment, when his anger had been pacified by strong feelings of love and compassion, revenge didn't seem to matter. He had the rest of his life to find Patrick if he absconded. All that mattered to him was that the woman he loved was safe. But that was tempered by the knowledge that she was suffering and he could do nothing to help or comfort her. He would slay all her dragons from now on, and nothing would ever hurt her again if he could prevent it, he vowed.

Every time Amber managed to stop crying it was only a temporary lull. She'd never experienced such deep and utter sadness, such helplessness and lack of worth.

Her bed seemed to be a mess in the dim light, as though all the clothing she'd been forced to

274

leave behind had been dumped on it. She burrowed under the pile of garments for warmth, huddling there, her mind seething with the horror of what had taken place. Now and again she was racked by shivering.

When she thought she might be able to sleep, the sight of Stephen Gould's body came to haunt her. He'd been looking at her, and for a moment she'd seen her own death sentence in them. They'd remained open when he'd dropped, and even though something had changed in them and she'd known he was dead the expression was so intense that she'd expected him to reach out for her in death. She hadn't been able to tear her eyes away from his body. It was the first time she'd seen a man die. It had happened so quickly. It could have been herself lying there dead if Benedict hadn't been so quick in her defence.

Her hunger returned, but she was too scared to leave the secure nest she'd made. She remembered the bowl of apples Stephen Gould had left on the dining room table, and although she began to crave them and her mouth watered with longing, she didn't have the courage to move, or to call out to Benedict.

A scuffling noise outside her door brought her heart up to her mouth. Beyond her door she could sense a presence, and thought it might be Benedict. She couldn't face him. Not yet. But she didn't want to think, just sleep. That escape seemed to elude her because every time she closed her eyes she remembered Stephen Gould's eyes and began to weep.

The moon rode high in the sky outside her window. Gradually it slid away from her and the shadows lengthened across the room. Amber's eyes began to ache with the effort of trying to keep them open. She allowed them to relax.

A knock at the door woke her. She sat upright in bed, rigid with fear, then gazed around her in bewilderment. It was morning.

Events of the night before flooded in on her and she cried out.

'Are you all right, Amber, dear?'

A woman's voice, kind ... the countess. Benedict had sent for his mother. 'I don't know.'

'Open the door, my dear. I've brought a maid of all work with me as well as Annie. And we've brought you some fresh clothes to wear. You might like to bathe and dress. It will make you feel better.'

'Is Benedict still there? I don't want to see him yet.'

'My son is downstairs. He's been to the farm and purchased some food. The housekeeper has cooked breakfast for the men. Come, my dear, don't keep me waiting any longer. You cannot hide in there for ever.'

Amber reluctantly opened the door, then gazed at the garments strewn about the room and over the bed almost incomprehensibly. Most had been ripped and tossed about. 'I don't know who did this,' she whispered, beginning to shake again.

Imogene's intake of breath was audible. 'It doesn't matter who carried out such a stupid act. You must try and put it from your mind, for

276

to dwell on it will only bring sadness. We'll throw everything away and you can start afresh. Oh, my poor girl, how ill-used you look. You must tell me what happened... I want to know everything.'

'Benedict killed Stephen Gould.'

'It was no more than the odious man deserved, and was a direct consequence of the threat the man posed to you, I understand the felon's shot missed your head by a heartbeat. If Bennet had not killed him you'd be dead and we'd all be grieving.'

Tears pricked Amber's eyes. 'But he stared at me so, afterwards. I thought he might be pretending to be dead, and would come for me in the night. I'm so hungry I haven't eaten or drunk anything except wine since he abducted me. He tied my feet and hands together, gagged and blindfolded me, then locked me in the cellar and starved me ... he won't come back, will he?'

'No, my dear.'

'Promise me,' she said, close to panic at the thought that he might.

'I promise. The authorities have taken his body away. Benedict sat outside your door last night to make sure you remained safe.'

Amber remembered the scuffing sound she'd heard.

A flap of Imogene's hand sent the maids scurrying about their business. 'Find a bath, bring it up here and fill it. The housekeeper will know where it is. And ask the woman – Mrs Phelps I believe Lord Hartford said her name was – to make up a tray of food for her mistress. Not too much. A small bowl of gruel perhaps. A coddled egg and some wafers of bread with butter on. Oh, and a glass of milk for extra nourishment.'

Amber could have done without the sympathy because immediately the tears she'd held back began to fall from her eyes. But then she was drawn into Imogene's arms and the words began to tumble out of her as fast as her tears, and in any order they wished.

The countess had been right. By the time she'd related to her what had happened, had break-fasted, bathed and been dressed in a dark blue day gown that Imogene had brought with her, she felt stronger and able to face what the day brought.

Annie brushed her hair dry and Imogene sighed over the missing locks. She took some scissors from her toilette case. 'I'll shorten the other side to match so you won't look uneven. Annie can curl the short pieces around your face and draw the rest into a bun and secure it with a bandeaux.'

When the maid had finished the countess smiled at the servant. 'How clever you are with your hands. No wonder Miss Hartford requested that you work for her.'

Annie flushed with pleasure as Imogene placed a silk shawl around Amber's shoulders. 'Do you feel confident enough to face the magistrate and make a statement now, my dear?'

'I don't know. Will everyone be there?'

'Men can be rather intimidating, can't they? I do feel it would be a disservice to my husband to exclude him from the meeting. He's a magistrate himself so nobody will attempt to manipulate your statement in his presence.'

Manipulate her statement?

'With your permission I'll also stay with you. If you feel the need to retire you need only to squeeze my hand.'

The countess's words puzzled her. She gazed at the maid. 'Would you excuse us for a few moments, Annie.'

When Annie had gone Amber gazed directly at the countess. 'First of all I would like to say that I'm extremely grateful for the help that you've given so generously to me. I'm a little perturbed though that you think a magistrate would attempt to manipulate my statement, any more than I'd expect you to.' Her voice softened. 'Or that you think I might allow it to happen.'

Shamefaced, the countess gracefully inclined her head. 'My dear, you're upset. I'm sorry. The welfare of my son is close to my heart and this business needs to be over and done with.'

'My mind's clear as to what happened. My statement will not be detrimental to Benedict in any way. Why should it be if I simply tell the truth? I do think it would be better if my cousin attended me. It would be more impartial.'

'But my dear, Lord Hartford cannot. Bennet has challenged him. They are to meet in the meadow at dawn. Kitt will act as your cousin's second since he has nobody else.'

'They cannot fight over this. I will not allow such a thing to happen. My cousin tried to save my life.'

'But he was part of the conspiracy to abduct you in the first place.'

'One man has already died. There will be no more blood shed here if it can be prevented.' She swept past the countess and down the stairs, where the representatives of the Costain family were gathered.

They stood as she came in, but she didn't return Benedict's smile. Patrick was standing alone. He looked pale and subdued.

'I believe you've been challenged to a duel by Lord Costain, Patrick.'

His eyes sharpened in on her. 'Don't tell me you care what the outcome will be.'

'I know what the outcome will be. You'll die ... and yes, I do care. You're my only relative and I've always believed you to have more worth than you consider yourself to have. But allow me to make myself very clear. Patrick, if Lord Costain dies you will never be welcome in my home again.' She then gazed directly at Benedict. 'I'm grateful for your timely intervention with regards to my welfare, My Lord. You do not have my permission to defend my honour in this manner.'

'I do not need it, Amber. You exchanged private vows with me in the eyes of God in front of an altar. Lord Hartford has insulted you and it's my duty to defend you.'

'The marriage was not a legal one.'

'In my heart and mind you're my wife, Amber. You committed yourself to me, and I to you.' He gave a tiny grin, adding softly, 'You know I am your husband.'

Colour crept into her cheeks at the reminder, and his meaning was not lost on the company for Kitt and Archie exchanged a glance and the earl frowned at his son.

'Such talk is unworthy in front of your mother, Bennet. You will apologize to the ladies before you say another word.'

'My pardon Amber Rose ... Mamma.'

He'd taken the wind from her sails, had made her feel as though she was in the wrong. She *was* in the wrong. He'd risked his life to save hers twice over. And as he'd reminded her, she'd committed herself to him body and soul. Yet her streak of stubbornness rose to the surface. She would not allow him to kill Patrick.

Quietly, she said, 'If you intend to go ahead with this duel you're not welcome here. And from this moment on you're no longer a guest.'

'I was never a guest, only one of the intruders. You're safe now, Amber Rose. You have your life and you have your fortune. You can also have the loan returned that my grandfather owed yours, and with interest. It appears that you have no need of me in your ivory tower now.'

When Benedict gave her a mocking bow and walked away with Kitt and Archie in tow her heart sank. She wanted to call him back and apologize.

Patrick gave a huff of laughter. 'So, it was you who bought the place. I should have guessed. You certainly know how to hit a man in his pride. You will excuse me, won't you? My pardon.' He nodded to the earl and the countess and began to follow after the other three.

'Where are you going, Patrick? We need to talk.'

'I'm going to the infirmary to visit Jonas. Thank you for your sacrifice on my behalf, cousin, but I didn't need it, and neither do I need a wet nurse. I hope to see you at dawn, where you can watch us duel over you from the safety of your window. No matter which one of us wins you'll be the loser. You always liked this house and now you have it. I hope it brings you joy. I've offered the use of grandfather's duelling pistols, by the way. Rather a nice irony don't you think?'

Stung by his sarcasm, she snapped, 'As far as I'm concerned you can shoot each other's damned heads off with them.'

When he'd gone Amber turned to the earl and his wife with an appeal in her eyes and a plaintive frustration in her voice. 'Men are so infuriating!'

The earl turned away with a slight grin when his wife said, 'I agree that men are not very sensible at times. But, my dear, you're not yourself at the moment and our son should have taken that into account. Bennet's behaviour was entirely reprehensible, but issuing such an ultimatum was not a good strategy. Even your cousin knew that, and he has the most to lose.'

She hung her head. 'I know, but I'm conflicted over this and something inside me refuses to withdraw my statement. How can I be wife to a man who kills my only kin, however unworthy he is? And how can I respect my cousin if he kills the man I love and honour above all others? I just want to rail at them both until they find

282

some sense.'

When the earl exchanged a smile with his wife Amber managed a wry smile. 'Oh yes ... I really do love and honour Benedict above all others.'

'Then all is not lost.'

Amber gazed around her in dismay. 'I do hope you will stay despite the dust. My hospitality does not extend to much since we lack servants, except for this mysterious housekeeper I must go and make the acquaintance of. I will send for someone to remove some of the boards from the windows of the main rooms so we can see what we're doing... I was going to ask Patrick to do it. It's about time this house saw daylight again.'

The earl gazed kindly on her, which considering the circumstances was most generous of him. 'I'll remove the boards after you've made your statement to the magistrate, who is waiting in the morning room with his clerk.'

She took the first step to making redress to the woman who'd been so kind, patient and understanding. 'I'd be grateful if you'd act as advisor to me, My Lord, and you as well, My Lady.'

Imogene's smile was one of great beauty, and her eyes were the deep blue of cornflowers, just like Benedict's. 'I'll leave that to my husband, who possesses much more wisdom. I'll occupy myself by familiarising myself with the house and preparing a room. Despite the dust the house has a comfortable, homely feel to it. No wonder you didn't want to lose it.'

'Oh, I wouldn't have minded losing it that much, though I would have missed it because it was my home. But Benedict said he liked this house, and that he was looking for a property that would support a horse stud, so I bought it for him ... a marriage gift. Only now things have changed. We have reached an impasse, since a situation has been created that neither of us can back down from.'

'A little bending from you would bring my son completely to heel.'

'And a little bending from Benedict would achieve the opposite, no doubt. I have no intention of being brought to his heel. Neither do I want him to grovel at mine, since he's not a dog.' Amber smiled. 'His arrogance can be endearing *sometimes*.'

The earl chuckled. Taking her hand in his, he kissed it. 'I'm sure a satisfactory conclusion will be reached in this matter, especially with the incumbent magistrate directing proceedings.'

'You mean the magistrate will officiate when two men attempt to kill each other. This is madness.'

'Someone must ensure that the rules of the Code Duello are observed fairly.'

Amber stared at the earl wide-eyed. For a moment she was speechless, then she said fiercely, 'If anyone steps into my meadow tomorrow I'll swear out a warrant and have them charged with trespass. That includes the magistrate.'

The earl held out an arm to her. 'Then allow me escort you in so you can tell him so face to face. I'll be most interested to hear his reaction.'

# NINETEEN

'*Trespass!*' The magistrate, a jolly round man, burst into laughter. Quivering all over he pinched her cheek and flirted with her, telling her he'd dangled her on his knee after her grandfather brought her home from Italy, and wouldn't mind doing so again now she was grown up.

His clerk, tall, lean and solemn cast a jaundiced eye over his employer's antics.

'Beware of being too familiar else Viscount Costain might call you out as well,' she warned, and he and the earl looked at each other and chuckled.

The reaction had been patronizing to say the least, and Amber felt put out by it. 'I don't find this affair at all funny.'

'It's a matter of honour between gentlemen, my dear. They know what they're doing. Trespass ... under such circumstances?' He began to laugh again, his jowls wobbling like jellies, so Amber had found it hard not to join in the merriment. But even while her mouth pulled up at the corners, she felt like slapping him for not taking the matter more seriously.

The statement was a truthful one. Yes, it was a matter of honour between gentlemen, she conceded. She'd been abducted for ransom by Stephen Gould. She had no reason to believe her cousin had been implicated, but if he had, he'd

285

repented of his transgression by seeking help. Yes, she'd been imprisoned in the cellar without food until Benedict came to rescue her. But the crimes had been committed against herself, not Lord Costain.

The man's laughter stopped and he leaned forward, his eyes avid with curiosity. 'I understand you were in one of the upper rooms being held against your will, and clad immodestly in a nightgown when the viscount and his companions arrived. Would you tell me exactly what occurred between you and the deceased.'

'When you're are abducted from your bed in the middle of the night, modesty is the last thing on one's mind,' she said tartly. Her face heated and she gazed at the earl with embarrassment. What was the magistrate implying?

'I'm satisfied from an earlier conversation my wife had with Miss Hartford that no serious impropriety took place,' the earl said blandly. 'Although Miss Hartford was ill-treated, Gould heard the rescue party arrive and used her as a hostage.'

'Exactly as I thought, My Lord. I believe Gould was about to shoot you when the viscount intervened, Miss Hartford?'

She shuddered. 'Yes.'

'Good, good. You were lucky the viscount was at hand to deal with him, since Gould was a crack shot by all accounts. I saw the body. It was a nice, clean shot through the heart. I would have preferred a head shot, myself.'

Caustically, she said, 'And I'd prefer death by natural causes, preferably in old age with my

286

children and grandchildren all around me.'

'Quite. You're a woman, after all.' He cleared his throat. 'Is there anything else you wish to tell me, Miss Hartford?'

'Such as?'

'The part that your cousin, Lord Hartford took in this affair.'

'I've already stated that I have no knowledge that he did. In fact, my cousin was very brave,' she said fiercely, even though she'd felt like killing him herself, earlier. 'He faced Stephen Gould with no weapons and tried to talk him out of what he was doing.'

'A foolhardy act.'

'But a brave one nevertheless, and one that must be taken into account.'

'Will you be swearing out charges against him?'

'Certainly not, and I absolutely forbid Lord Costain to do so.'

'Ah well, as for that, Lord Costain must decide for himself. As things stand I imagine the protagonists' actions tomorrow will settle the issue one way or the other.'

To stop herself from stamping her foot or committing other unseemly displays of temper, like breaking a pot over the magistrate's head, she said, 'Will that be all, sir? I'm suffering from the onset of an unpredictable headache.'

'Certainly, Miss Hartford. Your statement will need to be signed and witnessed. In half an hour perhaps, when my clerk has finished it.'

'How can you face this so calmly when your son and heir might be lying dead in the meadow tomorrow?' she demanded to know of the earl when they were outside.

'My dear, would you rather your cousin went to prison. I could have him charged, since he entered my home in company with Gould, and stole a document. Also a snuff box and a purse was stolen, of which only the snuff box has been recovered.'

She hung her head. 'I'm truly sorry, My Lord. I was thinking only of myself, and had hopes for his rehabilitation. To that purpose I would offer you compensation.'

A kiss landed on her cheek. 'My dear, sweet, girl, you cannot change the nature of a man, only he can. To take your cousin's burden on your shoulders would weaken him. Lord Hartford has yet to prove his worth as a man to himself. If it's any consolation to you I will not bring charges, for I have no wish to lose your friendship.'

'And if by some chance Benedict is killed? What then, My Lord. Will you still wish to retain our friendship?'

Contemplative eyes settled on her. 'I have the utmost faith in my son, since I know the man he is. We'll see what the morrow brings.'

But Amber knew what it would bring – instant death for someone. And having now been only an inch away from death herself, life had become very precious to her.

After a night of fitful tossing and turning Amber was hollow-eyed when the sound of horses brought her awake. It was still dark, with just a brushstroke of pale yellow light on the horizon to signal the coming dawn.

At the same time Annie came in with a candle and a jug of warm water in which to wash.

Mrs Phelps came after with a tray of tea, and a bowl of fruit which she placed on a side table. 'I thought it might help you wake up, Miss Hartford,' she said. 'Word has got around and there's a right goodly crowd in the meadow. The district has never seen the like of two gentlemen duelling before.'

And she couldn't have them all charged with trespass. No wonder the magistrate had laughed, she thought miserably as the woman left.

The hall clock struck six. Suddenly she remembered a John Donne meditation, learned at her grandfather's knee. *Never send to know for whom the bell tolls, it tolls for thee.*

She shivered, and scrambled out of bed in a panic. Quickly washing, she donned the blue gown Annie held out for her. A shawl was placed about her shoulders, for the morning had an autumn chill to it.

With no time to arrange an elaborate style, her hair was quickly tied at the nape of her neck with a blue ribbon. The short ends curled naturally against her skin, but Amber didn't care how she looked as she drank the tea offered to her.

What if Benedict should die? How could she live without him now? But how could she live *with* him knowing he'd killed her cousin? Patrick was no match for Benedict. Her heart lifted when she remembered it would be in Patrick's nature to have fled.

Her stomach suddenly roiled and she headed for the bowl with the washing water in and lost

289

the tea she'd just consumed. 'Goodness, what brought that on?'

'It's nerves I expect Miss Hartford,' Annie wiped her lips with a flannel. 'Do you feel all right now?'

'My stomach is a bit unsettled. I expect it's because I didn't have any sustenance except wine for two days.'

Annie picked up a small apple from the bowl. 'This will settle your stomach. My mother used to swear by it when she was with child. Reckoned she always knew because of the sickness in the mornings. Fourteen live ones she gave birth to, too.'

The sharp juice freshened Amber's mouth and settled her stomach. Fourteen children, what endurance, she thought as she headed off downstairs and out into the morning. She couldn't see the meadow grass for the mist rising from the ground. But then the sun came up beyond a row of beech trees and the morning lit up like a flaming torch.

Amber blinked. Women were huddled together in one group. Mrs Winter's glance fell on her. She nudged the woman next to her and whispered something in her ear. Immediately all heads turned her way. The group of men included Reverend Winter, whose glance was surprisingly sympathetic. Her presence had caused an animated buzz of whispers.

Patrick had a stubborn look on his face and was standing with Kitt, who was talking earnestly to him.

'God, please allow Kitt to talk some sense into

him,' she whispered, and she wondered which candidate the reverend would be saying his prayers over afterwards.

Her heart lurched when she saw Benedict standing with Archie. He must have sensed her presence for he turned and gazed at her, his eyes as blue and as deep as bluebells.

How imposing a figure he was, broad-shouldered and dressed all in black except for a silver grey waistcoat. Those eyes drew her into him and she felt her heart beat with the strength of his. If he took a bullet that silver waistcoat would be splashed with red as his life drained from him. If his heart stopped hers would break and she'd die with him.

She shrugged off her melancholy. He couldn't die. He was too alive. Clearly she recalled the ecstasy as they'd abandoned their outer skin of clothing and revelled in each touch on their naked bodies. She knew him well now, as he knew her. She blushed and grinned at the same time.

Benedict blew her a kiss and his mouth twisted into a faint smile, as if he was remembering it too.

'Don't die, I love you,' she murmured, not caring who overheard.

Immediately the women began to give each other knowing looks and whisper amongst themselves.

'You shouldn't be here, my dear,' the earl said.

'Yesterday I said things I shouldn't have. I was harsh and I wanted Benedict to know that I love him.'

'Believe me, he does know it.' The earl tucked her hand into his. 'Come, I'll take you inside until this is over.'

'No. I won't blame Benedict if he kills Patrick, but I'm hoping my presence will prevent it from happening.'

The doctor had arrived now, giving a cheery smile to everyone. He placed his bag on the ground. Things progressed quickly. There was a short conversation with all concerned. The seconds loaded the pistols in the presence of each other while the duellists removed their coats.

Patrick was offered his choice of pistols. He took one without looking and Amber's heart went out to him when she observed the beads of perspiration on his ashen face. God protect you, she whispered.

Pistols held at their sides the protagonists walked away from each other then turned. Pistols came up. Two puffs of smoke were followed by two reports, one immediately after the other.

Startled, the rooks circled up from the trees in the copse, cawing harshly.

Eyes wide, Amber stared from one man to the other. Patrick staggered a bit when a red stain appeared on his sleeve. The gun dropped from his hand.

Kitt moved towards him with the doctor and inspected the wound. After a moment or two he looked over to where Benedict still stood. 'Lord Hartford has been disabled and begs your pardon.'

Handing Archie the pistol Benedict advanced

towards Patrick and the pair shook hands while the doctor attended to Patrick's wound.

'Ah, yes ... that's what I thought they'd do,' the earl murmured almost to himself.

The relief was so palpable that Amber began to shake with it.

'Hussy,' one of the women hissed at her as the women filed by.

The men stayed around, talking amongst themselves. Benedict was having a conversation with the reverend as the earl led her back to the house.

She thought Benedict might come back to the house, but he didn't, and neither did Patrick. The earl and countess prepared for their journey home. Kitt and Archie intended to accompany them, but there was no sign of Benedict.

'Where's Benedict?' she asked Archie.

The pair gazed at each other. Archie shrugged, then Kitt mumbled evasively, 'I haven't seen him for a while. Don't worry about him.'

Patrick came by later in the day.

'Are you all right?' she asked him.

'It was just a scratch, the bullet grazed the skin. I've come to offer my apologies, then I'll be on my way. I was such a fool.'

'Thank you for not killing Benedict.'

'I'm a lousy shot. I didn't have a chance in hell of hitting Costain. My shot went wide. He could easily have killed me, but he spared me, and without making a fool of me. I won't forget that.'

She drew in a deep breath and offered him what she thought was right, considering that he was their grandfather's heir. 'If you'd like I'll give you the house back and some money. If the land is farmed properly it will support you, and there is an income from the rents.'

He smiled wryly as he gazed around him. 'I've never wanted the responsibility of this house. I still intend to go abroad, and I know your viscount would prefer it if I did. Kitt Foster knows a few people. He thinks he can find me employment with the British East India Company, abroad.'

'And will you take it up?'

'Since I've been offered a chance to redeem myself I'd be a fool not to. Don't worry Amber, I won't let him down. But first I'm going to take the girl who helped Stephen back to her father at the inn, and make sure Jonas is returned safely to his uncle. As for your money, I can't accept it. I'm already beholden to you for my life, something that became extremely valuable to me when I was gazing down the barrel of your viscount's gun. There, I never thought I'd say that.'

Amber tried not to smile at the sight of Patrick bristling with his new found pride, but she couldn't send him away penniless. 'The farmer still owes for the wheat crop he harvested when the house was yours? You're entitled to have that.'

'Is that the truth?'

'Go and ask him. He's probably hoping I've forgotten it. By the way, although I negotiated I couldn't push him up past a quarter of the sale price. But that's because I'm a woman. Fifty

294

percent would have been fairer. You might like to push him a little.'

He smiled at that. 'Thanks, Amber, I'll make sure I'll collect it.' When he awkwardly stooped to kiss her cheek she pulled him into a hug.

He gave an odd huff of laughter when she released him. 'I've never been hugged before.'

'I hope you don't die from it. Sometimes it's infectious.'

'It wasn't so bad.' Awkwardly, he hugged her back, then laughed. 'Goodbye Amber. It's unlikely that we'll meet again.'

'Good luck.' There were tears in her eyes when she watched him ride off down the drive without looking back.


## TWENTY

Amber didn't set eyes on Benedict during the next week and thought he might have decided she wasn't worth the trouble.

The house had been staffed in that time from an agency in Poole. The new servants were working under the authority of Mrs Phelps, who'd turned out to be efficient as well as pleasant. As a result the woodwork and furniture glowed with polish, the windows gleamed and every corner was free of dust.

The belongings Amber had left at Emma's house had been delivered, along with Jake. Now her house was in order she felt cut off from Benedict and his sociable family. Even Jake's arrival didn't assuage her loneliness.

'Have you seen Lord Costain?' was the first thing she asked.

He shook his head.

They sat at her grandfather's desk and wrote their thank you letters, then sent them off with a messenger. *Dearest, Benedict, I love you so much and I miss you*, she wrote.

A few days later Jake went with Annie on Samuel's cart into Bridport. They returned with huge smiles on their faces. From then on the pair exchanged secretive smiles or indulged in whispered conversations, which were cut off abruptly if she walked in on them.

On the second Sunday Annie was unusually fussy with her gown and hair. 'The cream one with the matching pelisse is so becoming, Miss.'

It was the gown Emma and Caroline had intended her to wed Benedict in.

'You should wear that, and the emerald set Lord Costain gave you with it. So becoming.'

And her hair arranged just so, with small curls and ringlets. To top it off was a straw bonnet trimmed with pink silk roses and ribbons.

'Wear this white silk shawl with the gown, Miss Hartford. And the white kid boots, I think.'

It was getting late. Jake wandered in, wondering whether his boots needed polishing. There was a secretive look in his eyes.

'I don't know why everyone is being so fussy today,' she said, pulling on white silk gloves. 'Your boots are fine, Jake. Come on, we'll be late for the service.'

Jake gave a wide smile. 'Lord Costain wishes to see you. He's in the morning room.'

Her heart nearly stopped beating. 'Lord Costain?'

Her head was full of humming birds, her stomach filled with butterflies.

'Tell him I'll be ready to see him in ten minutes. You may go on to church with Annie.'

She couldn't wait longer than three. He stood when she slid through the door. Dressed in dark blue cutaway jacket with a silver waistcoat, he looked splendid.

She found herself short of breath when he smiled, and looked into her eyes. 'We have things to say to each other. Would you like me to go first?'

When she nodded her crossed to where she stood and cleared his throat. 'I love you, Amber Rose. Will you become my wife?'

'I want to apol–'

He placed a finger over her lips and growled, 'Never mind apologies. Yes, or no.'

'Yes.'

'Come on then.'

'Where?'

'To the church, of course.' He drew her into his arms to gazed into her eyes, then his lips gently touched against hers.

'I've missed you, my love,' she whispered.

They walked off through the lane towards the church. Autumn was approaching fast. Leaves fluttered about them and were crunched underfoot. The chestnut trees were aflame, their nuts falling ripe from their husks to lie like glossy brown balls. She must collect a basket or two to roast.

They were in good time, for the service hadn't started. The church was filled with flowers. Benedict's family took up the two front pews. Jake offered her a cheeky grin.

As Amber knelt to pray, Benedict whispered in her ear, 'Whose soul are you praying so hard for ... yours or mine?'

She inhaled him with one deep breath, soap, leather and musk all in one swoop. Love for him swept through her and she experienced such exultation she wanted to shout with the joy of it. Her eyes met his and a smile curved her mouth up at the corners.

*Her hero. Her love!* She had an urge to lean forward and kiss the smiling contours of his mouth. Happiness burst through her veins and filled every space in her body with sunshine. 'Where have you been for the past week, you renegade?'

'At the inn.' His chuckle lifted the hairs at the nape of her neck. 'I thought a short time apart might give you the time you needed to think about the promises made between us, and to be sure in your heart that marriage to me was what you wanted.'

'Are *you* sure, Benedict?'

'From the first moment I met you.' He took her hand in his and gently traced the lines on the palm. 'I've missed you, Amber Rose.'

She closed her eyes, feeling complete now he was with her again. 'I've missed you, too.'

'Shush. You should be ashamed, disrupting the service like this,' Mrs Winter whispered crossly from the pew behind them.

Benedict quelled her with one look. 'I'm ashamed of nothing. Cease your tattling. A man should be able to declare his profound love for a young lady in the house of the Lord without being eavesdropped on and uncharitably censured for it.'

She should stop him, she thought, but then laughter bubbled up inside her at the thought that he'd risk making a fool of himself by displaying his feelings in public. And if he could do so, then so could she!

Amber placed a finger against his mouth, though when he tickled it with the tip his tongue it proved to be most distracting. 'You know I love you, Benedict.'

When she glanced round at the congregation, she saw his entire family was wearing encouraging smiles. Love for them all, and admiration for the way this family cared and supported each other touched her heart, for it was something she'd never known.

The reverend stepped forward, a smile on his face. 'Shall we begin the ceremony?'

The public declaration was a romantic gesture, one worthy of Benedict. Amber adored him for his thoughtfulness. She wanted to marry him because she loved him, but although she was not certain yet, she'd also begun to suspect there was another reason that they should wed. She remembered Caroline telling her about a gypsy foretelling that three sons would be born on the same day into the Costain family, and she smiled.

Placing her hand trustingly in his they moved

as one to stand in front of the reverend.

'*Dearly beloved, we are gathered together here in the eyes of God, and in the face of this congregation, to join together this man and this woman in holy matrimony...*'

This Large Print Book for the partially sighted, who cannot read normal print, is published under the auspices of

## THE ULVERSCROFT FOUNDATION